ST. JAMES PLACE

ST. JAMES PLACE

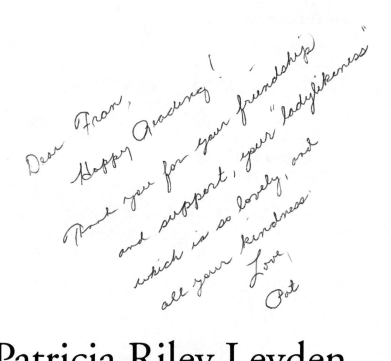

Dear Fran,
Happy Reading!
Thank you for your friendship
and support, your "ladylikeness"
which is so lovely, and
all your kindness.
Love,
Pat

Patricia Riley Leyden

Published by ᴡRITERS ROOM BOOKS
The Writers Room of Bucks County, Inc.
47 W. Oakland Ave.
Doylestown, PA 18901
www.writersroom.net
28204

Dedication

To the people of the past, the immigrants who came to the Lower East Side of Manhattan, and to their offspring.

To my mother, Rosemary A. Murphy, who loved me unconditionally in my past.

To the immigrants of today, a vital part of our future as a nation, just as immigrants always have been.

To my four beautiful daughters and dear son-in-law, Katharine M. and Richard A. Bergacs, Casey E. Leyden, Margaret A. Leyden, and Victoria A. Leyden, with love and thanks for their unfailing support in my today.

To my grandchildren (thus far), Richard Patrick Bergacs and Abigail Rose Bergacs, as they create the future.

Time present and time past
Are both perhaps present in time future,
And time future contained in time past.

T.S. Eliot

Acknowledgements

I would like to thank the following people and organizations for their help in completing this novel:

Two wonderful women: My sister, Leila Wright, and my friend, Dr. Prudence Cuper, both of whom spent hours reading and editing my manuscript and giving invaluable suggestions that I was so grateful to use; The International Ladies Garment Workers Union (ILGWU), who provided me with information about the fire; the Administration for Children's Services (ACS) in New York City for the information about social workers that I incorporated into my story (any inaccuracies are my fault, not theirs); Ben Cake, formerly of The Writers Room of Bucks County, who edited the manuscript and offered many powerful suggestions that improved this work; R. Foster Winans, writer, president and founder of the Writers Room of Bucks County, for his kindness and encouragement to me, and for his vision in creating a place like the Writers Room; and finally, Sr. Catherine Meighan, S.S.J., and Mr. Richard Heller for their help with the artwork on the cover.

MAY, 2002

Chapter One

The bright sunlight blinded her for an instant. She blinked, but the familiar sights of the noisy and congested New York City neighborhood were now altered. She blinked again, but the new images persisted. The street sign. It now read, "New Bowery Street," when only a moment ago it had read, "St. James Place." And it was different, old looking and strange. A young woman approached and stood directly in front of her. She was beautiful, but the expression on her face was stunningly sad. Her eyes seemed to be asking Elizabeth for something. Elizabeth instinctively put her hand out to the sorrowful figure.

Waves of nausea washed over her. She heard herself retching as she fought for control of her stomach. Perspiration dripped down her back, and her knees buckled. She reached for the lamppost to steady herself as the distressing episode began to subside. People on the crowded city street were staring at her.

And then it was all as it had been before-the Lower East Side of Manhattan bustling with activity on a warm May afternoon, honking horns, the relentless beat of a boom box, screams of excitement from children on the playground of the Al Smith housing projects.

But the beautiful young woman she had seen . . . She'd been wearing a long dress. Elizabeth glanced up again at the street sign. It was identical to almost all the street signs in New York City-green metal with white letters. It said, "St. James Place." And it was not the street sign of a moment ago.

What just happened to her? She tried to make sense of it. But there *was* no making sense of it. Her heart raced, and her hands shook. Her knees were still wobbly.

"Are you okay?" a stooped, elderly woman asked.

"Yes, thank you," Elizabeth said as she pushed back her shoulders and tried to regain some semblance of dignity.

She ran her icy fingers through her thick auburn hair. Her other hand was empty, her briefcase now on the sidewalk. She looked down at the skirt of her familiar suit. Elizabeth Charles, young, well-groomed, impeccably dressed professional social worker seemed to have had some kind of a hallucination followed by the public humiliation of retching in the street.

She picked up her briefcase and walked along St. James Place trying to imagine a rational explanation for what had just happened, but it did not come. She was still shaking and wanted to go home to Brooklyn, but it was important to her that she complete her last case of the day. A woman was seeking to legally adopt her nephew, and Elizabeth knew how anxious she was. She didn't want to postpone this appointment and add to the woman's stress. I'll think about the hallucination, or whatever it was, later, she thought. Now, she would just try to forget how frightened she was and do what she had to do.

The building she was heading for was on Madison Street. She walked there quickly, entered the lobby, and boarded the elevator. As she rode the elevator to the eighth floor, she pulled her brush through her almost impenetrable hair and popped a Tic-Tac into her mouth. She smoothed her slightly rumpled skirt and fussed with the buttons of her suit jacket. Stay calm, she told herself. But now she knew what the expression "sick with fear" meant.

The unpleasant odors in the elevators of the public housing projects, the ones that she thought she had become so accustomed to and barely noticed anymore, were now not agreeing with her still upset stomach. The halls were different though. She liked *those* smells. As she walked toward apartment 8E, she absorbed the pleasant aromas of various ethnic dishes and somehow felt comforted. Keep thinking these distracting thoughts and just get through this, she said to herself.

"Miss Charles, please come in." A carefully dressed African-American woman opened the door and Elizabeth entered. The apartment was meticulously clean. Elizabeth understood that her presence here was difficult for this young woman who was forced to prove to a largely white middle-class society that she was capable of caring for her own nephew.

"After all our conversations on the phone, I'm happy to finally meet you, Miss Harding," Elizabeth said as the two women shook hands.

"I'm happy to meet you, too, but I must admit I'll be glad when this is all over and Rory is truly mine. Would you like some iced tea?"

"Thanks, I'd love some. It's hot for the beginning of May, isn't it?"

"And you look like the heat's gotten to you," Carla Harding said, not unkindly. But Elizabeth was embarrassed, though not surprised that her efforts at freshening up in the elevator had not been successful. If this woman, who needed Elizabeth's approval, knew what Elizabeth *thought* she'd experienced on St. James Place, she'd probably throw her out of the apartment and call the authorities.

As she sat down in the attractively decorated living room, Elizabeth's eyes swept the home that Rory, a lively six-year-old, now shared with his aunt. Rory's father had died in a work-related accident just before his birth, and Rory's mother had recently died of cardiomyopathy after a virus had settled in her heart. Jenna Harding was Rory's mother's sister, and she had been eager to take care of him. It was obvious that she loved him. Clearly all was well here.

"Rory, I love your posters. You like Michael Jordan, don't you?" Elizabeth asked after Rory proudly showed her his room.

"Yeah, but I'm gonna play football instead of basketball."

Elizabeth wished all her cases could be like this one. It wasn't a traditional family home she was visiting, but because Rory was loved and wanted by his aunt, and because she could provide for him, Elizabeth knew they'd be okay.

It wasn't until she was back on the street heading for the Delancey Street station that she allowed herself to remember and try to process the strange experience she'd had on St. James Place. Her hands starting shaking again as she was swept down the subway stairs in the press of the crowd of commuters. She boarded the packed J train and tried not to cry. Her life, despite the usual challenges and a few failed romances, had been so good. Was a devastating mental illness going to mar it now? Or was it physical, a brain tumor maybe? For the first time in her experience, she felt a loss of control, and she was frightened.

The train crawled along at a snail's pace to Canal Street before she had to change to the R to get to the other side of the East River, to her apartment in a brownstone on Remsen Street in Brooklyn Heights. Remembering and reliving the strange incident didn't help; she was just as baffled and scared as she had been when it happened.

She walked from the subway platform up to the street and took a deep breath of Brooklyn. The Heights. She loved living here because of the tree-lined streets, the diverse ethnic groups, the rows of old brownstones. From the first time she walked on the Promenade and saw the Manhattan skyline, she knew she wanted to live in this historic place. So, when she'd graduated from New York University with her master's in social work and was hired immediately by the Administration for Children's Services, she went straight to a realtor in Brooklyn Heights. She wanted an apartment with the old gaslights on the walls, she had told him. And she was lucky enough to get one.

Her thoughts were interrupted by furious barking. It was Thunderball greeting one of his masters, Elizabeth's neighbor, Al, who was coming home from work. She waved hello. Al and his partner lived in the street level apartment of the brownstone. He turned away from his front door, which was under the high steps, a "stoop" as they called it in Brooklyn.

"How's it going, Elizabeth?" he called up as she climbed the smooth stone steps of the stoop above him to the main entrance of the brownstone.

"Fine, Al. How's Joe?"

"He'll be home any minute. Why don't you join us for homemade pizza and a little red wine later? We'll be eating at 6:30"

"I'd love to, but I'm bushed tonight. How about another time?"

"Sure, kiddo."

She opened the outside door at the top of the tall stoop and was soothed by the sight of the pale blue carpet in the hall inside that wound up the stairs to her apartment on the second floor.

The sharp contrast between the stark hallways of the housing projects and her own carpeted hallway never failed to jar Elizabeth after a day of work, and tonight was no exception. But the projects had something her building did not. Few comforting cooking odors ever reached her nostrils here. In this place, inhabited mainly by working couples, take-out food was the hallway fare. Mrs. Margolis was the exception.

"Elizabeth, hi," Mrs. Margolis said when she cracked open the door to her apartment, something she often did when someone came through the big door from the stoop.

"Hi, Mrs. Margolis," Elizabeth said. She stopped and chatted with her petite and wiry landlady.

"Wait here a moment, Honey." Elizabeth had been through this before. She knew Mrs. Margolis would return with a Tupperware container filled with warm goodies. "I always make too much for one. Enjoy."

As she entered her empty apartment Elizabeth suddenly felt lonely, and she thought of Rory and his dignified aunt back in the projects. She imagined them sitting at the spotless kitchen table having their dinner, chatting about his day at school, hers at the office. Maybe she should take Al and Joe up on the pizza invitation. She reached for the phone, but before she could pick it up, it rang.

"Hi, Dad." Twenty-eight years old and she suddenly felt like a little girl. She ached to tell her father about the incident on St. James Place, how she had seemed to be somewhere else, even though she knew she wasn't. She didn't want to worry him though. He would be as frightened as she was. More frightened.

"How about coming to dinner this week?" Elizabeth's father asked.

"Why don't you come here? I want to try out my culinary skills, newly acquired though they may be," she said.

"I didn't even know you had acquired cooking skills," he said.

"Actually, I haven't acquired any *yet*. I've been meaning to, but it just hasn't happened. How about being practice for me?"

The groan Michael Charles came back with was good-natured, and they both laughed, agreeing on the day and time.

Later, after nibbling on Mrs. Margolis's chicken cutlets, she walked into her bedroom in the old brownstone. She looked at the moldings on the high ceilings that she loved, the rather stark walls beneath them. Not only hadn't she learned to cook very well since she'd gotten her own apartment, but she hadn't done any decorating either. The exceptions were the Laura Ashley bedding and curtains she'd splurged on when she got this place at the end of last year.

As she was turning down the yellow and blue comforter, Elizabeth realized that she would now have to again confront the strange event of today and try to make sense of it.

She stretched out and lay flat on her back in her double bed. The white ceiling stared back at her. Her world seemed as normal and her future as promising as it had been yesterday. But what about the bizarre and inexplicable occurrence of today? She decided she'd try to forget it. In fact, maybe it hadn't happened at all; the sun in her eyes *had* been blinding. But then she clearly remembered the beautiful face of the woman in the long dress. Nevertheless, sleepiness eventually took over, and soon she was dreamlessly asleep.

Chapter Two

The next day Elizabeth was back in the housing projects on St. James Place for the first case of what would be the usual busy day. She planned to stick to her resolve and forget yesterday's whatever-it-was as she headed for the elevator to the tenth floor.

The Ruiz apartment was dimly lit with drawn shades, possibly to hide the filth she could smell, if not see.

"How are you, Mrs. Ruiz?" Two sullen brown eyes stared at her from a painfully thin and drawn face. "I'm Elizabeth Charles from the Administration for Children's Services. I'm here because we are concerned about Milagros. Some of her teachers have been worried about her because they saw bruises on her arms." She heard her voice echo somewhat as she spoke. She looked around her and saw that there was little furniture in the apartment.

"She's fine. We don't have any problems here," Mrs. Ruiz said. She motioned for Elizabeth to sit on the couch; she seated herself in the single chair next to it. A television set resting precariously on a kitchen chair and a shadeless table lamp sitting on the scuffed, bare floor were the only other things in the room.

"How is Milagros doing?" Elizabeth asked.

A grunt, then, "Okay. She's smart; she's a good girl."

"May I see her?"

"Why do you want to see her? She's a kid. She has nothing to say to you."

"Nevertheless, I would like to talk to her."

The mother got up and shuffled wordlessly to a closed door off the hall, opened it, and gestured to the child inside. A fragile-looking little girl with fine black hair and brown eyes appeared in the doorway to the living room.

Elizabeth's heart went out to the tiny girl. Her mouth turned up slowly in response to Elizabeth's own friendly smile.

But the smile never fully materialized as her mother gave her an unnecessarily rough shove into the living room.

"May I speak to Milagros alone, please?"

"I'll stay," the mother barked. She remained standing with her arms folded across her chest as Milagros slowly walked toward Elizabeth.

"Milagros, my name is Elizabeth Charles. Will you come and sit next to me?"

Milagros lowered her eyes and Elizabeth sensed her shyness when she took the little hands in hers and squeezed them gently before she sat down on the couch.

"Milagros, how are you?"

"I'm fine, Miss Charles."

The child's studied courtesy belied her surroundings. Where did she learn it, Elizabeth wondered.

"Do you like school?"

"I love school, and I love to read. I love gym, and I'm going to sing in the school play, too." Milagros's large brown eyes burned with excitement as the shyness disappeared. Elizabeth guessed that an avalanche of words was only barely being held at bay.

"What do you like to read?" Elizabeth asked.

"I just finished *Green Mansions*," Milagros said. A book that took her far from the Al Smith housing projects, Elizabeth thought.

"What did you like about *Green Mansions*?" Elizabeth asked.

This was the question Milagros wanted to hear, it seemed, because a torrent of details poured forth as Milagros told Elizabeth the story. Elizabeth was as amused by Milagros's enthusiasm as she was touched by the little girl's identification with the main character in *Green Mansions*, an isolated young girl living in the trees, deep in the jungles of South America.

Elizabeth asked Milagros more questions about school and her friends and was impressed at the articulate answers given by the eight-year-old. She was clearly a highly gifted child whose language skills far surpassed those normally possessed by a third grader.

As Milagros spoke, Elizabeth looked discreetly for signs of physical abuse. The long-sleeved dress, too warm for the unseasonably hot May, was a possible indication of abuse. The child's arms might be bruised as her teacher had reported, but Elizabeth could not tell. The child's thinness was also a possible sign of abuse, in the form of neglect.

"Do you like to eat, Milagros?" Elizabeth asked when Milagros stopped talking.

"Oh, yes," she answered at once. She named the junk foods of which she was particularly fond. Elizabeth noticed that the child glanced nervously over at her mother from time to time during the interview, but was nevertheless able to focus back on Elizabeth and the subject at hand very easily.

"Okay, Milagros. You can go back to your reading now because I'd like to talk to your mother. Do you want to say anything to me?"

Milagros looked older than eight years suddenly as she frowned and looked at her mother. Unexpectedly, she kissed Elizabeth lightly before dashing into her room.

"Mrs. Ruiz," Elizabeth began, "as I explained to you when I first came in, a complaint was made to my office that Milagros has come to school with bruises on her arms and one on her face. I have been sent here to investigate how Milagros got those bruises, to find out if they are the result of abuse in the home."

When there was no response, Elizabeth tried again.

"Mrs. Ruiz, how many people live here, and what are their names?"

"There is only one child, Milagros. Me. And I have a friend." The woman's icy demeanor dissolved in front of Elizabeth's eyes. "Don't take my child. She is all I have. I love her. I have not taken good care of her, but soon it will be better. It will. No one will hurt her."

"Your friend, does he live here with you?" Elizabeth asked.

"Yes, sometimes, but he doesn't hurt Milagros. He doesn't. Soon he will be gone anyway."

The mother opened up a little about her friend, apparently her boyfriend. His name was Chet King, and his work, if any, was vague.

Despite the mother's protestation of love for her daughter, Elizabeth had a bad feeling about this home. The sparsely furnished living room did not contain photographs or personal items that reflected the personalities of the inhabitants. What she could see of the kitchen from her vantage point was not promising. The whole place was bare, dirty, and depressing.

"Mrs. Ruiz, you said your friend doesn't hurt Milagros, but have you or your friend had a problem with your tempers with Milagros?"

The mother's body went limp, she slumped into the chair in the living room, and put her head in her hands. "We would not hurt Milagros. We would not hurt Milagros."

Elizabeth's stomach churned, and she felt sick. If the abuse were clear cut, she could remove Milagros from this toxic home right now. But it was not clear cut. Maybe her mother was a loving mother who was just beaten down by life, by poverty. Maybe it was the boyfriend who was the problem. In any case, there *was* a problem, she was sure. She did not know how she could bear to leave this child here. But she had no direct evidence of abuse in the home, so for now she was powerless to do anything. Her thoughts turned to the countless children throughout the city in similar situations, and she felt sicker still. She resolved to follow this case closely as she headed for the next home visit.

Her feet were aching from pounding the pavement of the Lower East Side when she finally returned to the offices of the Administration for Children's Services at the end of the day. With over fifty thousand cases of abuse and neglect reported each year, the agency had its hands full. Elizabeth spent one day out of five in the office for paperwork. The rest of the week consisted of home visits and court hours. As she began to tackle the reports, Elizabeth thought of Milagros and sighed. The sorrowful little girl had been transformed into the vibrant spirit she was meant to be when she talked about the book, *Green Mansions*.

Back at the office, she began to write up the Ruiz case after making it through the backlog. She would soon make a follow-up visit to Milagros's school and a surprise visit to the home. Her cell phone rang.

"How about a spontaneous dinner tonight? No slaving in a hot kitchen. Our charming restaurant with Ralph the waiter after work instead of cooking and dishes? What do you think?"

Elizabeth couldn't resist her father's invitation. They agreed to meet at the Hungarian restaurant on Montague Street that they favored since Elizabeth moved to Brooklyn Heights last year. It was only blocks from her apartment where they could go for coffee afterwards.

The phone on her desk rang. "Stay away from my place or you'll be sorry." The caller hung up. Social workers who worked for the Administration for Children's Services sometimes got calls like this. She'd fill out an incident report and give it to Angela, her supervisor. Elizabeth wrote down the time of the call and the man's words. She'd never personally received a call like this. It was disturbing. Which family had the threatening call come from, she wondered.

She deliberately turned her thoughts to the dinner date with her father and another disturbing thought. Should she tell him what had happened on St. James Place? She had told him almost everything about what was going on in her life for as long as she could remember. She was only three when her mother died; Elizabeth had no real memories of her. Her father had always been her best friend and confidant. She turned back to her work and sighed again.

The restaurant was on the second floor, and her father was already seated when she arrived. His tall, lean frame unfolded from the chair when he saw her approach.

"We're lucky today," he said as he embraced her. "Our favorite table by the window was empty when I came in. We can look down on the street below at the colorful characters you have here in the Heights."

"Like you don't have colorful characters in Manhattan. I love the Heights, colorful characters or not," Elizabeth said, smiling over the old argument between them.

Ralph came to the table and they ordered their favorites. "You look happy, Dad. Is anything new?" Elizabeth always hoped her father would find someone to love, but it hadn't happened. He dated often, but he never got serious with any of the attractive women he escorted around the city.

"Yes, I think there is something new," he said. "I'm flying to Chicago in the morning to a financial planners' conference, and then I'm taking a short vacation. Which is why I asked you here tonight. Can you join me for the weekend? I'm staying at a friend's house in the Bahamas. It's a huge villa on the ocean with an in-the-ground pool, a tennis court, a fun place." Michael took off his glasses, rested them on the table, and lifted his thick eyebrows expectantly as he waited for Elizabeth's answer as Ralph brought their food to the table.

"My caseload's heavy, and there's one child who may be in trouble. I have to follow through so she doesn't fall through the cracks." Elizabeth's face showed both her interest and her disappointment. "I wish you were going in a few weeks."

"Don't worry; soon I'll be taking vacations all year round. I've decided to retire and get out of the rat race. It's time to travel and learn how to enjoy leisure time."

"That *is* news." She was surprised. She scrutinized her father as they ate the delicious meal. At fifty-nine, Michael was at his peak, it seemed. With a full head of wavy brown hair with only the slightest sprinkling of gray, he was fit and full of physical and intellectual vigor.

"I can't imagine you slowing down, much less retiring. Something *has* changed," she said as she leaned toward him across the table and took both his hands in hers after Ralph cleared away their dishes. Her father flushed slightly. He was about to speak when the waiter interrupted.

"How about some dessert and coffee, you two?"

"No, thanks, Ralph. We're going to my daughter's for dessert and coffee tonight," Michael told the waiter. He turned to Elizabeth, "We'll talk more about it at your place."

Elizabeth took his cue and steered the conversation in another direction, "Will you be selling the business?" Elizabeth asked.

"Of course not. Don't you think I would consult you first, as my only heir, and perhaps try to convince you to take it over? I should say, give you one last chance to take it over."

They both laughed, knowing that Elizabeth would never take over her father's financial planning business. Michael Charles, whose concern for his fellow humans was not limited to writing tax-deductible checks, had been the example that Elizabeth had followed when she decided to be a social worker.

"Of course my huge, plush office, with its magnificent view of the city, doesn't interest you. I guess you like bleak offices, case overload, lousy press, and all the inconveniences of working for an organization that suffers from a perennial budget crisis instead." He sat back, his hands still in hers, a smile on his face. "Seriously, though, Elizabeth, I want you to know how truly proud I am of you. You *are* such a special woman. I know that the work you do is hard, but I know that you've made a real difference in the lives of many kids."

His words warmed her. Throughout her life her father had made many choices available to her, and he always had faith in her judgment and her instincts when she made a decision. Which she realized she would have to do tonight. Not about the business-he knew where she stood on that, and obviously that was more than fine with him. No, tonight, she'd have to decide whether or not to tell him, and of course worry him, about her "hallucination." She wasn't having much luck forgetting about it, as she had promised herself she would.

"What's the matter, Bethie?" He could see the conflict on her face and knew it was serious, or he wouldn't have used his childhood name for her.

She couldn't do it. He was going to Chicago tomorrow and on to the Bahamas for a great weekend. Besides, he was about to tell her something momentous at her apartment. She'd wait until he got back before she told him what had happened or had not happened on St. James Place. "Oh, you made me all misty with your proud father stuff. I love you, Dad."

He didn't look fooled, and was about to speak when Elizabeth's cell phone rang. She left the dining room to take the call in the lobby.

When she returned to the table, he had already paid the check and was placing a generous tip on the table. "No coffee at your place?"

"No coffee at my place. A child has been abused, and I have to take him to the shelter tonight."

Her father shook his head.

"I wish I could take each of them home with me, Dad. I go to these homes when the police are there, quickly pack the few things they may have, and then leave them in another cheerless place, a shelter usually, where they know no one."

Michael hugged his daughter. "I know, Honey."

"I wish we had some time tonight, Dad." She wanted very much to know what it was that he had been about to tell her when Ralph had interrupted. It was more than just his retirement, and now, suddenly, she did want to confide in him about the incident on St. James Place.

"We'll have all the time in the world," he said with his usual cheer; her father never fussed over things that couldn't be helped.

He put her in a taxi, and Elizabeth directed a very annoyed driver to Manhattan, the Lower East Side projects. She watched her father waving on the corner of the bustling Brooklyn Heights street, the lights of the restaurant blinking behind him until her cab turned, and he was out of sight.

It was the last time she would ever see him.

Chapter Three

It was almost two a.m. when the cab flew across the Manhattan Bridge. Elizabeth was tired. Was it only six and a half hours ago that she and her father were finishing dinner at the Hungarian restaurant?

When she'd arrived at the projects, she found that the child she'd been called to help, a little boy named Johnny, had numerous bruises and abrasions that needed medical attention. They'd sat in the emergency room of NYU Downtown Hospital for two and a half hours before he was treated and released.

Throughout the ordeal the child had remained silent, his brown eyes listless and vacant. Elizabeth's gentle questions had gone unanswered. He did allow her to keep her arm around him as they sat and waited in the ER though. She'd stroked his hair occasionally, and when he wasn't dozing, she told him stories that he seemed to be listening to.

She had seen other children like this before. They become unresponsive on the surface. Something dies in them from the hatred and violence they experience routinely. She'd winced when the doctor went over the seven-year-old's body. The scars from old injuries were a chilling reality, a rebuke to her, she thought, because she couldn't make his life what it should be, or the lives of the other children who suffered like this.

While she was helping him to dress, she'd tried to reassure him that he would be okay, make new friends, and have something good to eat. Later, as his eyes scanned the bleak surroundings of the city shelter she brought him to, she felt like a liar. She succumbed to tears for Johnny during the cab ride home.

"Lady, you gettin' outta the cab, or what?" the driver asked her. She hadn't realized that they were in front of her apartment on Remsen Street. She paid him, and barely slammed the door of the taxi before he screeched away from the curb and into the night.

The stoop of the brownstone loomed high above her in the darkness. Her head snapped around at the unexpected sound of a footstep on the deserted street. She thought she saw movement in the shadows near the entrance to Al and Joe's ground floor apartment. Did Thunderball, their dog, have to make a middle of the night trip outside?

"Al, Joe, is that you?" she called out. There was no answer. Instantly awake and alert, she raced up the steps of the stoop to the front door of the brownstone. Her heart was pounding, and she panicked as she fumbled with her key ring for the key to the big outside door. The key ring slipped from her fingers, clattering onto the granite. There was someone watching her from the shadows at the bottom of the stoop. Would he rush up the steps and overcome her? She quickly picked up the key ring, and holding the door key firmly, unlocked the door. She was finally safely inside. She took the carpeted stairs two at a time and was pressed against the inside of her apartment door in an instant. The pounding of her heart resounded in her ears as she tried to catch her breath. It wasn't like her to get spooked like this.

What am I doing in this job that keeps me out at all hours of the night, she asked herself for the hundredth time, even though she knew the answer. She thought about Johnny and her failure to help him tonight. In the past two years that she'd been working for the ACS, there had been too many kids like Johnny.

But then there were the kids that she had helped. She had to remember them. It was possible that Johnny would be one of them eventually. She couldn't allow herself to get discouraged. And Milagros Ruiz, she was another child she would try to help.

Milagros is a survivor, Elizabeth thought, as she got ready for bed. If she's being abused, she isn't going to let it destroy who she is. She's only eight years old, but she has some special ingredient that enables her to keep dreaming of something better. Her books must be giving her the material to dream on. That's why I'm doing this job, Elizabeth thought.

Yet, she'd really been frightened just now. Could it have been her imagination that created a monster in the dark tonight? She hurriedly put on her nightgown, tied her bathrobe tightly around her waist, and walked to the front of the apartment. The curtains in her dark living room were open and she strained to see any movement on the street below. The street lamp illuminated a small patch of concrete in front of the brownstone, but she saw nothing and closed the curtains quickly. She was tired and upset, two ingredients that could have conjured up a nonexistent threat. She climbed into bed, but lay awake for some time thinking about Johnny and Milagros, the incident on the street just now, the hallucination on St. James Place, and the threatening phone call she'd gotten at the office. There were too many demons racing around in her mind for her to sleep peacefully.

Chet King stood in the shadows. He stared at the windows on the second floor of the brownstone. He walked away when she closed the curtains.

The next morning she wrote some case notes and assembled papers for her court appearance in support of the little boy, Johnny Jackson, whom she'd taken from the projects last night. Family Court was packed as she'd anticipated. She looked around at the sea of suffering humanity in the courtroom and felt as discouraged as she did early this morning during the cab ride home from the shelter. She opened her briefcase.

"Ms. Charles?" Elizabeth looked up. A fit looking man with glasses who appeared to be in his early thirties was standing in front of her. As she was enjoying his warm and solid handshake, she noticed his brown eyes, thick black hair and broad shoulders. She felt an unmistakable current. What was this, she wondered. "I'm Mark Lewis, with the D.A.'s office. I'm here about the Johnny Jackson case."

"Yes," Elizabeth nodded. She forced herself away from the tumultuous feelings meeting Mark Lewis had brought on as she remembered the grim scene she had witnessed in the projects last night. "There isn't much that could be worse about Johnny's home."

"I read the police report. Johnny's only seven years old. He's been beaten and neglected his whole life," Mark said.

"I know. I was there and saw the kind of life he has."

"He'll be placed in a good foster home," Mark said as he shook his head sadly.

When the formalities of the court proceeding were over, Mark Lewis approached Elizabeth. "You had a rough night last night. How about a cup of coffee to revive you?"

If this was a line, Elizabeth didn't care. She felt at ease with Assistant D.A. Lewis and gratefully accepted.

"How do you feel when you see these children?" she asked him.

"They break my heart too," he admitted. "I grew up in a family where we were as close as could be. We still are. Our parents were wonderful. I know what a good home is."

Elizabeth knew too, and she nodded in agreement. "Why were we so lucky; why do these kids have to suffer like this?"

"I've tortured myself with that question a million times too," Mark said.

Elizabeth put out her hand simply because she wanted the sheer pleasure of his handshake again. "I guess I'll see you in court," Elizabeth said as they parted. She hoped she'd see him outside of court too. The attraction she'd felt for this man was like nothing she'd ever experienced. And it was wonderful. This was another thing she'd think about later.

She headed for P.S. 1 on Henry Street, the school where Milagros attended the third grade. A conference had been scheduled between the Acting Assistant Principal, Mrs. Fellingham, one of the school guidance counselors, Ms. Raffaele, and Milagros's teacher, Mrs. Rivera. Elizabeth would lead the meeting as the case social worker.

"I feel that Millie is being abused," the teacher said. Her mouth was set firmly as she glared at the Acting Assistant Principal.

Elizabeth noticed a look of exasperation on the Acting Assistant Principal's face.

"Please go on, Mrs. Rivera," Elizabeth said to the teacher.

"She sometimes even has bruises on her face. The long sleeves, the tights, and the pants she wears conceal her arms and legs, but sometimes I've seen scratches on the backs of her hands. She often looks tired, and she's always poorly dressed," the teacher said. "Although she seems clean," she added.

"And I've been bringing in clothes I've picked up, so she has some decent things to wear to school," the guidance counselor said.

"You are *not* supposed to do that, Ms. Raffaele. Please don't do that again. And none of this is proof of abuse anyway. I don't see how the school can get any more involved," the Acting Assistant Principal said. "There will be a permanent principal coming next week; I think you should bring it up with him or her. I don't see how we can deal with this now."

Elizabeth would never cease to be amazed at the fear, selfishness, cowardice, and ignorance of people.

"Mrs. Fellingham, this cannot wait. If we determine today, and in fact, the determination, one way or another, must be made today, that Milagors is being abused, we have to remove her from her home immediately."

Mrs. Fellingham, clearly unmoved, made an excuse, and left the room.

"Thank you for your input, Mrs. Rivera, Ms. Raffaele. You both have been very helpful. If it weren't for dedicated professionals like you, some of these kids would never be rescued," Elizabeth said.

"We don't know for sure, Ms. Charles, but we both fear the worst as far as the Ruiz home is concerned," Mrs. Rivera said.

"Thank you for coming," Ms. Raffaele said. "I'll go get Milagros for you."

The rap on the door was very soft. The carved oval brass doorknob from an earlier time dwarfed Milagros's small hand as she entered the room and closed the door gently behind her.

Elizabeth was reminded of Alice in Wonderland when the world was big and Alice was small.

She looked almost eager when Elizabeth asked her to sit down. "Did you bring your lunch today?"

"No, not today."

"How would you like to be my guest at McDonald's for lunch?" Elizabeth signed Milagros out of school and they went outside.

They walked along the warm crowded streets of the Lower East Side and talked about Milagros's favorite books without stopping.

When they went back into the school, Elizabeth asked Milagros questions about her home life. Usually with a child this young there were other ways of getting the information she sought, but Milagros's level of maturity allowed Elizabeth to be direct. At first the child was hesitant and fearful. It was obvious that she was ashamed of her home life, although her loyalty to her mother was pathetically evident. Elizabeth now viewed the recent as well as the older bruises. By the time she returned Milagros to her class, there could be no doubt that she was being physically abused by her mother's boyfriend.

As they parted, Milagros turned to Elizabeth, "I like to be called Millie, for short," she said quietly.

Elizabeth went into the Principal's office and called the New York State office in Albany to report the abuse. Then she called her own office, to set into motion the procedure to immediately remove the child from the overt danger of violence and abuse in the home.

The sunlight blinded Elizabeth when she stepped out onto the street in front of P.S. 1. She rubbed her eyes and focused upon another time. The street and its buildings seemed newer, cleaner. Before her was Henry Street. The people were dressed in the clothes of a bygone era, long coats on the women, bowler hats and suits with vests or heavy overcoats on the men. She saw a horse and cart. The street was crowded. A newspaper stand was within close range. She strained to see the date. *The New York Sun*, March 26, 1911. The headlines screamed of a tragic fire in a factory.

Nausea rocked her as she struggled for composure amid curious stares. She couldn't suppress the retching, and again she found herself drenched in sweat. Truly frightened, Elizabeth prayed that a cab would materialize. She reeled and almost fell from dizziness.

"Señorita, come and sit down." A young Hispanic man led Elizabeth toward his store and guided her to a folding chair.

"Are you all right?" His eyes were kind and concerned.

"I'm okay, thank you. I just need to go home."

"I'll get you a taxi," he said.

The cab pulled up in front of Elizabeth's apartment on Remsen Street. Her still shaking hands fumbled with the fare. She saw the cabdriver look at her strangely as she got out of the taxi. She was glad that he pulled away quickly and didn't see her tripping up the steps of the brownstone. She barely answered Mrs. Margolis's friendly greeting.

The shower was hot and steamy, but it could only wash away the perspiration, and not the confusion that fogged her mind.

It must be a form of epilepsy, or, and she had to face the possibility, a brain tumor. If her father were home, she'd tell him now. He'd go to the doctor with her. Maybe it was better that he wasn't home; he'd be worried, too worried.

She was scared. She'd call her family doctor in the morning and make an appointment.

Chapter Four

"Sorry if this hurts," the Mount Sinai Hospital technician said as she tightened the tourniquet on Elizabeth's arm. Elizabeth shivered in the thin hospital gown. "Keep still, please; it'll only take a minute." Elizabeth concentrated on not shivering again in the frigid air conditioning as the needle pierced her skin. Her clothes were in a cubicle several corridors away, and she longed for them now. First one tube and then another quickly filled as the technician deftly finished drawing her blood.

Elizabeth's mind wandered as the technician labeled the tubes and gently placed a band-aid on her arm. Dr. Ellis hadn't even wanted to see her in his office when she called yesterday and told him her symptoms. "I'll set up a full battery of tests at Mount Sinai. Be there tomorrow morning at 9:00 a.m.," he had said.

The technician was smiling at Elizabeth. "You're a million miles away. Don't worry too much. All the tests your doctor ordered are routine, except for the brain and C-T scans," she said.

"Thanks," Elizabeth said. She was glad that the day would end soon. At 3:30 she was scheduled for a complete physical with Dr. Ellis.

It was all over by 4:00. "Call my office for an appointment and we'll go over the results. Everything looks fine so far," Dr. Ellis said before Elizabeth left.

Elizabeth was glad she'd made a date for dinner with her friend and former college roommate, Jane. It had been some months since they'd gotten together, and she missed Jane. The dinner would be a respite from child abuse, and her health concerns.

Elizabeth walked into the Hudson Café a few minutes early. Jane wasn't there which didn't surprise Elizabeth even though the downtown restaurant was close to Jane's loft apartment nearby in

Tribeca. The haunting rhythms of the three-piece jazz ensemble playing softly in the bar held her attention while she waited. Jane finally walked into the restaurant ten minutes late. Elizabeth smiled at her, taken with her beauty and the colorful silk Armani dress which graced Jane's lithe figure.

"How's the mad world of advertising?" Elizabeth asked after she greeted Jane with an embrace.

"How's the mad world of beaten-up kids?" Jane countered. "You look tired. I knew seeing those kids every day would get to you."

"I *am* tired, but just today. Normally I feel great and love the work I do."

"You sure?"

Elizabeth hesitated. "I'm sure, I think." Elizabeth smiled sheepishly and squeezed Jane's hand.

"We'll order, and then we'll talk," Jane said.

The restaurant was alive with sounds-the jazz ensemble, the tinkle of crystal and silver, and the buzz of conversation among the patrons. It was all so normal, Elizabeth thought, looking around the crowded restaurant at the mostly happy faces of the other diners, who seemed to be a dichotomy of both the Wall Street financial types and the artsy who populated this part of the city.

The waiter brought the bone-dry white wine they'd ordered. She felt herself smiling as she relaxed; the trepidation she'd felt about her physical condition when she was at Mount Sinai only a couple of hours ago was gone. Elizabeth decided not to tell Jane about the possibility of a brain tumor. She wanted to simply enjoy this evening with her friend.

"What would you say if I told you that my father is retiring?"

"I wouldn't believe it. Why? When?"

"I'm not sure why, and soon, I think."

"Your father seems too young to retire. I'll bet he's finally met the woman of his dreams."

"I'd like that," Elizabeth said.

"He deserves it," Jane said. She picked up her wine glass and took a sip. "Why haven't we been closer in the last few months? I've missed you."

"I don't know, but I've missed you, too. Let's not let this much time pass again without getting together."

Jane nodded. "We're a long way from Middlebury, aren't we, Beth?"

"Not that long; to me it seems like just yesterday that we were in the dorm, washing each other's hair, staying up all night studying," Elizabeth said.

"Nobody on the floor thought we'd stay roommates for all four years. They said we'd drive each other crazy." They both laughed.

"But they were wrong. They forgot the expression, 'Opposites attract,'" Elizabeth said. "And we couldn't let it go at that. Planning the trip after graduation helped us keep our separation anxiety at bay."

"Yeah, gallivanting around Europe together during that first summer after graduation kept us kids a little longer," Jane said.

"We've shared so much," Elizabeth said.

"It's one of the best things that ever happened to me," Jane said looking into her wine glass.

Elizabeth's eyes burned, and she quelled the tears she felt coming. She knew Jane was gently working her way around to the enigmatic remark Elizabeth had made earlier about her career. Little did Jane know that that was not the only thing that was going on in Elizabeth's life. What if she did have a brain tumor? She knew Jane would be there for her. But she couldn't tell her.

"Me too," she said simply.

"Tell me about your job; you never talk about it when we're together," Jane said.

Elizabeth smiled. She was right. Jane had gotten her relaxed talking about college and their friendship so she could now unload about her job.

"Is it true you took the child specialist position when you could have earned more money as a supervisor or administrator in a position that required the Master's in Social Work?"

"My desire to get an M.S.W. was always geared toward direct practice, not supervision or administration," Elizabeth said.

"Was it worth it?" Jane asked.

"I thought it was worth it; I still want to think it is worth it. I only wanted to work in the field. But it's the kind of job where you can't expect miracles too often." Elizabeth told Jane about Johnny Jackson and Milagros Ruiz and what they'd had to endure. She told Jane how Johnny was now in the system; she told her about Millie's interest in reading. Jane was saddened to hear about Johnny, and fascinated by Millie's interest in books and Jane asked if she could give Johnny and Millie some books.

"Johnny's already in foster care. Millie was removed from her home. She's in a shelter now, waiting for placement in a foster home."

"So she has no place to keep things of her own?"

"Right. But I'm taking her out this weekend. Maybe we could visit you."

They agreed that Elizabeth would bring Millie to Jane's loft apartment on Sunday. The waiter brought their dinner and all the serious conversation was over. Jane entertained Elizabeth with stories of the characters in the advertising agency where she worked. As they left the Hudson Café an hour later, they passed by the live jazz trio featured every Friday night. The trio was playing a soulful rendition of "You Came to Me From Out of Nowhere." The bearded bass player smiled at Jane and Elizabeth as they passed.

Millie was scheduled to go to her own foster family in a few days. The hearing at Family Court had gone smoothly, but Elizabeth had noticed the smoldering hatred in the eyes of the mother's boyfriend as Elizabeth testified and gave her evaluation of the home life of Milagros Ruiz. When she described the abuse Millie had suffered at the hands of Chet King, the mother's boyfriend, he had jumped from his seat screaming obscenities. It had taken two court officers to restrain him. Elizabeth was grateful she'd gotten Millie away from this violent man.

Their weekend together finally came.

"Millie, your cheeks are pink," Elizabeth said as they hugged. Millie jumped up and did a little dance at Elizabeth's words.

"But she hasn't gained any weight yet, Ms. Charles," the nurse on duty at the shelter said. "The doctor was here, and he said there were ketones in her urine, a sign of starvation, and she should be encouraged to eat anything at all, for now."

"Anything?"

"Anything, just as long as she gets calories. She's such a super kid. We're going to miss her this weekend. This child has brought so much life to this place," the nurse said. "And the most amazing thing, Ms. Charles," she whispered, "one or two of the people who work here with the kids are, well, a little burned-out, you know, kind of hard, not really great with kids. She even has *them* smiling sometimes."

"I'm not surprised," Elizabeth said, but she couldn't smile. The shock she felt that such people were working with kids who needed love and protection disgusted her. They started out for Macy's. When they arrived at the corner of Eighth Avenue and 34th Street, Elizabeth put her finger under Millie's chin and directed her gaze upward. She was rewarded by Millie's astonishment at the size of the store.

"See these old wooden slats on the escalators?" Elizabeth asked Millie. "They were exactly the same when I was a child."

"They're very old-fashioned, but I like them," Millie said smiling.

Millie's excitement was contagious, but she became quiet when she saw the endless choices in the large children's department. Elizabeth thought about the bureaucratic Acting Assistant Principal at P.S. 1, and how she didn't want the school guidance counselor to buy Millie any clothes. Elizabeth's conscience pricked her. Was this trip, were the purchases in Millie's best interests? She didn't know if she was doing the right thing or not.

It was not easy to get Millie to accept anything, but finally she allowed Elizabeth to help her pick out some underwear and socks, new jeans, tops, and sneakers. Elizabeth wanted to get some nightgowns, and a dress, but Millie would not allow it. Elizabeth honored her pride and didn't insist.

Millie was obviously pleased, though, with the wardrobe she would bring to her foster home. "I like the cool jeans and the tops. I don't know what I like the best," Millie said when they walked out of Macy's. Millie's excitement made it seem okay, and Elizabeth decided to stop thinking about it and just enjoy the child's pleasure in her new clothes.

Elizabeth smiled at Millie. "Let's try everything on again when we get to my apartment, and maybe you can decide."

"When do we go to your apartment, Miss Charles?" Millie asked.

"Right now, and we're going to have what we call a 'sleep-over,' Millie."

"What's a sleep-over?" Millie asked wrinkling up her little nose.

"A sleep-over is when you eat popcorn and stuff like that, maybe stay up late watching movies, and of course, you have fun."

Al and Joe were walking Thunderball when Elizabeth and Millie arrived at the brownstone on Remsen Street. It was hard to tear Millie away from Thunderball. The two hit it off right away. Mrs. Margolis's head popped out of her door when she heard them come in, but only for an instant. She was gone and then back in a flash with an aluminum foil package of freshly baked chocolate chip cookies for Millie.

When they finally got settled in the apartment, Elizabeth brought out some snacks and a video to watch. Millie was capable of consuming endless cups of sweet tea, Elizabeth learned. The chocolate chip cookies were a big hit as well. Elizabeth put out carrot and celery sticks and sandwiches cut in little triangles, but Millie didn't touch those. At least Elizabeth didn't feel guilty giving Millie junk food. A healthy diet would have to come later. They watched *An American Tail*, and Millie cried when the main character was reunited with his family in the end.

During the night the phone rang, startling Elizabeth out of her sleep. "You're not too bright, Lady." She hung up immediately. It was the same voice she had heard in her office. She hadn't remembered to file the incident report with her supervisor. Now he had her home phone number, she realized with a chill. It was probably Chet King, Millie's mother's boyfriend. She remembered the hatred radiating from his eyes in Family Court. She checked on Millie and was grateful that she had slept through the ringing of the phone.

The visit with Jane on Sunday was as lively as only Jane could manage. The wildly colorful loft with the odd furnishings and huge canvases of Jane's art hanging on every wall fascinated Millie.

"These are my paintings. I painted them all myself. Painting is my hobby," Jane said.

"I wish I could paint like that," Millie said, her eyes shining as she looked at Jane's bright geometric canvases.

"I'll teach you sometime. We're going to be great friends and we'll do fun things together."

"You don't look like a hard-nosed advertising executive in this setting, Jane," Elizabeth said, and Jane just laughed.

Jane never kept junk food in the house, and Elizabeth was doubtful when Jane insisted that Millie try both her scallops sautéed in extra virgin olive oil, as well as her specialty-mushrooms stuffed with crabmeat.

"I'm sorry, Jane. I don't like these," Millie finally said with tears in her eyes.

"Of course you don't, Millie. Don't feel bad. What was I thinking to give you this stuff?" A grilled cheese sandwich was quickly made and devoured by a hungry Millie. The sweet tea was now replaced by a glass of milk. Progress.

"It's time to go," Elizabeth finally said. She had to take Millie back to the shelter. She remembered the nurse's words, "one or two of the people who work here with the kids are, well, a little burned-out, you know, kind of hard, not really great with kids." Please, God, don't let anyone be unkind to Millie, or any of the kids in their care, she prayed.

Millie, Elizabeth could see, was trying very hard not to cry when they arrived at the shelter. Elizabeth squeezed the tiny child gently and told her she'd see her soon. Millie smiled, and Elizabeth helped her to take the shopping bags with her new clothes to the bedrooms in the back. Elizabeth watched the tiny eight-year old proudly unpack the bags. Elizabeth felt like her heart was breaking.

Millie would only be there for a few more days, but what if her foster home wasn't a good one? She thought of her father and how he would tell her that worry was a waste of time. "Wait and see," her father would say.

The only way she could cheer herself was with the thought that her father was coming in tonight from the Bahamas. She had so much to tell him. Even though Ray, his driver, would be picking him up, and he had told her not to meet him, she called the airport to find out if his flight would be on time.

"I'm sorry, that flight is delayed; it's still on the ground in the Bahamas," she was told when she called. Now she wouldn't be able to figure out about what time he'd be home, and therefore when to expect his call telling her that he'd arrived safely.

Knowing him, he'd probably book a different flight, if that were possible. He hated waiting around. She went to bed. He'd call whenever he got to his apartment. She thought about Millie before she fell asleep.

Elizabeth wasn't in a deep sleep when the phone rang and woke her. She hoped to hear her father's voice. Or maybe, and she was afraid when she thought of it, maybe, it was Chet King.

"Miss Charles, this is Ray. The plane your father was supposed to be on has crashed. Maybe he wasn't on it though. I think you should come down to the airport to wait."

Her hands shook as she dialed the number of the cab service which would take her to J.F.K. Airport. She prayed as she had never prayed before on the ride to Kennedy.

The terminal was packed with the families and friends of the passengers. Reporters and camera people from the news media were there too. It was announced that the flight had developed engine trouble and had crashed on the runway while landing. There were over two hundred people on board, and it was known that there were survivors. The airline ground personnel attempted to reassure the waiting crowd, but they did not have information, so no real reassurances could be given.

For two hours, Elizabeth sat or paced, occasionally offering comfort to another distraught family member waiting for word about a loved one. She prayed that her father had changed his plans when the flight was initially delayed, and was not on this plane. Ray, her father's driver, sat grimly, waiting with her.

The news came at five a.m. The names of the dead were posted, and printed sheets were handed out to the people waiting. The tense silence in the crowded waiting room was broken by sobs as a woman seated near Elizabeth became the first person to realize she had suffered a loss.

Elizabeth became the second. Michael Charles was listed among the dead.

Chapter Five

The bridge across the Delaware River from Stockton, New Jersey was a welcome sight but it was the view of the hills and the steeples of Pennsylvania on the other side of the river that filled her with peace. She was almost there, home.

But the familiar feeling of anticipation about going home evaporated as she turned north onto Route 32 in the rented Ford Taurus she was driving. The sickening realization that she was in Pennsylvania without her father, that he would never be with her again, landed with a thud in her stomach.

She tried to concentrate on the narrow river road as it twisted and turned next to the little canal that ran parallel to the great river. Finally she was in Lumberville where she soon made a right, crossing the wooden bridge over the canal to her home. The bridge creaked loudly as the wheels of her car thundered on the wood. She thought fleetingly of Jessica Savitch, the newswoman who had drowned in the canal many years earlier. Her father had told her about that tragedy as a caution when she was getting her driver's license.

The driveway of her home in Lumberville opened before her, and she imagined the old BMW her father used to own sitting parked at the end of it. But, of course, it wasn't there.

She looked up at the stately old fieldstone house. This was where she had spent each of her childhood summers and vacations, winter weekends too. Her father had taught her to swim, ski, tube, and ride horseback here.

A light rain began to fall as she got out of the car. She grabbed her bags from the trunk and looked quickly around at this peaceful place. It was all as it had always been, and that was a comfort to her right now.

She needed to be here to rest. The viewing at Campbell's and the funeral service at St. John the Divine for her father had been simple but had drained her. Michael Charles's prominence in the New York City business community was carefully documented in the *New York Times* obituary, and dozens of business associates had come to offer their condolences. They had no family, but friends like Jane from college, and Ellen, her childhood friend, and many other friends and acquaintances had come to the service too.

After the ordeal of the funeral, she decided to take two weeks off and go to their home in Pennsylvania to begin to heal from her loss and to try to understand that he was gone.

"Elizabeth, Elizabeth." She turned at the sound of her name. The barking of Moss, the big black Labrador Retriever who lived in the next house with his now very flushed mistress, almost drowned out the rest of Ellen's words.

"I'm so glad you came home," Ellen Sanderson, her childhood friend and next-door neighbor, said before she burst into tears and hugged Elizabeth. They walked arm-in-arm toward the house.

"I've aired the place out and put fresh linens on your bed." Ellen began carrying the bags upstairs over Elizabeth's futile protests.

Elizabeth walked into the kitchen, her favorite room in the house. It was an enormous country kitchen with a pale blue ceramic tile floor, two skylights and the original fireplace with a high mantle that her dad had refurbished with Delft tiles. She ran her fingers over the gleaming oak dining set, pulled out one of its sturdy Windsor chairs, and sat down.

She stared at the breathtaking view of the Delaware River through the wall of glass at the back of the kitchen. Moss nosed his massive black head under the hand she had resting on her knee and looked at her expectantly. She got up and opened the French doors, and he bolted through them into the misty rain toward the stream that flowed gently down the hill from Ellen's house onto their property. Her property. Her father's only heir . . . .

Ellen came noisily down the stairs, and her chatter interrupted Elizabeth's thoughts, ". . . upstairs and the cleaning lady has been here every week, just yesterday, in fact." She began laying logs on the fireplace after putting the copper kettle on the range for tea. Elizabeth was grateful for her friend's presence in the house.

"I'm going into New Hope for dinner tonight, Ellen."

"Do you want me to go with you?"

"No, tonight I have to be alone."

"Why put yourself through that? Is it because of the ritual you and your dad had?"

"I don't understand it myself, El. But my father and I always went to Martine's as soon as we got here from the city, and I have to go."

Ellen shook her head. "I think you're giving yourself needless pain, but maybe it's something you just have to get over with somehow. Won't you let me come with you?"

"No, but thanks for understanding," Elizabeth said. They finished their tea in silence.

"I'm going home now; you try to get some rest. If you change your mind and want company tonight at Martine's, just call." They hugged and Ellen was gone.

Later Elizabeth had to swallow the lump in her throat as she entered the quaint and old establishment. Their favorite table in the nook looking out on the little street that ended at the Delaware was occupied, so she sat down at a table close to the fireplace. May in New Hope did not necessarily eliminate the need for a fire which roared and sent forth the fruity aroma that was peculiar to Martine's. The fire soothed her from the chill of the damp, rainy night. The sweltering heat of only days ago in the city seemed far away. The last time they had been together they were in a restaurant; they'd gotten their favorite table.

The proprietor offered his condolences to Elizabeth, and Jenna, their favorite waitress, brought her a glass of Pinot Grigio immediately. Elizabeth was touched by their obvious sorrow at her father's passing. She ordered Martine's famous French onion soup and a salad, but she had no appetite, so she barely touched the food. The magnitude of her loss began to dawn on her, and she didn't know how she would bear it.

The logs in the fire crackled and spit. She looked at the bright orange flames which seemed to be getting brighter and brighter. The sounds of the other diners' voices, the creaking of the old wood floor as the waitresses hurried to serve customers, and raucous laughter from the bar in the front of the restaurant faded as the fire hypnotized her and roared with a life of its own. She couldn't turn away. Her heart began to race as she recognized the onset of one of her hallucinations. But this was different somehow. Suddenly the knowledge that her father was with her, not close by, but truly with her, came to her as surely as any truth she had ever known. She couldn't see him or hear him, but his presence was as palpable as if she could put her arms around him again. Awe and peace replaced her sorrow.

She didn't question the gift she'd received, but she knew that something powerful had injected itself into her grief. Her loss would now be missing her father as if he were away, not that he was gone forever. Her mind reeled as her surroundings came back into focus. She felt none of the nausea or other symptoms she had felt on the other occasions.

On the drive from New Hope back to Lumberville she marveled at the change in her emotional state as she realized that she had work to do at home. The children whose lives might depend on her actions or non-actions needed to be closely monitored. She'd go back and follow up on Johnny, make sure he had a good placement. Millie must miss her, and Elizabeth wanted to be sure she was safe in her new foster home. Michael's estate and business would require her attention too. Home to Brooklyn. Next time she came here, it would be home to Lumberville for a vacation. It was not time for a vacation now. She didn't need to be here to mourn her father's death either. His spirit had been with her tonight and it would be with her always, wherever she was.

The phone was ringing as she entered the warmth of the big fieldstone house. She sat down on the couch in front of the fireplace in the living room as she picked it up.

"Elizabeth, this is Mark Lewis from the D.A.'s office. I'm sorry to interrupt your time away, and I'm sorry for the loss of your father." Mark took a breath, "I read your report on this case and spoke to your office. We all agreed you'd want to know. Milagros Ruiz was taken from school today by her mother's boyfriend and beaten severely. She's in Downtown Hospital in a coma. She's on life support and may not live."

Chapter Six

The child in the bed in the Pediatric Intensive Care Unit at NYU Downtown Hospital did not look like Millie. Endless tubes and the hoses on the respirator obliterated her features. Animation was gone, and the only movement was the rigid up and down of her chest as the respirator pumped air into and out of her lungs.

Elizabeth took the little hand in hers. She closed her eyes and pictured Millie telling her about *Green Mansions*. Tears streamed down her face. Nothing she had ever felt, including Michael's death, could compare with the feeling of utter horror at the near destruction of this innocent child who lay helpless in the bed.

She felt a hand on her shoulder and she turned to see Mark Lewis.

"I'm glad you came. I can only imagine how hard this is for you. There really isn't anything to do here. Will you come with me, and we'll talk?"

Elizabeth nodded and wordlessly followed Mark Lewis through the winding corridors of Downtown Hospital to the street where he hailed a cab. They soon arrived at his office.

He took her jacket and hung it on a hanger on the back of his door. Elizabeth sat down on one of the chairs in front of his desk.

"I'll be right back," he said and returned a moment later with coffee for the two of them. He handed her a steaming cup, "Dark, no sugar, right?"

She wanted to smile to acknowledge that he had remembered correctly, but she couldn't. Her hands started to shake, spilling coffee on her skirt. He took the coffee from her and put it next to his on the front of his desk. He sat in the other chair next to her and took her hand.

"We have to make sure justice is done. We have to lock this guy up for what he did."

Mark explained how there had been an eyewitness to the beating. It was Millie's mother.

Elizabeth told Mark about the phone calls she'd received and her suspicion that they may have been made by Chet King. Elizabeth told him everything she knew about Millie and her mother. Mark took many notes. A half hour later, Mark called the detectives on the case only to learn that Chet King, the boyfriend of Mrs. Ruiz, had not yet been picked up.

"Don't worry, we'll get him," Mark was assured by Detective Dominic Gentilli.

"I'm going back to the hospital," Elizabeth said.

"Okay, I'll put you in a cab, and I'll meet you there later. There are a few things I have to finish up here first."

"Please don't come to the hospital, Mark. You wouldn't be going there again today."

"I would, Elizabeth. I want to be with Millie, and you too." He put his hands on her shoulders. "I know I'm a stranger to you, but I'd like to be your friend. I can see you're taking all this very hard. I know you just lost your father. I'd like to be with you if you don't mind."

She hesitated. "Thanks," she said.

Elizabeth remained at the hospital all day. The feeling of horror at the child's condition alternated with rage at the man who had done it. She prayed for Millie as she tried to quell the anguish she felt looking at the tiny form in the hospital bed. There was no sign of Millie's mother nor were there any other visitors.

"Are you the social worker on this case?" a young doctor who approached Millie's bed asked Elizabeth.

Elizabeth nodded.

"I'm afraid the prognosis often isn't too good in these cases." He paused and scratched his head. "For some reason I feel hopeful though."

Elizabeth's spirit picked up at the doctor's words and his kind smile. He then went on to list Millie's injuries which ranged from bruises and abrasions to swelling of the brain due to several severe blows to the head with a blunt instrument.

A nurse who looked well-seasoned whispered to Elizabeth, "Dr. Piscali can't face reality; he won't admit anyone will die."

Elizabeth refused to be discouraged by the nurse, however, and said quietly, "Well then, God bless Dr. Piscali."

Looking at the grave injuries suffered by Millie, she thought of her own health. At Michael's wake, Dr. Ellis had come up to her. "I know you haven't had time to call. Your tests. All of them came back negative. From them and my examination, we have learned that you are a particularly healthy young woman."

The information hadn't meant anything then. But now she looked at Millie wishing that her own health could be taken into the small body.

"Hi." Mark entered the room and approached Elizabeth. As she turned fully to face him, the sunlight which was pouring into the room blinded her. She tried to reach for his hands to experience again the warmth and comfort that seemed to emanate from them. But the physical reality of Mark Lewis began to fade slowly.

She was on the street in an unfamiliar place. Young women were jumping out of the windows of a building above. A body crashed to the concrete inches from her feet. She stared at the broken and lifeless form of a beautiful woman in a long skirt and high collared blouse. She was no more than twenty years old. Her face was smudged with dirt. Wisps of hair loose from the Gibson hairstyle circled her face. Elizabeth screamed in horror at the tragic death. She saw another body on the sidewalk, dead from the fall from many stories above.

She felt as though her own body weighed tons. She was unable to move her arms and legs. She opened her eyes cautiously and saw Mark Lewis's anxious face above her.

"You screamed and passed out. Has this ever happened to you before?"

Elizabeth sat up slowly. She was violently nauseated but managed to suppress the urge to retch. "I'm sorry; I've been having peculiar spells of some kind lately. I want to tell Millie I'll be back, and then I have to go home."

"Let me get a doctor to look at you," Mark said.

"No, no, Mark. I have to get home," Elizabeth said.

In thirty minutes she was in her apartment sitting on the couch, a hot cup of tea in her hands, and telling Mark Lewis the entire story of the hallucinations she had been having.

He listened quietly, only his eyes and face expressing his feelings of sympathy and support. He occasionally squeezed Elizabeth's hand when she faltered.

When she was finished talking, she was spent. She didn't care if Mark Lewis thought she was mad. She had to tell someone.

Mark silently stood up, and placing his hands on her upper arms, drew her to her feet. He put his arm around her and led her to her bedroom. He helped her into bed and pulled the comforter over her. It wasn't long before he could hear her breathing softly. He left the room and closed the door behind him.

He picked up the phone in Elizabeth's kitchen and punched in a familiar number. "Doris, it's Mark. I have a new friend; she's been having problems that sound like just your thing." They talked for a few minutes before hanging up.

Chapter Seven

Doris Fisher was in her late fifties. Her forehead was very high, a feature that was attractively played down by a wisp of bangs. A long, thin, aristocratic nose added to the impression of wisdom and scholarship.

Elizabeth felt an instant rapport when she looked at the woman's kind face despite her inability to see into her eyes which appeared as crinkly slits when she smiled.

"It's temporal lobe, Miss Charles," she said when Elizabeth described the hallucinations she'd experienced.

"Do you mean that there is a tumor there that was undetected by the medical tests I took?"

"No, the temporal lobe is the part of the brain referred to as the great integrator. It takes in all of the perceptual information our senses have to offer and mixes in our emotions and memories. There is a great deal of electrical activity in this area of the brain which we do not understand."

"You think this was some type of seizure, an electrical disturbance?"

"I'm not sure yet, but if you are willing, I'd like to try to find out."

Elizabeth hesitated. She wanted to direct her attention to Millie.

Doris seemed to know she was thinking, "We can work around your schedule," she said quietly. They spent the next hour beginning the job of trying to find out about Elizabeth's hallucinations.

Dominic Gentilli stared at the case on his desk at the 5th Precinct. After twenty-seven years on the force, he still wasn't inured to the brutality that surrounded him in his daily work. He often wondered why he had chosen it, a foolish reflection he too often indulged in the older he got. This would be his last year. The youngest of his three children was now finished with college.

Marie had been begging him to retire. Ten years ago they bought a beautiful piece of land in North Carolina; three years ago they started building a house on the wooded acreage. Marie had spent the last year going back and forth, buying furniture, and putting the finishing touches on decorating the place. They had saved and planned for this for so long, and now they would be able to realize their dream. He'd wrap up his career after this case.

That poor little girl. He remembered his visit to the hospital at the beginning of the investigation. Mark Lewis had been there at the time. He saw the anguish he himself felt at the sight of the little girl reflected on the younger man's face. At fifty-two he had long since learned to hide his feelings.

"Morning, Dom, any progress?" Dominic looked up at his young partner with his perfectly trimmed moustache and bright brown eyes. Miguel Martinez had stepped into the squad room, his crisp appearance a sharp contrast to everything inside the shabby office, including Dominic himself.

Dom watched as Martinez stripped off his jacket revealing his shoulder holster and 9MM automatic against a shirt so white and starched that it looked like it belonged on a Wall Street executive rather than a detective on the Lower East Side. It was fitted to his muscular body and seemed to shine against his light brown skin. Martinez turned around and smiled at Dom. Like a son, this kid, Dom thought with affection. He had no doubt that Marty would be the Commissioner some day.

"No, Pardner. We got no new leads." They sat over the case and planned the strategy for the day. Despite the alerts, the NYPD had not yet located Chet King.

"Let's go back to the building and hit the apartments where no one answered yesterday," Dom said.

"Good idea; let's go." After an hour of knocking and bell ringing, they had about as much as they did the first time they had visited Millie's building on St. James Place.

"Let's go to Lewis's office and tell him what we have," Marty said.

"You mean what we don't have," Dom said.

Marty nodded, and a few minutes later they were in the offices of the District Attorney.

Chapter Eight

"Your work is suffering, and I'm afraid you'll have to immediately stop seeing the Ruiz case. It was entirely unprofessional of you to get emotionally involved in the first place. I've never heard of a social worker taking a child out of the shelter or group home. You even bought clothes for the case. What you did was inappropriate."

Elizabeth burned under the criticism. She believed that each child was important and not just a "case." She knew that most of the child specialist workers felt the same way, but that there were a few heartless bureaucrats sprinkled throughout the system. She could even understand that the tragedies of this work could burn people out and that the appearance of cold indifference may be the way Angela Simms protected herself.

"You're right about my neglecting my work, Angela. I'd like to request a temporary leave of absence," Elizabeth said.

"I know your father's death has made your work poor and your judgment worse, but you of all people realize what a burden that puts on the other child specialists. If you were on a temporary leave, we wouldn't be able to fill your position because it wouldn't be a true vacancy. You know what our budget is like. We'd have to split up your cases among all the social workers and they have too much already. Our ability to help the children would be compromised even further than it already is. I must insist that you resume your duties or resign."

Elizabeth sighed. She knew Angela was right. But it was so hard to let go of this job. She'd dreamed of making a difference here. "I'll let you know what I decide in the morning," she answered.

It was five p.m. and Elizabeth headed straight for the hospital. Millie lay exactly as before.

A middle-aged man was seated next to the bed. He looked clean but untidy somehow. His wrinkled jacket stayed wrinkled as he stood and turned toward to Elizabeth. She saw faded blue eyes shining out of a tired but friendly face. He extended his hand. She put her small hand into his meaty one.

"I'm Dom Gentilli," he said. His deep voice was subdued and Elizabeth saw how affected he was at the sight of Millie. "You must be Elizabeth Charles."

"You're the detective. I heard Mark Lewis speaking to you on the phone when I was in his office."

Gentilli nodded and looked over at Millie, shaking his head sadly. "We have an eyewitness to what that monster did to this child but we have no leads on where he is."

"King," Elizabeth breathed. "Millie will never be safe while he's free." Elizabeth remembered the violence of the man and started to shake at the thought. She told the detective about the phone call at her office, the feeling someone was watching her outside her apartment the night she brought Johnny Jackson to the shelter, and the phone call to her home when Millie was there for the weekend.

Dom knew about these events as Mark had already told him but he listened to Elizabeth.

"It's okay, it's gonna be okay." His voice was husky and soft. She felt comforted somehow by his words. She knew she was missing her father in this crisis and this man was a welcome substitute at this moment.

Marty came into the room silently. It was obvious that he had something to tell his partner, but Dom wouldn't allow the formalities to pass unobserved despite the urgency on Marty's face.

"Miss Charles, this is Detective Miguel Martinez; Elizabeth Charles, Pardner."

Marty's eyes sparkled with intelligence and warmth, and Elizabeth liked him instantly.

"Elizabeth," she said extending her hand.

"Marty," he said as he clasped it.

"King has been spotted. We've got three units on the way."

"Let's go," shouted Gentilli. "It's gonna be okay, Honey," he said to Elizabeth.

She held Millie's small hand for over an hour, talking and singing softly to her and stroking her cheek and forehead, wondering what was happening with the detectives.

"Don't you sometimes think she hears you?"

Elizabeth hadn't heard Dr. Piscali enter the room.

"Do *you* think she does?'

"I don't know if she does, but I believe, I like to believe, she does. Right now her condition is the same."

A caring doctor. Millie had a caring doctor. Thank God. She told him that the police had a lead on the man who put her in this condition.

"I hope they get him," Dr. Piscali said. Elizabeth noticed his hands tighten into fists.

The apartment where King lived had been under surveillance since the beating. Millie's mother had not been seen entering or exiting since they questioned her initially. Several police units were in front of the projects with their red lights flashing brightly when Gentilli and Martinez arrived.

"We lost him," the officer reported.

The detectives couldn't hide their disappointment.

"Come quick," one of the other officers shouted.

They ran into the lobby of the run down building on St. James Place. The super of the building was standing in the middle of the lobby wringing his shaking hands. The dark skin of his face glistened with perspiration as he spoke in a mixture of Spanish and English and told the young officer that he had found a body in the garbage room in the basement.

"Dead, the lady, she is dead."

"Show us, Señor," Gentilli said.

He was obviously reluctant to return to where he'd found the body but he led the officers to the garbage room.

The detectives entered the filthy room. A blend of odors, mostly of spoiling foods, assaulted their nostrils. The nude body was carelessly wrapped in black plastic garbage bags. They'd have to wait for the Medical Examiner, but they could see bruises on her throat and neck. She had probably been strangled. Her body was bruised and lacerated elsewhere too. Her face was partially caved in from the beating.

"It's the girl's mother," Gentilli said.

Gentilli and Martinez looked at each other. "Now we have him for homicide," Marty said.

"We gotta get him first," Dom said.

Chapter Nine

"Here's my resignation, Angela. You're right; I can't concentrate now. I'm not giving the agency my best."

Angela took the letter from Elizabeth. "You're a fool to throw your career away over one case," she said before spinning her chair around to face the computer behind her. She began to type, immediately dismissing Elizabeth.

Elizabeth was glad she hadn't responded. A confrontation would have been pointless. She threw the few personal possessions she kept in her cubby into a box and went through each of her cases, bringing them up to date and making additional notes on each one for the child specialist who would get them. She felt a stab of remorse that she was leaving these kids but resolved to find a way to help abused kids that was outside the bureaucracy. She realized suddenly that because of her father's hard work, she was a woman of considerable means which would free her to do almost anything she wanted to do.

After a couple of hours of work and a few goodbyes to her colleagues, Elizabeth went to the mail room and mailed the box with her personal things to herself. She left the building then, her emotions over leaving this part of her life in a frenzy of sadness, anger, regret, and relief.

She hopped on the subway for the short ride uptown to New York University where she was meeting Jane. They had spoken on the phone but she hadn't seen Jane since Michael's funeral. Jane wanted to go to the hospital to see Millie and they had agreed to meet at Washington Square Park, have a quick dinner, and go to the hospital together. When she ascended the subway stairs at West 4th Street, she was blinded by bright sunshine. A quick call to the hospital on her cell phone revealed that Millie was the same.

She began to walk. Elizabeth was startled when a sudden downpour drenched her. Darkness replaced the clear sunny skies of only a moment before. She lowered her head against the torrential rain and ran toward Washington Square Park.

Soon she had difficulty walking because of the congestion of people. She began to feel disoriented by the mass of people that filled the street and the park. A sea of black umbrellas and a crowd numbering in the thousands filled every inch of space.

Elizabeth raised her head and looked toward the sky where she saw hundreds of women leaning out of the windows of buildings and standing on the roofs. A wailing, screaming cry began somewhere near her and rose to a deafening crescendo as it swelled undiminished through the crowd walking in the teeming rain. There were dozens of policemen in long black raincoats lining the streets, their faces full of concern.

Elizabeth saw a group of young women supporting one who had swooned. She recognized her with a start. It was the beautiful young woman in the long dress. Her red hair was in disarray as it wisped out of the bun on top of her head. Grief and anguish distorted her face. Through the disorientation of knowing she was hallucinating, Elizabeth heard the woman groaning, "Killed my friend, killed my friend." The slight figure shivered in the chilling downpour that soaked her coat. The icy wind tugged fiercely at her hair and the thin garments she wore. Mud oozed out of her shoes.

Elizabeth needed to help the girl who was so obviously distressed. She walked to her side. The lovely face turned up to her, and she reached for Elizabeth's hand. Elizabeth felt as though she were falling as the scene seemed to be getting smaller and smaller. Fleetingly she noticed a streamer flying in the wind, "We Demand Fire Protection," it read. The lovely young face grew blurry and dim as Elizabeth felt herself moving farther and farther away.

"Probably drunk or on drugs," she heard as she woke on her back to bright sunshine in Washington Square Park with a crowd of curious on-lookers surrounding her and murmuring.

She hoped Jane would forgive her for not showing up as minutes later she jumped into a cab to Doris Fisher's office.

Chapter Ten

Doris Fisher never took her eyes off Elizabeth as she told her about her day from the time she left her job in the morning to the events in Washington Square Park in the afternoon. She described the last hallucination, the rain, the marchers, and the young woman with the red hair.

"After you were here the last time I tried to check on the article you'd seen in *The Sun* on March 26, 1911. I couldn't get that article, so I checked *The New York Times* of the 26th. There was a terrible fire the day before, on March 25th. One hundred and forty-six people were killed. It was a fire that took place in a factory where mostly young immigrant women, girls actually, worked." She paused and looked at Elizabeth carefully. "Many of them died from jumping out of the building. The building is near Washington Square Park. Do you know anything about that fire?"

Elizabeth began to tremble. She vividly remembered the young woman crashing to the sidewalk close to where she was standing. "Is it possible that the hallucinations are some way of seeing actual events of the past?"

"That's what I think. Such things have been reported by many others." Doris came from around her desk and sat next to Elizabeth. "It has been referred to as a 'time slip' by some. A person's environment suddenly disappears, and he or she is in a scene from the past. Sometimes the hallucination or vision only lasts a moment; sometimes it can last a half hour or more. That part is unpredictable. It can also involve some kind of encounter and interaction with those people from the past."

Elizabeth had not moved.

"You are deeply upset and frightened by what I just told you." She picked up Elizabeth's hand and squeezed it gently. "You've been through a lot lately. You've suffered through the unexpected loss of your beloved father, the grave injuries to a little girl you love, and you feel responsible for that in some way, I think. You've even lost your job. All these things have happened since you've been having the hallucinations. That much stress is a great deal to cope with." She stopped speaking, a thoughtful expression on her kind face.

"There are things happening that we don't understand, yet. But we will, we will learn what is going on with you. I'll be working on it every day, and I have many clues to use. You must have faith that you will be able to go on with your life-that there's an end to this.

"In the meantime you must be very good to yourself. You must get plenty of rest and recreation. I don't say this lightly. You must reduce the stress. I know this sounds impossible because of Millie's condition, but you must try. Use the opportunity of not working to do things you enjoy."

Elizabeth knew Doris was right. She was feeling the stress of these recent events and was overwhelmed.

"I would like to see you every day if there is a way you can swing it. If not, you must call me every day. I will continue my research and let you know what I have learned."

"Every day," she repeated. "What about your practice?" Mark had told her that Doris was a physician who also had a doctorate in psychology. She was seeing Elizabeth, not just as a patient, but because she was a friend of Mark's. Elizabeth knew Doris wanted to see her every day for a reason. It alarmed her.

"Your problem is of great interest to me, which is why I wanted to see you when Mark told me about you. Now that I know you, I feel compelled to get this resolved as quickly as possible."

Elizabeth felt and saw the concern Doris had for her behind her formal explanation and was grateful that despite the losses in her life, she still had people who cared about her.

The intercom beeped and Elizabeth saw Doris's face crinkle into the smile that always made her eyes seem to close. She said, "Send him in."

"Mark is here."

Mark Lewis walked in and Elizabeth's heart began to beat faster. He came toward her after smiling and nodding to Doris. He pulled her out of the chair gently and put his arms around her. She returned his warm embrace with feeling.

"I called Doris's office and her receptionist said you were here. I told her not to let you leave before I got here. I got a cab right away. I called the hospital before I left the office too. There's no change. Can I persuade you to go out to dinner with me? We can go to the hospital after dinner."

"Go, my dear," Doris urged.

"I think that's just what the doctor ordered," Elizabeth said.

They headed for Greenwich Village. "The place is bring-your-own-bottle so we'll stop and buy a good bottle of wine to go with Antonio's meal."

A bell tinkled softly as Mark opened the curtained glass door to the tiny northern Italian storefront restaurant called "Antonio's." Elizabeth's sagging appetite was stimulated by the aromas coming from the kitchen.

"Antonio, I brought a special friend," Mark said as the proprietor stepped from the back in response to the bell.

The immaculate white apron actually crackled from the starch in it when Antonio extended his hand to Elizabeth.

"Welcome to Antonio's, Signorina. You must tell me what you like, and I'll make it special for you."

Antonio led them to a table by the window where they not only had an excellent view of a row of the elegant old brownstone houses across the street, but also of the strolling Villagers enjoying the beautiful day.

Elizabeth looked around the tiny restaurant which had but ten tables. Two other couples were eating with obvious enjoyment. Italian opera music played softly. The marble topped tables and the antique oak sideboard with its cloudy mirror near the entrance to the kitchen in the restaurant delighted her.

"You like it here, I see," said Mark.

"It's enchanting," she said.

Mark was enchanting too, his face and form, his voice, his smile, his hair which she wanted to run her fingers through, the slight limp when he walked, his warm handshake, his moustache. She felt that current, the same thing she'd felt when she first met him. In the middle of all this stress, during this brief respite in this quaint and lovely restaurant, she would pretend life was normal.

They asked Antonio to select something for them that he thought they'd like. He scrutinized the bottle of wine and nodded in approval.

"Something for this fine wine, I think."

Antonio prepared a glorious pasta and a veal dish. This was after serving a few different appetizers, giving them plenty of time to talk and unwind.

"You look almost happy," Mark said after Antonio brought the espresso. "I've never seen you look happy before. You've always been cheerful or friendly or businesslike, but I've never seen you happy."

Elizabeth laughed. "It's being here with you right now that's making me happy, Mark. Actually, I almost always, I always used to, I mean, feel happy, truly contented and satisfied, but lately . . ."

"Lately, has been rough, Elizabeth Charles."

"Yes, lately has been rough. My father, Millie . . . But having you as a friend, and Doris and Dominic and Marty . . ."

"Dominic and Marty?"

"Yeah, Detectives Gentilli and Martinez. I really like those guys. I never dreamed I'd make so many new friends all of a sudden. Oh, no," Elizabeth said suddenly. "I'm talking about new friends and I forgot all about Jane." She explained about her date with Jane at NYU when she had the inexplicable episode in Washington Square Park and went to Doris's office.

They thanked Antonio who was pleased at the tribute they had paid to his superb meal. Once outside Elizabeth called Jane on her cell phone. There was no answer on her cell phone or at Jane's loft, so Elizabeth left a message on the answering machine. They decided to take a cab to the hospital and then to Elizabeth's apartment in Brooklyn Heights where Elizabeth would try to reach her again.

They were disappointed to find Millie exactly the same. Elizabeth stroked her forehead and talked to her softly, but there was no response.

As they were going over the Brooklyn Bridge, Mark put his arm around Elizabeth and kissed her gently.

"I think I'm falling in love for the first time in my life," he whispered. She almost asked him if that was the line he used on all the women he met, but when she looked into his eyes, she realized he meant the words, words that were so welcome but confusing right now.

He read her thoughts. "I just want you to know how I feel. For now I'll be your friend and help you through this time. Later we'll see what happens, if that's okay with you."

"I want to touch your hair." They laughed at the non sequitur. She imagined that his thick wiry black hair would be almost as impenetrable as her own abundance of auburn hair if she tried to get her fingers through it.

They kissed some more, but they didn't speak for the rest of the trip.

Mark insisted on walking her to her door but stopped where the pale blue carpet ended at the threshold. She'd forgotten to lock the top deadbolt lock, she realized. She opened the bottom lock in the doorknob and turned around.

Mark kissed her lightly. "I'll email you when I get home tonight."

"I love emailing," she said. I feel like we have so much to talk about."

They couldn't resist some more kissing and then Elizabeth went inside.

After hearing the deadbolt turn from inside, he ran quickly down the stairs, his thoughts full of Elizabeth and the evening they had spent together.

The first scream caused him to freeze for an instant. It was followed by unrelenting screams of pure terror, Elizabeth's pure terror. The front door of one of the apartments on the hallway opened as he bolted back to Elizabeth's apartment door. She didn't stop screaming as he pounded on the door calling her name begging her to open it. An elderly woman in a faded housedress ran up the stairs as fast as her arthritic knees would allow and handed Mark a key.

"Open it, open it," the landlady ordered. Mark fumbled with the key and got the two locks open. The woman was behind him when they got into the living room to find Elizabeth standing over the body of a young woman, a young woman lying in a pool of blood, an apparent knife wound in her chest.

"Oh, Jane," the old woman said, "Poor Janie, poor Janie." The woman fell to her knees and continued to cry as she rocked back and forth.

Elizabeth's screaming had not diminished. Sirens screamed in accompaniment as Mark tried to pry Elizabeth out of the room. Her eyes were opened wide with pupils dilated as she finally turned from Jane's body and looked at him. Then she fainted in his arms.

Chapter Eleven

She woke up on her bed. Mark was sitting on one side holding her hand and Mrs. Margolis, her landlady, was on the other, crying softly. The horror of seeing Jane lifeless, her beautiful, vibrant friend, murdered, began to wash over her slowly.

A uniformed police officer entered the bedroom.

"There's a doc here, Mr. Lewis, a Dr. Fisher. She said you called her."

"Doris," Elizabeth whispered.

"Let her in," Mark said abruptly. Doris entered with her bag and began to speak soothingly to Elizabeth as she prepared a syringe. Mark rolled up her sleeve as Doris swabbed her arm and gave her an injection. Elizabeth was out immediately.

"She needs to be out because she can't handle this right now."

"I'll be right back," Mark said. "I have to give my statement to the detectives." Doris took Mark's place on the bed. Mrs. Margolis slipped out of the room quietly.

"Did we contaminate the crime scene in any way?" Mark asked the first officer he saw as he walked into the living room and watched as the NYPD did their work. Jane's body was being photographed.

"No, I don't think so," the officer said. Although he hadn't known her, Mark had to look the other way as an officer photographed the body which was outlined in chalk. It would be removed after the ME had done the preliminary examination. The place was also being dusted and anything which might provide clues or act as evidence was bagged, labeled and removed.

"Dom, Marty," Mark said as he shook the hands of the two detectives just entering the apartment.

"Glad you called us, Mark," Dom said solemnly.

The 5th Precinct was not involved in this case. The 76th Brooklyn precinct had jurisdiction, but Mark believed that there may turn out to be a link to Chet King and felt that Dom and Marty should be here.

"How's Elizabeth?" Dominic asked in his gruff voice.

"She's under sedation."

"Elizabeth, under sedation?" Dom Gentilli frowned.

Mark told them how Elizabeth discovered Jane's body. Dom just shook his head, and Marty looked around helplessly and walked toward one of the Brooklyn detectives.

"Can I talk to the witness?" he asked the detective.

"Sure, man, we can use all the help we can get."

Marty and Dom approached Mrs. Margolis gently. "I know you're upset, Mrs. Margolis. But would it be all right if we asked you some questions now?"

Two men entered the apartment. They went to Mrs. Margolis and hugged her.

"This is Al and this is Joe; they live downstairs, in the apartment under the stoop," Mrs. Margolis said to the detectives.

"Please tell us Elizabeth is okay," Al said.

"She'll be okay. Right now I have to take Mrs. Margolis's statement. You can stay with her if she wants you to."

"Yes, please, I would like them to stay with me. I'm ready to give my statement now." Mrs. Margolis sat up straight and threw back her shoulders as far as her osteoporosis would allow. The proud gesture was not lost on Detective Martinez. "You want to help, don't you, Mrs. Margolis?"

She nodded and the pain of the experience showed on her face as she began to speak.

"Jane rang my doorbell . . . ," she paused. Marty decided not to interrupt by asking her the times or anything else. He didn't want to break her concentration and he could always get the details later.

"She was cheerful, but she seemed a little anxious. She was looking for Elizabeth. Elizabeth and she were to meet at NYU, she said. She'd gotten tied up at her job and couldn't get away. She never made it to NYU. She couldn't reach Elizabeth on her cell phone. She thought she'd come straight here and wait for Elizabeth. She thought they'd go to dinner . . ."

All this had been said very rapidly when Mrs. Margolis suddenly stopped, her shoulders now hunched over once again as she started to cry.

"I knew Jane. She was Elizabeth's best friend. I told her I'd let her in to Elizabeth's apartment. We walked up the stairs together, and she told me about the funny commercials she thinks up. She always wears such pretty things too. She asked me how I was. What a sweet girl she always is, like Elizabeth, polite and doesn't talk down to me because I'm old. She knows I am a woman inside this old wrecked body and she treats me like that. She's so young. If I hadn't let her in, she would be alive."

By now Mrs. Margolis was barely able to remain calm. They'd have to question her later. Al and Joe comforted her, and Marty sent a patrolman for Doris.

"It wasn't your fault; it wasn't your fault," Dom said over and over to Mrs. Margolis, wondering how many times he'd uttered those words in his twenty-seven year long career. Marty held her hand and noticed a number tattooed on her arm. A Holocaust survivor. Here was a woman who had had enough suffering. How could he possibly help her? Nevertheless, he tried, too, to assure her that it was not her fault.

Doris spoke to Mrs. Margolis and the two detectives discreetly left the room. Al and Joe remained by her side.

Dom and Marty went back into Elizabeth's bedroom where Mark was seated by the bed. "She looks like Sleeping Beauty," Dom said. The three men looked at her, each thinking his own thoughts, when they turned to each other simultaneously.

Gentilli expressed what was on their minds, "We gotta have her wake up good." The simple thought was understood by all of them.

"That's right, Gentlemen," Doris said as she entered. "She's a strong woman, but right now she's in a fragile state." She sighed.

"What should we do, Doc?" Gentilli asked.

"Let's bring her to my apartment," Mark said.

"Okay, for now," Doris agreed. "Mrs. Margolis is back in her apartment with her two tenants to take care of her. I've given her a sedative if she needs it; let's go."

They got Elizabeth on her feet and bundled her into the detectives' unmarked car. Doris would follow in her own car.

Mark held Elizabeth tightly through the ride. She stayed asleep.

Chapter Twelve

She didn't know where she was at first. An unpleasant metallic taste in her mouth nauseated her. Drugs, sedatives, she thought. She looked around and saw masculine effects around the double bed she found herself carefully tucked into. Elizabeth knew then that she was in Mark Lewis's bedroom.

Then the memory of finding Jane assaulted her. The sight of Jane's bloodied body would stay forever in her mind. She checked the sob that caught in her throat. She heard low voices outside the room.

She rose from the bed and had to steady herself. She felt weak and dizzy. She was wearing her dress which was now wrinkled and uncomfortable. A chill went through her body. Mark's bathrobe had been placed at the foot of the bed. She gratefully wrapped it around herself.

The door of the bedroom was ajar and she heard Dom Gentilli's voice, "Ya gotta face it, Mark. She's in real danger. I think King is after her." She heard Dom talking to Mark about the two phone calls and the night she came home late and thought someone was in the shadows outside her brownstone.

"You think he surprised Jane and he had to kill her to avoid . . ."

"Yeah, I do."

Marty nodded in agreement.

They all looked up as she came through the door. They rose as a group as if on cue.

"Sit down; I'm okay." She smiled shakily.

Mark moved forward and put his arm around her protectively as he led her to a chair in his comfortable living room. She didn't remember coming here.

"How do you feel?" Doris asked.

"I'm fine. I feel fine."

"Sure," Dom said to Elizabeth. "And don't you guys scare her," he added as he slipped into the kitchen. He returned a few minutes later carrying a steaming cup of tea for Elizabeth.

"I told you not to scare her," he said.

"I wanted to know about all of it, Dom; really I did. I'm glad they filled me in," Elizabeth said.

Mark had told Elizabeth that they suspected Millie's mother's boyfriend, Chet King, of Jane's murder. Fingerprints had been found at the scene which they hoped would identify King as the murderer. He had probably gotten into Elizabeth's apartment by picking the lock, entering, and then waiting. Instead of Elizabeth, Jane had surprised him.

"He was after you," Gentilli conceded, "but maybe this bungled attempt and his having to murder Jane will be the end of it. How many risks can he take? The phone calls, being outside your home, he's been stalking you. He wanted to get revenge on you for taking Millie out of the home."

"It is more than likely that he'll be looking out for himself and concentrating on hiding or disappearing," Marty added.

"We can't take any chances though. Elizabeth, I'd like you to stay here with me until we catch this guy," Mark said.

"No, Mark. I realized when I woke up in your room where I want to be."

"You mustn't go back to your apartment now, Elizabeth," Doris said softly.

"I'll never go there again, not ever," Elizabeth said firmly. "I'm going to move into my father's apartment. I'm going to move in there permanently."

"Where is his apartment?" Marty asked.

"Fifth and 72nd."

The four of them looked at one another. As one, they knew this was a good idea—a building with security, a twenty-four hour doorman. Mark wouldn't be able to stay with her all the time anyway. And his place was on E. 92nd between Madison and Park, only a cab ride away.

"Marty and me'll go back to Brooklyn and ask Mrs. Margolis to put together some of your things. We'll bring 'em to your new place tomorrow," Dom said.

"I've got to see Millie in the hospital," Elizabeth said.

"We'll go. Dom and I will visit tonight and call you and let you know how she is," Marty said.

"I'll go too," Doris said.

"Please stay here for tonight, and I'll take you there in the morning," Mark added.

Elizabeth agreed to stay with Mark and thanked the two detectives and Doris. She gave Dom the address of her father's apartment.

Doris turned to her as she was leaving, "Here's some sedation if you need it, but I think you'll be okay. Call me if you need me, or if you have any more psychic experiences."

"We don't call them hallucinations?" Elizabeth asked wryly.

"No, we don't," Doris said as she kissed Elizabeth on the cheek.

"Hallucinations or not, they're better than real life," she whispered.

Mark closed the door and threw the deadbolt. Their eyes locked for a moment and they were in each other's arms.

Elizabeth's fragile mental state and Mark's concern for her made anything more unthinkable. The time was not right for true intimacy, and they both knew it.

Mark walked Elizabeth into the bedroom and lay down beside her on top of the covers. She knew he'd wait until she fell asleep before he left the room to sleep on the pullout sofa in the living room.

She heard her own screams, but they seemed far away and she couldn't wake up right away. Breathless, she realized she was in Mark's apartment. She heard him running to her. He held her tightly and spoke her name over and over until she was calm.

"Jane was begging me to save her. I saw King stabbing her, and she was begging me to help her. I was frozen and couldn't move." She sobbed quietly now as Mark caressed her hair, stroked her back, and gently rocked her in his arms.

"It was a nightmare; it's okay. It's all over." Her breathing became regular and she felt herself drifting back to sleep.

"Don't turn off the light," she said.

"I won't, and I'll stay with you."

"Yes, thank you," she said.

"I'm here," she heard him say before she fell asleep.

Chapter Thirteen

It was seven a.m. when he rolled over and found her gone. He jumped up. She was on the phone, and he was surprised and relieved to see that she was her business-like and confident self.

"Dr. Piscali tells me that Millie is okay, the same. I'm going to petition the court for custody and have her moved to a private hospital for coma patients."

"That will take time, but it's do-able," Mark said.

"I hope we can take a few short cuts. We have to get it done. I've spoken to my father's lawyer, and he'll handle everything. My father's co-op on Fifth Avenue is owned jointly with me, as are most of his assets, so the lawyer sees no problems in that area. I have to have my things packed and moved from Brooklyn to Manhattan," Elizabeth said.

"I'm sure Mrs. Margolis will do that for you," Mark said.

"I've made coffee," she said. "I hope your don't mind my nosing around in your kitchen." His smile told her that he didn't.

Over coffee she told him about her last phone call. Dom said that Jane's body would be released from the medical examiner's office later that day. He told her how he had notified her family last night and that arrangements had been made for services and interment.

"I'm going to attend the service, of course. Jane and her parents have been like a second family to me since college."

Mark marveled at the change in her. Her command of her emotions under these circumstances was remarkable, but also worrisome. The doorbell rang and it was Dom and Marty with two suitcases.

"Mrs. Margolis packed the things she thought you'd need for a few days."

Elizabeth's eyes filled up. "It was so kind of her; I don't know how she faced the apartment."

"She cares about you, and she's quite a tough lady," Marty said with admiration. "How about a ride in a broken down police car to your new digs?" he added to lighten the moment.

Elizabeth looked through the suitcases and hurriedly selected some clothes and got dressed. Mark would shower and go to his office and call her later.

Dom whistled softly when they stepped into the vaulted marble hall of Elizabeth's father's apartment. The decor was simple and elegant yet utterly masculine in browns and other earth tones. Elizabeth had her own room there still, although she'd moved out after completing her Master's in Social Work at NYU.

"We lived here during the school year, but for the summers and many of the holidays we went to Pennsylvania," she explained.

Marty looked concerned as his eyes perused the apartment. "I hope you will feel comfortable here."

"I'll make my space," she said, smiling. She squeezed his arm, touched by his sensitivity.

She gave them a tour of the duplex. The downstairs had a living room, a large formal dining room, a kitchen, den, powder room, and maid's room with a bath. There were two staircases to the upstairs, one in the marble hall, the other in the kitchen. Upstairs included three bedrooms, each with its own bath.

Five bathrooms. Dom thought of his humble house in Queens which he considered luxurious because it had one and half baths instead of just one. Somehow this unaffected girl did not belong in this kind of opulence.

Elizabeth quickly affirmed his impression. "Let's put my stuff in the downstairs bedroom. I'd like to be on the first floor. My dad never had a live-in maid, so the room has never been used."

The room was airy and spacious with a lovely view and Elizabeth felt at home in it. As soon as possible, she thought, she'd fix it up with her curtains and comforter from her apartment in Brooklyn. Then maybe she'd feel at home.

Dom and Marty dropped Elizabeth at Doris's office with a promise to see her soon.

"I'd like to hypnotize you, Elizabeth. Are you up to it?"

"Yes, I'll do anything to take my mind off Jane, even if only for a few minutes."

Elizabeth was an easy subject and was soon in a hypnotic state. Doris gently asked her about March 25, 1911 and if she knew what had happened that day.

Elizabeth saw the now familiar redheaded woman.

"The young woman who spoke to me is speaking to another young woman. They both look so young. They are good friends. My lady is crying now and talking frantically to the other one. They look very distressed."

Doris could see Elizabeth's distress as well and brought her quickly out of the hypnotic state.

"Are you okay?"

She nodded. "I can still see them. Did I tell you?"

"Yes, but tell me more."

The one who appeared in the first hallucination and the last one, her name is Catherine. The friend's name is Sarah. Elizabeth started to cry. "Something awful will happen to them, won't it?"

"I'll try to find out. If my research is fruitful, we may get some answers. We have two names now," Doris said.

"Doris, suppose there are no such people as Catherine and Sarah. Suppose I'm . . ."

"We will find Catherine and Sarah, I think." Doris Fisher got up from her desk and came around to Elizabeth. "I'm worried about you. I want you to call me if you have any more paranormal experiences. It doesn't matter what time. Even if you are only scared or upset, or thinking about Jane, I'd like you to call."

Elizabeth could only nod. The determination she woke up with this morning in Mark's apartment, never to lose control again, was still there. She was just not sure how she would manage that knowing Jane was murdered in her stead. But somehow she would have to learn how to live with that unalterable fact. She was glad she had Doris.

"I will, I will call."

Chapter Fourteen

Jane's brother Gordon opened the door of his parents' home in Bay Ridge, Brooklyn before Elizabeth and Mark quite reached it. His wife Estelle was standing beside him. Elizabeth hugged Gordon first. She was startled when she embraced Estelle and felt her baby kick against her. A thrill went though her as she felt the new life.

"Soon your baby will be here," Elizabeth said. "I'm happy for you."

"Twins, Elizabeth, we are having twins," Gordon said. A flicker of a smile passed over Gordon's face, but soon disappeared.

"Jane was so excited about becoming an aunt," Estelle said. Two tears slid down her face. "You should see all the things she bought them," Estelle said.

"My mother is anxious to see you. Let me find her," Gordon said.

Elizabeth dreaded seeing Mrs. Levin. The guilt she felt over Jane's death almost overrode the sorrow.

"I am okay, Elizabeth. I'm calm, and I'm okay," Mrs. Levin said as they looked at one another a moment later. Elizabeth hugged Jane's father who was unable to speak.

The limousine pulled up to the house and they all went to the memorial chapel for the funeral service together. Despite their grief, Jane's parents and brother made Mark feel welcome. The fingerprints had turned out to be King's, Mark told them. He assured them that they would get King.

Elizabeth went to the podium in the packed little chapel to speak about Jane to a large community of her friends in the advertising business and the art world. "Jane's special gift was her love of others. She showed every individual she met how special and interesting he or she was. She felt the pain of the negative people she met and gave them something of herself that was good for them to walk away with. Her life as an artist was full of friends and people to whom she gave her love and her help."

Elizabeth's eyes swept over the people gathered for Jane's funeral. Mark sat next to Jane's parents and her brother and sister-in-law. He smiled his encouragement when their eyes met. She knew that he didn't know where she got the strength to eulogize her friend when she was under such a physical and emotional strain herself from guilt and grief. She didn't know either, but she had to do this.

Elizabeth almost made it through the eulogy but her voice broke as she said the final words. The Rabbi took the podium. He spoke movingly about Jane's life and it was then finally time to go to the cemetery. The Rabbi sought Elizabeth out at the end of the service. His kind eyes penetrated hers. "You spoke beautifully about your friend. Thank you. I'll see you at the house."

Jane's mother beckoned Elizabeth upstairs to Jane's old room. "I'd like you to take any of Jane's things you would like. Gordon and Estelle have taken a few trinkets, but they don't want anything else. I have always kept her room as it was when she left home for college except for the things she took when she moved to Tribecca after graduation. I think she enjoyed having her room the same when she came for a visit and stayed over night."

"She did; I know she did," Elizabeth said.

"Please," Mrs. Levin continued, "I know she'd want you to have anything of hers you would like."

Elizabeth looked at Jane's tiny mother, dressed all in black, looking so earnest in making this request.

"Mrs. Levin, it's my fault Jane was murdered. That man was after me. I don't know how I can live with that. Surely you know this; you must be so angry with me."

"No, no, dear, Elizabeth. Of course it isn't your fault. It was a tragic accident. I am not angry with you. Please don't blame yourself. Please." Mrs. Levin reached up and hugged Elizabeth. "Don't cry, Honey. Sit down on her bed with me." Mrs. Levin took both of Elizabeth's hands. "It is not your fault. None of this."

Elizabeth didn't know what to say.

"Now, tell me you will take something of hers; that will be a comfort to me," Mrs. Levin said.

"Yes, I would like to have something of hers. I will," Elizabeth said.

"Her desk, I'd like you to go through her desk too." She pointed to a desk across from Jane's single bed and went to it, turning on the lamp that sat on the top, bringing the old wood to life in an instant. The browns and reds in the mahogany gleamed in the lamplight.

"It's beautiful," Elizabeth said.

"It's been in the family for years. Jane always had a special love for it. She wouldn't even bring it to the loft because she was afraid of paint getting on it." She paused and looked at Elizabeth, "She said she'd bring it to her home in the country someday when she decided to marry and settle down."

They cried together as they walked toward the door of Jane's room, the place where Jane had once dreamed as a little girl of her future life.

"I'm going downstairs. Stay here for a moment, if you want to," Mrs. Levin said.

Jane's mother slipped out of the room and Elizabeth sat on Jane's bed again. She fingered the colorful patchwork quilt that rested on top. She smiled at a stuffed walrus next to the pillow, the Barbie dolls and a Teddy bear on a shelf on the wall. The grief she felt over Michael's and Jane's deaths and Millie's condition was too much to bear. She put her head in her hands but held back the tears.

"Hi," Mark said. She hadn't heard him enter Jane's room.

"Hi," she answered reaching for him.

"The Rabbi is here," he said.

Elizabeth nodded, and they rose together to go downstairs. She wanted to see the holy man again and take comfort in his words. She turned around at the threshold before leaving the room. Her eyes took in the whole comfortable room, but then they settled on the quiet majesty of the shining mahogany desk.

Chapter Fifteen

A few mornings after the funeral, Elizabeth opened her eyes only to feel the leaden weight in her chest that had found a home there in recent days. Recent days. They were packed with activity. Her twice-daily visits to the hospital nursing facility that specialized in coma patients that she had found for Millie comforted her though. She'd sit and talk to Millie and read passages from *Green Mansions* aloud. Rubbing Millie's little hands and feet, caressing her cheeks, she talked of their future as a family. Discouragement wasn't an option, she told herself when she watched Millie's still figure, unchanged, day after day.

Challenging hours each day at her father's office kept her mind off Millie, Jane, and King for brief periods. Although he had shared his business activities with her all her life, her father had not taught her how to run his business. She still had everything to learn. A further distraction, one she had devised for pleasure, was her attempt to make her father's apartment her home. Thank goodness for shopping on line. All new curtains and comforters for the bedrooms had begun to arrive. Millie would want to pick out her own decorations, and though she was tempted to have it all decorated when Millie came home, she resisted. Millie should be surrounded with things she herself had selected.

She was not being unrealistic about Millie's chances of recovery; she was just choosing to stay in the present moment where Millie was stable. It wasn't necessary to allow negative thoughts in. In the present moment it was okay to plan a future with Millie well and happy.

The phone rang.

"Hi, Sleepy Head," Mark said. "Did I wake you?"

"No, just putting off getting up," she said. Her heart beat just a little faster, she noticed, when she heard his voice. They had been emailing each other each night, something that gave her less sleep, and Mark too. But the emailing turned out to be a great way to get to know one another. They shared so much, especially the way they felt about their jobs. Mark was as burned out and discouraged working in the D.A.'s office as she had been working at the ACS. They each longed for meaningful work outside the rat race, but neither knew what it might be.

As she began to heal from her losses, she hoped she would be more of a friend to Mark. As it was now, he'd been the giver and she the receiver. She wanted to reciprocate by giving him back the caring and interest he had shown her during the last weeks.

"How about dinner at Antonio's tonight?" Mark asked.

Elizabeth thought for a second.

"Am I insensitive?" Mark asked. "I guess since we were there last on the day Jane died, that maybe it's not such a good idea."

"No, Mark, I don't associate Jane's death with Antonio's. Instead, it was a place where I felt happy and optimistic, before the nightmare of Jane's murder."

Several hectic hours later, they entered the little restaurant. Mark opened the door and they both looked up at the tinkling bell and smiled. As though it were mistletoe, they kissed spontaneously beneath it.

Antonio's effusive greeting warmed them as he sat them at the marble topped table by the window where they had sat before. He took the bottle of Bardolino that they had brought back to the kitchen to uncork it.

They talked of the future. Elizabeth told Mark that she planned to take Millie to Pennsylvania to recover.

"That sounds like a good idea for you and Millie, if you could be safe from King there, but what about the paranormal experiences? How is it going with Doris?"

"She's discovered more about the fire. Doris believes we can resolve this and the episodes will stop."

"But you haven't had any episodes recently, have you?"

She lifted her wine glass and looked at the dark red wine. "No. I have dreams, though. I don't remember them completely, but they are upsetting."

"My money's on Doris. I believe that she's right, and the episodes will stop. In the meantime, I want to fix this for you, and I can't. It's so frustrating to see you go through this."

"I'm so grateful to have you in my life, Mark. I know I can get through this because of you." They talked and talked as they finished Antonio's delicious meal.

Monday morning came. It was time to get back into a normal routine. Her doorman tried to hail a cab for her, but he was having no luck. None were in sight. "I'll go inside and call for one, Miss Charles."

"No, Bruce, I think I'll walk the few blocks. It's a beautiful day."

Bruce touched his cap as Elizabeth began walking toward 71st Street on Fifth Avenue. Almost as soon as she left her own block she began to sense an eerie presence. Relax, Elizabeth told herself. She glanced over each shoulder and saw nothing, but she felt as though someone were watching her. She quickened her pace and wondered why she had decided to get such an early start this morning. The streets were almost deserted. It was a full hour before the hustle and bustle would begin and the streets would be flooded with people rushing to their offices, even the early birds.

She heard a low whistle. It was long and soft but unmistakably a wolf whistle. What should she do? Was it a harmless whistler, a rapist, or King toying with her? She broke into a run, kicking off her high-heeled shoes, oddly remembering how she'd forgotten to put on her Nikes this morning, her usual footwear for traveling to work, even by cab. She heard a laugh behind her and the footfalls of a runner. He was gaining on her. She would reach Madison Avenue in a moment. Her breath came in bursts from her overtaxed lungs, and she wondered how she'd be able to scream if he overtook her. As she rounded the corner onto Madison, she saw with relief that there were two persons walking on the otherwise deserted avenue. She ran to an apartment building with a doorman. He looked at her expensive suit, bare feet, and terrified face as he opened the door for her.

"Did someone attack you? Should I call the police," the old man asked as he pulled Elizabeth through the door.

Sitting in the beautifully appointed lobby of the Madison Avenue apartment building with no shoes, torn panty hose, and panting like a dehydrated dog, Elizabeth suddenly felt ridiculous. She was so jumpy lately the whole thing could have been her imagination, yet she knew instinctively that it wasn't.

"No, I'm sorry," she gasped out. "I think I just scared myself."

"Can I get you a cab, then?" the doorman asked. He looked anxious to get her out of his building now. Elizabeth gave him a shaky smile and nodded yes.

His whistle quickly brought a cab, and he politely held the door for Elizabeth. She gave him a tip and she heard him mutter before he walked back inside.

"No one would believe the things I see on this job," he said. "A scared rich kid with no shoes on." Elizabeth wanted to laugh when she saw him shake his head.

Mercifully, the building where her father's offices were located, her offices, she supposed she ought to think, was still virtually empty. The security guard didn't seem to notice her shoelessness, and she got into the office unseen by anyone else. She kept an old pair of flats in the office closet and a package of panty hose in her desk, so within moments she was back to a relatively normal appearance.

She sat down at her father's huge cherry desk. As usual, she felt like a fraud. She pictured him sitting there as she had seen him dozens of times, his smile, his laugh. She wanted to tell him about her almost mugging or whatever it was, another hallucination for all she knew. A lump formed in her throat, but she willed it away. She went through her in-box and made a list of priorities for the day. Then she got up to make the first pot of coffee that she and

Annette, her secretary, would consume when she arrived in about an hour.

The phone startled her. "Charles and Associates," she answered.

"Howya doin', Honey?" Dom's gruff voice asked. He sounded hoarse and sleepy. He was probably still at home. "I figured you'd be in the office when I couldn't get you at home."

She felt the stinging of her feet which smarted uncomfortably from her run on the concrete.

"You're not going to believe it, Gentilli," she said somberly. Then she gave him a self-deprecating account of the morning's incident, downplaying it and telling him how it was probably her over stimulated imagination.

There was silence on his end for a moment. "It sounds pretty scary to me, kiddo."

She knew he was worried.

"No surveillance. We can't afford it. And that's final."

Gentilli hung up and looked across the kitchen table at Marie, his wife of twenty-six years and his soul mate.

"I guess the captain said no," Marie said pushing stray strands of her salt and pepper hair out of her eyes.

"Yeah," Gentilli said.

Marie got up from the table and tightened the cord of her terrycloth bathrobe before pouring them both another cup of coffee.

"Why don't you do it on your own? You and Marty could split it."

He reached across the table and took her hand. Their eyes met in an understanding that had grown out of the love they shared through both the good times and the bad in their marriage. He gulped down his coffee and picked up the phone to call Marty.

Chapter Sixteen

"As we already know, the fire took place on March 25, 1911. One hundred and forty-six people were killed, mostly young women. The factory was located in the Asch Building near New York University. You attended NYU, did you not, Elizabeth?"

"Yes, I got my Masters in Social Work there."

"I believe the building now belongs to the university. It's called the Brown Building. Do you know it?"

"Yes, and it has a plaque on the outside. Something about the fire, I think."

"The Triangle Shirtwaist Factory was a sweat shop. They made blouses or 'bodices' for ladies," Doris said.

"How did the fire start?" Elizabeth asked Doris.

"Some of the scraps of fabric left over from making the blouses ignited. The great loss of life, though, came from some of the doors being locked. Many of the workers couldn't get out. The owners were afraid the girls would leave early or take their profits by stealing some of the fabric. Some of the fire doors were deliberately locked to prevent that. The girls even had to open their purses for inspection when leaving the factory at quitting time to ensure that they weren't stealing. The working conditions were crowded and miserable."

Doris pressed the fingertips of her hands together. Her elbows were on the edge of her desk. "It became an inferno in there. The girls were screaming to get out but many of them couldn't because of the locked doors. It was because the heat became so unbearable that many of them jumped out the windows to their deaths on the street below. So what you saw, *did* happen, Elizabeth."

Doris watched Elizabeth shudder. She knew that Elizabeth was remembering the horror she felt at the image of the body of the young woman falling from the burning building to the sidewalk in front of her. It was a while ago since she was in that particular time slip. But how could she ever forget it?

Doris handed her photos of the young women lying in neat rows next to the building where the firemen had placed them. She watched Elizabeth scrutinize the pictures.

"Look at the Gibson hairstyles, the clothes, the horse drawn fire trucks. They are just as I saw them in the episodes. Was there a Catherine or a Sarah?" Elizabeth asked as she handed the photos back to Doris.

"There were a number of Sarahs, two different spellings of the name."

"And Catherine?"

"There was only one Catherine who died in the fire. Catherine Maltese. A Catherine Sherlock shows up in the paper too, but it is unclear whether she died in the fire or not. She may have survived. I'm not even sure she was a Triangle employee," Doris said as she scrutinized the photos once again.

"Sherlock, . . . how odd; that name seems so familiar. Maybe my grandmother's name or her maiden name."

Doris's head shot up.

"Do you think there's a connection?" Elizabeth asked breathlessly.

"Could be. We'll have to check. We'll have to take a look at your family tree."

Elizabeth explained how her mother had died when Elizabeth was three years old. She didn't remember her grandmother.

"Do you have relatives you can ask?"

"My father and I had no one but each other."

"Did he ever speak of family, his parents, brothers or sisters, or your mother's family?"

"No. He rarely spoke of his childhood and school days, or of his parents who died when he was a child. I vaguely remember something about my mother's side. That's why the name Sherlock rings a bell. We have an attic in the house in Pennsylvania. There are boxes of old things up there."

"Maybe you should take a look, Elizabeth. It may have nothing to do with the fire, but it should be interesting to find some roots."

Doris could not imagine not knowing the names and details of the lives of her immediate family's parents and grandparents. She felt so enriched by her relatives and the memories of family celebrations and the warmth of all their homes from her childhood. She wondered about Elizabeth's childhood.

"What did you and your father do for the Christmas holidays?"

"We went to our home in Pennsylvania. For Thanksgiving and Easter too. My father always fixed a big meal, all the trimmings. He'd invite neighbors and friends. There was always a house full of people, kids, dogs."

They talked for almost an hour, and Doris found that Michael had truly created an environment that resembled a large extended family to the best of his ability. His efforts had paid off since Elizabeth was a warm and open person who seemed to naturally trust others.

They ended the session with Elizabeth's interest in her family history peaked. "I'll get right to it," she told Doris as they hugged and said good-bye.

Millie was a doll-like figure in the long bed. She was completely motionless, the covers in a perfectly straight line across her shoulders, her black hair framing her face on the white pillow. Elizabeth pulled the covers back and reached for Millie's hand. She squeezed it gently but no squeeze came in return. She opened *Green Mansions* and began to read. Every once in a while she'd touch Millie's face and speak directly to her. She rubbed her forearms and her hands and told her how much she loved her. Elizabeth prayed silently, "Please, please let Millie live." She prayed these words over and over and they gave her comfort.

"Miss Charles," Elizabeth was startled when a young woman came into the room. "I'm Nancy Cabello, Millie's physical therapist."

Elizabeth shook Nancy's hand and felt cheered by the warmth of her smile.

"We have Millie on an exercise program to prevent atrophy so when she wakes up . . ." she smiled again and Elizabeth responded with her own smile, "... *when* she wakes up," Nancy repeated, "she'll be strong enough for a speedy recovery."

Then Nancy expertly put Millie through the routine. Soon Millie was back as before, her thin form barely visible under the covers.

Before she knew it, it was time to leave. Elizabeth kissed Millie on the forehead. The heaviness in her heart was somewhat lifted by Nancy Cabello's words of hope.

Chapter Seventeen

Elizabeth invited Mark to her house in Pennsylvania to help her explore the attic. He liked the idea. "Just what we both need, a weekend away."

"We'll leave the city on Friday night after dinner and return Sunday morning. I wouldn't feel comfortable leaving Millie longer than that." They looked at each other and wondered how they would feel leaving her that long, even with the shifts of private duty nurses Elizabeth had hired.

"Dom visits every day and Marty almost every day."

"They do?"

Mark nodded. Elizabeth was moved. Tough veteran cop, Dom, and Marty, the glamorous bachelor—they could still be captured by a little girl.

"Elizabeth, I recently found out that Dom lost a child, a little girl about Millie's age, years ago. He started drinking heavily afterward and almost got fired from the force."

"What happened?"

"It was a family day on the lake, somewhere in New Jersey. They rented a house there for a week every summer. The rest of the family was doing other things that day. Dom took his little girl out on the boat, and she fell overboard. He hadn't put her life jacket on her."

"Oh, God," Elizabeth said. She thought of Dom, that first day she met him, keeping watch over Millie in her hospital room. No wonder he wanted to save this child.

The traffic was heavy going out of the city but non-existent as they went across New Jersey. The Delaware River glistened in the moonlight as they crossed the bridge from Stockton.

Ellen had the house ready. The refrigerator was stocked with milk, juice, and butter. A package of English muffins and a can of coffee rested on the kitchen counter. Wood was laid out in front of the fireplace and Elizabeth started a fire immediately.

"A fire in June?" Mark said.

"It's cool this evening," she said. "But really, Ellen knows me; I love a fire, and any excuse will do to have one."

Elizabeth took Mark on the tour of the house. She gave him Michael's bedroom, with its large four-poster bed.

"This is a beautiful home. Have you ever thought of living here permanently?"

"We always considered it our real home and we're actively involved in the community here. New York is where my father worked and played too. New York is where I went to school. But this is home."

They sipped their wine staring at the fire.

"I would love to live outside the city," Mark said softly.

Elizabeth knew he was about to confide something important, something he had thought about a lot. She put her hand on his.

"I told you a little about how I feel in my emails. The work I do is, is . . . so meaningless. One criminal after another, so many victims. The system doesn't help either. The plea bargaining, the politics. I don't feel good about it. I thought I could help, or make a difference, but I realize I can't."

"Taking children out of abusive homes makes a difference in their lives."

"Maybe from beatings or further abuse, maybe not, but many of their young lives are already destroyed by the time I see them, and if I hang around long enough, chances are I'll see them again, when they've committed a crime themselves."

"Mark Lewis, I had no idea you were such a pessimist!"

"I'm not really," he laughed. He pulled her into his arms. "I've dreamed of living a simpler life, though. I've thought about it intensely for the last two years. At first I used to think about retirement, planning my retirement."

"You sound like Dom, his house in North Carolina . . ."

"Yes, but then I realized that I'm so many years from retirement that I'm wishing my life away." He put his hand under her chin and kissed her lightly. "I've thought about moving to a rural area, of leaving the D.A.'s office. Doing something that makes me feel good about myself."

Elizabeth thought about her job at the ACS. "I understand how you feel."

She knew that he understood how she felt too. He pulled her close and began to kiss her, gently at first, and then more and more intensely. He put his hands in her thick hair, pulled it up and kissed her neck and throat.

The phone rang softly. It rang again and again. Reluctantly, Elizabeth picked it up.

"We've got King, Honey. You can rest easy tonight. He's in jail," Dom said.

Chapter Eighteen

Dom and Marty headed for the local coffee shop after King was booked and safely incarcerated.

They passed the unofficial precinct cops' bar on the way and saw a couple of their fellow officers heading in the door for a couple of beers after their shift.

Dom and Marty smiled at each other. Dom had been sober with the help of AA for sixteen years. Marty never touched alcohol. He'd seen it ruin too many lives.

The restaurant was shabby but homey. The smell of both this morning's eggs and bacon and lunchtime's greasy hamburgers greeted them as they entered the brightly lit coffee shop.

"A light decaf and a regular," Marty ordered for them both.

"How can you drink regular coffee at this hour and go to sleep, Pardner?"

"I'll sleep like a baby now that we got King. I can drink all the coffee I want."

"Yeah, we don't have to worry about Elizabeth now."

"I could never have forgiven myself if anything happened to Elizabeth," Marty said.

"It was the right thing to do, keeping an eye on her when we were off duty. King would have gotten to her eventually."

"Do you think he would have killed her in cold blood?"

"After what he did to Jane, sure."

"I don't know why I'm so attached to these two, the kid especially. I guess she reminds me of the little girls I grew up with in El Barrio. She's had it rough, and it's really gotten to me. I know why you feel the way you do about her, Dom."

Dom turned his head away. "Yeah," he said. "Anyway, we were lucky King didn't get to Elizabeth. We were lucky."

Marty suddenly grinned and opened his palms on the table. Dom stared incredulously at Marty's perfectly white, starched shirt cuffs and wondered how after a day on the streets and in the filthy office doing paper work, he had managed to stay as fresh as he had been in the morning.

"Lucky?" Marty whistled. "Gentilli, how can you say we were *lucky*? It was not luck but crackerjack police work that got us King."

"You're right, Pardner." Dom smiled and slapped Marty's hand and they shot their thumbs up simultaneously.

"I lost my head when I said 'Lucky.' Batman and Robin we ain't, but it was hard work, and Marie encouraging me . . ."

"And me," Marty said.

" . . . to work on our own time that got us our man," Dom finished.

They relived the capture of King blow by blow. The best part was when he walked out of the heroin dealer's apartment and they were there waiting.

"Yeah, then the squad car got there, and the rest was routine."

They kept talking over a couple more cups of coffee before they went home.

"I wish we didn't have to leave," Mark said. "It's beautiful here."

"I'm so glad you like it. I love this place," Elizabeth said.

"I can hardly concentrate on the road," Mark said.

Elizabeth laughed. "I know; the scenery is breathtaking."

"That's not what I meant," Mark said. He reached for Elizabeth's hand.

The drive along River Road with its twists and turns along the sparkling Delaware was soon over.

"Let's stop at Martine's in New Hope for lunch before we go back to the city," Elizabeth said.

The waitress seated them outside on the patio of the historic restaurant. The table Elizabeth and her father had always chosen was not visible. That part of her life was over, and Elizabeth accepted that fully now.

Mark took Elizabeth's hand across the table. "I not only like it here in Bucks County," he said, "I love being with you. I wasn't referring to the view when I said I couldn't concentrate."

"I feel the same way," Elizabeth said.

Two and a half hours later they were back at Elizabeth's apartment in the city. Mark had to go back to his apartment. They agreed to email later.

Elizabeth skimmed through the mail and threw most of it on the hall table. A letter from Jane's mother was among those waiting for her. She opened the envelope eagerly.

> Dear Elizabeth,
>
> Larry and I have decided to move to Florida. I know you haven't had time to come over and look through Jane's things. I'd like you to have Jane's desk as I know you will cherish it. It gives me comfort to know that a piece of furniture that has been in our family for so many years will be cared for by you always. Perhaps you will pass it on to one of your own children someday.
>
> Please accept this desk and know how much Jane would have wanted you to have it.
>
> A moving company has crated it and picked it up from here and will deliver it to you at your convenience. Enclosed is their business card with the number to call to make the arrangements.
>
> I did not go through the contents of Jane's desk. I apologize for leaving this sad task to you. I hope you understand.
>
> Larry and I will be leaving New York in two weeks. The house is slowly being packed up and we are leaving the sale of the house and other legal matters to the real estate agent and our lawyer.
>
> I would like to see you before we leave. Will you call me and we can meet either here or in the city?
>
> My love to you, dear Elizabeth.
>
> Francine Levin

Elizabeth pressed the letter to her face and cried. When she composed herself she called the moving company in Long Island City and arranged for the delivery of the desk for Tuesday afternoon. She'd leave work early to be there. She called Jane's mother to tell her that the arrangements had been made, but there was no answer at the Brooklyn home.

She showered and quickly dressed for a visit to the extended care facility to see Millie.

Dom was standing by Millie's bed when Elizabeth arrived. His tired, fleshy face lit up, and he lost ten years when he smiled and embraced Elizabeth.

"Honey, it's so good to see you."

The affection she had felt for Dom before was deepened by the knowledge of his own tragedy.

She stared anxiously down at Millie desperately searching for some change in her, some sign of improvement.

But Millie was much as she was the last time Elizabeth had been there. The only change was that one of the nurses had fixed her hair into two braids which extended from her shoulders down onto her chest. Elizabeth picked up one of the braids and twisted it gently in her fingers.

"Hi, Millie. It's me, Elizabeth. I'm here and I love you. I went to Pennsylvania this weekend, and we're going to go there together when you get better."

Dom moved away from the bed to let Elizabeth sit down. "I have to go back to the station," he whispered. "Do you want to hear about the arrest before I go?"

"I do," she motioned to the door and they walked out into the hall. "I believe Millie can hear, and I don't want to upset her," Elizabeth said.

Dom told an astounded Elizabeth about the relatively easy collar of King.

"Dom, I know how much all this has taken out of you. You've been working around the clock trying to get this guy. I can't tell you how grateful I am to you."

"Hey, you're a special kid." His voice got husky, and Elizabeth knew he understood how she felt.

"What am I interrupting here? It looks like a mutual admiration society."

They both grinned as Marty joined them in the hall. "You look very probably like your old self," Marty said to Elizabeth. "Of course, I didn't know your old self, but you know what I mean."

"I accept the compliment."

"How's Millie today?"

"Same."

They all looked at each other. The light mood was now broken by reality, but the bond of friendship among them was solid.

Chapter Nineteen

Elizabeth decided not to go into work so she could be home to receive Jane's desk. She sighed with bittersweet pleasure as the moving men uncrated it. The red in the mahogany seemed to glow as she rubbed her hand lightly over the rich wood.

She had decided to place the desk in the small den she used to read, watch T.V., write letters and emails, and listen to music. It was a warm and cozy room decorated in burgundy and hunter green. She pictured Millie sitting on the couch in her nightgown munching chips and reading. She even pictured Mark sitting in the plaid wing chair. The den was the only place for the desk. The very formal and stuffy living room was never used, and it would be lost in there.

The moving men finished. Elizabeth tipped them, and they left. She sat on the loveseat and stared at Jane's desk, thinking about her friend, thinking about her father. Doris had said it was okay to grieve, that the losses were real and painful and all that was happening to her, the tears, the sorrow, the emotions were normal and healthy. The competent business woman persona that she sported, even in front of Mark on the morning after Jane's murder, could not be sustained all the time.

The desk looked stately and beautiful in its new home. She got up from the chair to open the slant top. The old key turned easily. She laid the top down gently. Inside was an intricately carved gallery with slots for envelopes, letters or papers. There were tiny drawers. There was one little door in the center of the gallery that had a carved shell design on its facade. She pulled it open by its tiny knob. Inside were plastic sandwich bags filled with dried roses and some other dried flowers. A little tag was inside of each bag. She opened one and read the tag, "Junior Prom June 4, 1989."

Each bag was a memory, the tag inside documenting the occasion, "Graduation from high school, June 23, 1990, flowers from Mom and Dad." "Date with Jeremy Milford, September 20, 1990, Annual Blue Jug Dance." No wonder Jane's mother could not go through this desk.

She closed the little door and lifted up the slant top. Her hands seemed to freeze as she turned the old key. A charge flowed through her as her knees began to buckle. She was dizzy and lightheaded. Was another hallucination about to start? She couldn't remove her fingers from the key.

She was in an apartment. The woman she had come to know as Catherine was urging her to look at something. She was pointing and nodding. Elizabeth could see her lips moving but heard no sound. Elizabeth did not want to look. She resisted with all her strength. She had to look away from Catherine because Catherine's face was desperate, desperate for Elizabeth to look.

She was retching, back in her den now, her fingers no longer on the key and the desk. She sat weakly down in the chair, shaking hard. What was happening to her? Doris. She'd be seeing Doris tomorrow.

She had to do something. She couldn't sit here and think about these bizarre incidents or she'd go crazy. She picked up the phone and called Jane's mother. "The desk has arrived. When can you come? I'd like to meet here so you can see it before you go," she said breathlessly, hoping Mrs. Levin wouldn't notice how distressed she was. Jane's mother said she could come later that same afternoon.

Elizabeth still felt restless. The hallucination, time slip, whatever it was, was so close to her. She didn't know how to shake it. She walked from room to room, always returning to the den. This big apartment wasn't home. She lived here, but it wasn't home.

She entered the living room. Her father had furnished it in elegant oriental designs. It was an impressive room but to Elizabeth it was sterile. She remembered parties at the apartment and guests gathered in the living room, eating, drinking, laughing. She couldn't ever remember sitting there herself though. Sitting, talking to her father in the living room, no they had never done that. The dining room was equally unavailable to her. It was as she imagined a refectory in a monastery would look. The dining room with its heavy oak table, impossibly long with ten high backed chairs, seemed austere in its furnishing and decorations. She ran her hand along the sideboard. How many dinner parties had they held at this table? She remembered the witty conversations, her father joyfully presiding at the head of the table, her own excitement at being present with the Beautiful People, Michael Charles's highly successful and sometimes, celebrity friends. But she and her father had never dined alone in this room.

She looked at her watch. Jane's mother wouldn't be coming for another three hours. She walked into the kitchen to make a cup of tea. The kitchen was a friendly room like the den. Here she and her father had shared meals, late night snacks, and dreams. She looked at the very old enamel stove and the long white cabinets with their glass doors. Her father had not wanted to modernize this room, and she was glad. The tea was hot and soothing. If only it could wipe out the memory of the latest paranormal experience.

She finished her tea and changed quickly. She had time for a visit to Millie before Mrs. Levin arrived.

Millie was the same. Sometimes Elizabeth fancied that she saw movement, but she always finally realized that it was her imagination. The physical therapist came in again. Nancy Cabello was warm to Elizabeth and talked to Millie nonstop as she put her through her paces during the therapy session. It didn't matter that it was a one way conversation; Elizabeth believed Millie heard everything Nancy said. Elizabeth watched again with interest as Nancy gently put Millie's muscles through the exercise program that would keep them from atrophying.

Mrs. Levin rang the doorbell at four o'clock. Elizabeth opened it and found that her friend's mother had become thinner and appeared drawn. It was probably an ordeal for her to even come here.

They embraced, and Elizabeth led Mrs. Levin into the apartment. She brought her to the den to see the desk. Mrs. Levin smiled sadly. "It pleases me that you have this, my dear. It looks lovely in this room."

"How are you doing, really?" Elizabeth asked Mrs. Levin as they sat down.

"Everyone says that time will dull the pain. It's a cliché and it's hard to believe. But losing a child is something beyond pain. Something like your losing your mother when you were three must have been, my dear."

"Although I barely remember her, I sometimes feel an aching longing for her."

"With your father gone, it must be so much worse."

Elizabeth heard the selflessness in this grieving mother who cared about Elizabeth's loss. Before long she found herself telling Mrs. Levin the whole story of meeting Millie, the beatings and abuse Millie had suffered at the hands of her mother's boyfriend, and the murder of Millie's mother. The shock and horror on Mrs. Levin's face was not lost on Elizabeth as she recounted the background of the monster King who had murdered her Jane. It seemed only natural that Elizabeth should tell Mrs. Levin about the hallucinations. Elizabeth watched as the expression on Mrs. Levin's face changed to astonishment as Elizabeth told her the whole story.

"Elizabeth," she whispered when Elizabeth finally finished. "My grandmother died in that fire."

Chapter Twenty

Doris assembled all the facts she had surrounding the fire on March 25, 1911. Two women, one named Catherine and the other named Sarah, had been in Elizabeth's episodes. A Catherine Sherlock appears in some accounts of those who died, but not in others, and she was not on the official list. And then there were the unidentified bodies. She may have been one of those. There was one other Catherine, too, Catherine Maltese. There were several Saras or Sarahs. She also knew many of the details of the fire, but how would that help? She went over them again.

It was almost quitting time at the Triangle Shirtwaist factory when the fire struck on the eighth floor. The fire quickly spread to the tenth floor, and the factory soon became an inferno. Dozens jumped out the windows to certain death on the street below rather than endure the searing heat and suffocating smoke. Catherine Sherlock was identified by a friend as one of the victims, but then the friend recanted and said it was not Catherine Sherlock.

Something was wrong. Doris could feel it. What was it that wasn't ringing true? She picked up one of the books that gave a detailed account of the fire. She looked at the photos with renewed horror; so many young people lost their lives working in that unsafe sweatshop. One of the photos showed Broadway during a heavy rain-women marching, women in the windows of the buildings holding signs. These were women who worked in the sweatshops protesting the needless deaths of their co-workers, deaths caused by greed and the class system. The class system, the ethnic groups. Sherlock is a Celtic name. All the workers at Triangle were Eastern Europeans or Italians.

That's not all. There was something else that was wrong.

The day Jane was killed Elizabeth had had an episode where Catherine was marching in the rain. That was it. How could Catherine have been killed in the fire and march in protest two days later? Catherine Sherlock had not been killed in the fire. She'd eliminate Catherine Maltese and concentrate on Catherine Sherlock.

Her thoughts were interrupted by her secretary's buzz. "Mr. Lewis is here to see you, Dr. Fisher."

"Send him in, please."

"Doris, how are you? I'm here to ask you if there is anything new with Elizabeth. I'm worried about her hallucinations, leaving her alone . . ."

"Have you spoken to Elizabeth about your fears?"

"I don't want her to know how worried I am. Now that King is behind bars, I guess I'm beginning to focus on these episodes, but I haven't spoken to Elizabeth about it."

"That doesn't make for good communication between people who care for each other, does it?" Doris asked.

"You're right, of course, and it goes against everything I believe in by not talking about it. I haven't wanted to upset whatever little peace she has right now. She seems so strong and I wonder if it's real."

"I can understand that, but I think you know what you have to do."

Mark sighed, "Yeah, I'll talk to her."

Doris's face crinkled up and her eyes became slits as her face fell into its characteristic smile. "I think you and Elizabeth are lucky to have found one another."

"We are. And I'm so happy I knew where to go when Elizabeth first told me about the hallucinations; I thought of you immediately. How many discussions have we had about parapsychology over the last few years of our friendship?"

"It impressed me that a young assistant D.A. would be so open to the possibility of psychic experiences." They both smiled as they remembered their first meeting.

"Frankly, I wasn't that open when the detective told me he wanted to use a psychic to find the murder victim's body in the

Franklin case. But the detective convinced me that it was worth a try. I didn't want to inadvertently hire a quack so I did my homework and found you, a respected and eminent physician and psychiatrist with an interest in parapsychology. I wanted to consult with you about psychics and for a referral, if there was anything to it."

"It was right here in this office," Doris said.

"And I got to see first hand that at least *you* weren't a quack." They both laughed.

"The psychic you recommended helped us find the body that time, and I no longer had prejudice against psychics or anything else I don't understand."

Doris believed she knew what was troubling Mark. "But *this* thing that you don't understand, this one, is too close for comfort, isn't it? You've fallen in love with Elizabeth and her episodes are bizarre and incomprehensible."

Mark nodded. "Do you have any idea what's going on, Doris? Can a person become a conduit to the past, to past events? Is Elizabeth going back to 1911 when she has these visions? Are the events of 1911 still going on now? Is she being haunted by a ghost, this Catherine?" He almost laughed as he asked the last question, and his handsome face contorted in its struggle to be reasonable in this unreal situation.

"I don't know all the answers, Mark. I just know that this is real. Elizabeth is going back into the past into a 'time slip,' if you will, something others before her have experienced. I wish I knew why her, why now, but I don't. I think we will find the answer to that eventually too, though."

Doris filled Mark in further on what she had learned of the fire at the Triangle Shirtwaist Company. She pushed the fingers of her hands together tip to tip as she always did when thinking.

"We don't understand time." She took a deep breath as though knowing that what she was about to say would be shocking. "I do believe that the woman Catherine is trying to communicate with Elizabeth."

Mark paled and his hands shook slightly. "Did she tell you about the episode with Jane's desk in her apartment yesterday?"

"No, I'm seeing her today at four. I was wondering when the next episode would occur."

Doris was focusing ahead, lost in thought. "Today is going to be another hypnosis. Maybe we'll place another puzzle piece on the board."

Chapter Twenty-One

Elizabeth could barely contain herself as she told Doris about Mrs. Levin's visit and her revelation that her own grandmother had died in the Triangle fire.

"Jane's great grandmother . . ." The articulate Doris was speechless. Their eyes locked, both of them full of wonder at this coincidence. Could it actually *be* a coincidence?

"What did you learn about the grandmother? What happened to Mrs. Levin's mother? What did . . . ?

"Doris, she didn't know many of the details. She couldn't even remember her grandmother's first name. She only knew that her maternal grandmother died in the fire, nothing more."

"How did you leave it with her?"

"She's going to try to find out the details and then she'll call me."

Excitement and tension sparked the air in Doris's office. They both felt it.

"How am I going to relax you for hypnosis? How am I going to relax myself enough to hypnotize you?" she added in a whisper.

But Elizabeth felt herself go under immediately. It was even quicker than the last time. She heard Doris's soft voice and the steady ticking of the clock on her desk. She felt her body melt into the cool leather of the comfortable chair.

A large dark apartment. Catherine. She was speaking to a child, a little girl of little more than five. The little girl's lip was trembling and there were red blotches on her cheeks. Tears were beginning to spill out of her eyes. Catherine was crying now too. The little girl lifted her arms up and Catherine stooped over to pick her up. The child drew up her knees the way a baby does when it is being picked up.

Catherine held her tightly in her arms, the little girl's head burrowed in between Catherine's neck and shoulder. This was not a child being comforted for a scraped knee, but for an anguish so great Elizabeth felt it in her own heart.

Doris was alarmed by Elizabeth's expression and her voice and quickly brought her out of the hypnotic state. She woke up exhausted. Doris led her to the couch where she lay down. She covered her with a blanket while Elizabeth haltingly told her of what she had seen. She began to describe the furnishings she had fleetingly noticed and then stopped. "The furniture doesn't matter . . ." She was breathing deeply and was focused on the memory of the episode.

"Catherine feels for that little girl what I feel for Millie. I knew it; I felt it."

Doris wondered how long this would take and what the resolution would be. Elizabeth was a strong woman, but this was draining her. She'd have to see this through and do what she could to get it done quickly. The family connection possibly. Elizabeth's search in the attic at her Pennsylvania home had been forgotten in the excitement following the news that King had been caught. She'd have to go back there and look for some connection, connection to what? To the fire, to someone named Catherine or Sarah, the Lower East Side? She didn't know.

Elizabeth stirred. She opened her eyes suddenly. "Doris, I want to have a party. A dinner party. Something happy, a celebration. I want to use my father's dining room table. I'll cook a big meal. Will you come?"

Doris knew that this strange outburst was Elizabeth's mind trying desperately to escape the anxiety and the unhappiness she was feeling. Her psyche had turned to this sudden idea as a coping mechanism.

"Of course. I'd be delighted." Her face crinkled, her eyes disappeared, and Elizabeth smiled in return as Doris gently squeezed her hand. "It's going to be okay."

Hours later Elizabeth sat down at the kitchen table and began to make a menu. No, she should start with a guest list. Mark,

Doris, Dom and his wife, Marty and a date, Nancy Cabello, Millie's physical therapist, Ellen, of course, if she'd come into the city from Pennsylvania, Mrs. Margolis, Al and Joe, and she'd tell them to bring Thunderball. She missed Thunderball. Jane should be on the list she thought with a pang.

She blinked back the tears and took out a five by eight index card on which she would write out the menu. Should she have a buffet or a sit down dinner? A sit down dinner. Like her father used to have. She busily wrote out the menu and the accompanying shopping list. Later she would call everyone and set the date for next Saturday night.

Chapter Twenty-Two

Saturday arrived and Elizabeth was organized and prepared. She was expecting ten for dinner, not counting Thunderball and Moss, whom she'd also invited, to Ellen's delight. If only Millie were here too; she'd love being with all the people and the dogs.

Ellen had come from Pennsylvania early in the day and filled the usually quiet apartment with her cheerful chatter. Elizabeth brought Ellen's bag to the guest room upstairs with Moss dutifully following. Ellen also wanted to see Elizabeth's old bedroom where they had so many good times as kids.

"I'll bet you're going to give this room to Millie," Ellen said, smiling.

"You're right, Girlfriend; that's exactly what I'm going to do," Elizabeth said.

"Remember when we were kids and your father would take us to a fancy restaurant and then to a Broadway show?"

Ellen's face glowed with the happy memories. She swung her long straight hair from her shoulders to her back where it hung almost to her waist. Ellen was only twenty-eight but she was a child of the 60's in spirit. Elizabeth always thought that the artsy, albeit aging hippy population of nearby New Hope had been a strong influence on Ellen in her flower child style.

"I remember," Elizabeth said. The bittersweet memories of her father and the fun he always was that would never be again started up the ache inside her. But it felt good to listen to her childhood friend, the one person who knew her history, her family life.

"It's good to have you here."

"I'm glad you invited me. I miss seeing you at home on the weekends. I didn't even meet Mark or talk to you since Jane's death. You left in such a hurry the last time you were there."

"I think it's time I filled you in on a few things . . ." Elizabeth sat down in the little rocking chair in the guest room, and Ellen plopped down on the bed, her eyes wide with expectation.

Elizabeth began with the first hallucination, meeting Millie, the facts surrounding Jane's murder, and all the succeeding events. She watched Ellen's face, lovely and expressive, absorbing the information and relating it to her feelings for Elizabeth. She was speechless for a moment after Elizabeth was finished.

"When can I meet Millie?" was all she said finally.

They headed for the private nursing facility by cab. Ellen was uncharacteristically quiet when she saw Millie in the hospital bed, and Elizabeth knew her mind was racing furiously trying to think of ways to help. They returned to the apartment in short lived silence and spent the balance of the afternoon discussing the strange events and the strong hope they had for Millie's recovery while making the final preparations for the dinner party.

Mark and Doris were the first to arrive. Nancy Cabello phoned just then to say that something had come up at the last minute and she wouldn't be able to make it.

"Millie's okay, isn't she, Nancy?" Elizabeth asked.

"Oh, yes, of course. Don't worry, Elizabeth. I'm so sorry I won't be there tonight. Have fun."

Despite the physical therapist's reassurances, Elizabeth was worried.

Ellen was happily meeting Mark and Doris when the doorman called announcing a third guest. The doorbell rang a moment later and Ellen went to answer it. Marty was standing there all starch and polish, glowing with friendliness and good looks. Ellen seemed electrified for a moment. "You are Marty."

"Yes," he agreed.

Marty was currently without a girlfriend and had told Elizabeth he would not be bringing a date, but Elizabeth hadn't considered a match with Ellen. She was glad to see the spark of interest between her friends.

Elizabeth brought Doris into the den and showed her Jane's desk. Her heart was pounding because she was afraid she'd have an episode right then and there as the desk had a powerful pull for her in a way she did not understand.

She opened the slant top gently and showed Doris the carved gallery inside. Nothing happened, and she breathed a sigh of relief.

"It is beautiful, Elizabeth. In mint condition after all these years." She couldn't resist running her fingers over the gleaming surface either.

"Do you think it is a coincidence that I had an episode from touching this desk the first day?"

"I wish I knew," she sighed. "Come now; let's enjoy this party. I think you'll find there is much to enjoy," she added with a twinkle in her eye.

"I never thought of you as a matchmaker," she joked, sure Doris was referring to her growing relationship with Mark.

The buzzer from the lobby sounded, and Elizabeth headed for the door to greet her guests. A few moments later, Mrs. Margolis, Al, Joe and Thunderball walked into the apartment.

"You are so safe here, darling," Mrs. Margolis said. "When we walked into the lobby and told the doorman that we were going to your apartment, he asked us our names and then checked his list and crossed us off."

"Your apartment is beautiful, Elizabeth," Al said. Thunderball ran over to Moss and the two mature male dogs went about introducing themselves to each other before settling down.

"I'll get drinks for me and Al and Mrs. Margolis," Joe said.

The first round of drinks was almost finished when Dom and his wife arrived. Dom looked more tired than usual, but he was wearing a pair of gray slacks with a sharp crease and a freshly pressed shirt so unlike his usual rumpled suit that he seemed like an entirely different person.

Dom didn't look at Elizabeth or Mark as they greeted him nor did he look at Elizabeth as he introduced his wife, Marie.

Elizabeth felt uneasy, but the feeling was dispelled as Marie smoothed the awkward moment with her charm and friendliness.

Her brown eyes radiated maternal warmth to which Elizabeth immediately responded.

With Mark helping, Elizabeth began to pass the hors d'oerves. Ella Fitzgerald's voice from the c.d. player filled the room.

"I never thought of this luxurious apartment as homey, but you've made it homey tonight," Mark said.

They finally sat at the huge dining room table for the appetizer which was a big hit. Only Ellen knew how nervous Elizabeth was about the food since her entertaining career was in its infancy.

Her father had always tried to interest her in cooking, and she dutifully watched and worked with him in the kitchen all her life. Her lack of interest made her believe she could not cook, but the years of watching had paid off. When the cooking bug bit her, she was ready and full of knowledge she didn't know she had.

Doris seemed to be studying Elizabeth. Every time Elizabeth glanced at her, she smiled mysteriously.

When the main course of salmon steaks done in champagne sauce with shallots was finished and raved over, the party headed back to the living room where Elizabeth fed the waning fire and got it blazing again. They all teased her for having a fire in June. She confessed to being a diehard where the fire season was concerned.

"You did a great job on the dinner; you really did," Marty said as he and Ellen sat down. He winked knowingly, and Elizabeth realized that Ellen must have told him how nervous she was.

Doris was sitting in Michael's favorite chair, a great wingback, twin to the one in the den. "Well, we have some news to report tonight. As you know, Elizabeth has been up against a deadly enemy, the live-in boyfriend of Millie's mother, Chet King. This man has killed Millie's mother and Jane Levin. We believe he has been stalking Elizabeth. He did so on at least one occasion before and one occasion after killing Jane. We know he wanted Elizabeth dead but fortunately Dom and Marty got him in jail."

Elizabeth looked at Dom and saw him shift uneasily in his place on the couch. His wife's hand reached over and touched the top of his lightly. He looked at Marie quickly, and Elizabeth saw his knuckles whiten as he gripped his glass of club soda more tightly.

Elizabeth shifted her eyes to Marty. He was studying Dom too. Marty's forehead was creased, his eyebrows close together. He seemed to be concentrating intensely. Elizabeth knew why. Something was wrong with Dom, and his partner knew it. Marty's mind was probably racing, as Elizabeth's was, wondering what it was. Mark, Elizabeth noticed, had picked all this up too.

Doris continued, "The news is, that despite all this sorrow and fear, we can now be joyful because Millie began to show signs tonight of coming out of the coma."

Doris's eyes disappeared as her face crinkled up into the usual smile. Elizabeth stood up. Her arms dropped to her sides and she stared at Doris in astonishment. She felt a bolt of joy and hope flood through her as she burst into tears of happiness and relief.

Mark had her in his arms in a flash, and she continued to sob as each of her friends except Dom got up and hugged her, sharing her joy at this wonderful news.

"How, when," she finally stammered. "Ellen and I were visiting her earlier, and there was no change."

"I stopped on my way here tonight. I had the cab wait while I went up to see Millie for a moment. Nancy Cabello was there. She said Millie's finger had moved. She said her eyelids were fluttering, both signs of a slow return to consciousness. It could be many days before she is fully conscious, but now we believe she will return to us."

"I need to go there now."

"No, Elizabeth, Millie is sleeping now. It is 10:30. Even coma patients have definite sleep patterns. You may disturb her rest if you go now. I didn't tell you earlier because I knew you would run there and not eat. But I guess it's hopeless, trying to keep you away tonight."

Elizabeth fell limply into the chair Mark guided her to. Ellen and Marty headed for the kitchen. Moments later they were serving coffee and dessert to the guests.

"And that's why Nancy didn't come?"

"Yes, she wanted to stay with Millie for the evening."

"How kind of her, but I should be there. She can't stay all night. I'd like to sit with Millie tonight."

Elizabeth noticed Dom still sitting miserably on the couch. His eyes were hollow, and his skin was pale. There was a slight tremor in his hands. He squeezed Marie's hand, shifted his position, and then stood up.

Elizabeth's elation became apprehension as Dom approached her.

"She's not alone tonight, Honey," Dom said as his eyes finally fully met Elizabeth's. "There is a police officer with her, protecting her, captain's orders. Just before Marie and I left the house tonight, the precinct called and told me that King had been released from jail, on a technicality. I don't know the details. Anyway, the judge let him go. We had plenty of evidence to re-arrest him, but he has disappeared. King is gone."

Chapter Twenty-Three

There was no keeping her away. When everyone had left, Elizabeth, Mark, and Ellen gave the mess a lick and a promise, called a car service, and went to see Millie.

They sat with her for awhile seeing no change but were greatly encouraged when the nurse read from the chart, "Patient's left index finger was raised several times; rapid eye movement."

Before they left, Elizabeth lifted one of Millie's thick black braids and stroked her smooth cheek. "I'll soon be brushing these braids and putting ribbons in your hair," she promised.

The nurse reassured them that Millie needed her rest and would be fine. Elizabeth agreed to leave to be better rested for the morning when she would return bright and early. They spoke to the police officer who was on duty, and he also assured them that he knew his job and would protect Millie with his life.

Mark brought Elizabeth and Ellen to the door of Elizabeth's apartment but declined her invitation to come in. They were all whipped.

"I'm going to walk Moss," Ellen said as she went inside to get the big Labrador.

Mark took Elizabeth in his arms and kissed her.

Finally they pulled apart slightly and looked into each other's eyes. "I love you."

"I love you too," Elizabeth whispered.

They embraced again. "We have a lot of plans to make."

"Yes."

They laughed now, the absurdity of standing in the hallway of the elegant Fifth Avenue apartment building declaring their love suddenly amusing them.

Mark became somber first. "King."

"I know."

"He'll have to be dealt with before . . ."

"Before there is peace and happiness for us."

"Let's try not to think about it for now. We'll get through this." They parted almost happily, choosing to ignore for once the shadow of danger that followed close behind.

The next day, Elizabeth packed a picnic lunch for herself and Ellen, and they headed for the nursing facility. The change in Millie was immediately apparent. She appeared to be sleeping naturally. Elizabeth squeezed her hands and rubbed her forehead gently from time to time as she read to her softly. Millie stirred occasionally, causing excitement in Elizabeth who quickly looked at Ellen grinning back at her.

Elizabeth never left Millie's side as various nurses, Nancy Cabello, the physical therapist, and others came and went. Ellen seemed restless and announced that she was going out shopping for a while. The police officer who stood guard was a friendly man who confided in Elizabeth that he had a daughter Millie's age, and it broke his heart to see Millie so sick.

Dom and Marty stopped in for a visit too. They noticed the change in Millie immediately. They talked to her and encouraged her to get better. Elizabeth noted with interest that Marty seemed disappointed that Ellen wasn't there.

He brightened moments later when Ellen did walk into the room carrying big shopping bags that she could barely manage.

"Presents for Millie?" he guessed.

"You bet." She winked at Marty. Elizabeth began to unpack the bags, gleefully describing each item for Millie's benefit. There were long, lovely, feminine nightgowns trimmed in lace in pale pink and mauve, underthings of various colors, a casual dress, a dressy dress, stretch pants and tops, tights, and socks.

There was also a bag of books. Ellen had guessed well at Millie's taste, Elizabeth thought as she read the titles to Millie—*A Light in the Attic*, *A Tree Grows in Brooklyn*, *Roll of Thunder Hear My Cry*, *The Adventures of Huckleberry Finn*, and *The Clan of the Cave Bear*. Well, maybe Millie was a little young for *A Tree Grows in Brooklyn*.

Elizabeth hugged Ellen, touched by her generosity and thoughtfulness. "How'd you get all this in only two hours?"

"I got a cab to Lord and Taylor's and then one to Barnes and Noble, no problem. But wait, I've saved the best for last. I saw a little store on Fifth Avenue near Barnes and Noble."

She lifted the first bag up onto the bed and took out a big, soft teddy bear with real looking brown eyes and big pink bow around its neck. Then she reached into the bag again and pulled out a small wooden music box with a picture of a lush green forest on the top.

"Like *Green Mansions*," she said to Elizabeth as she wound it up. She opened the top and it began to play an old sad song called "My Buddy." The tinkling notes filled the room and Elizabeth whispered the refrain, "Your buddy misses you."

She looked up from the box in time to see Mark enter the room and stop dead on the threshold, staring at the bed. Elizabeth turned and saw Millie's big brown eyes gazing at her, a slight smile on her face as she reached for the teddy bear.

Chapter Twenty-Four

She came into the office at the crack of dawn each morning. It was the best time to get the work done because the phone didn't ring, and no one was there to make demands on her attention. She refused to let herself be frightened by the thought of Chet King on the loose. She took normal safety precautions and went about her life.

She found that she enjoyed the job at Charles Planning Services and had a flair for business. The company was flourishing under her direction. Even though she was not a certified financial planner, she was a good manager. Like cooking, she found she had learned a lot about this business through absorption over the years. Of course, her father's staff, the Certified Financial Planners, did the real work of the company. Her job was to handle all the details that could take them away from that work.

The early hours enabled her to get to see Millie too. She got to the office at 6:15, worked until 10:00, took a cab to the nursing facility, stayed until 2:00, then back to the office until 5:30. A visit to Millie in the evening completed her day.

She looked forward to the day when she could go home to a fully recovered Millie, not that she wasn't grateful for the progress that Millie had made so far. Gratitude was the cornerstone of her life now. She never wanted to lose sight of the many blessings that surrounded her. The friendships she'd made were some of them. She thought of her old friends, Ellen, Mrs. Margolis, Al and Joe, and her new ones, Dom and Marty, Doris and of course, Mark.

The ringing of the phone startled her. "It's Francine Levin, Elizabeth." Elizabeth glanced at the clock, 6:39 a.m.

"Are you okay?"

"Yes, you told me that you get to the office before seven and as I am an early riser also, I thought this might be a good time to call. We've been surrounded by boxes since we moved. I hadn't forgotten my promise to you about looking for information about my grandmother's death. The odd thing is that my grandmother didn't work for the Triangle Shirtwaist Company."

"She died in the fire, but she didn't work for the company?"

"She didn't work at all. She had already had my mother at the time of the fire. She used to work there, before my mother was born, I guess, but she definitely wasn't working at the time of the fire."

"How do you know she died in the fire?"

"We always knew. It was an interesting but sad part of our family history. My grandmother's mother wrote about it in her diary. I've had the diary for years, but it is in Yiddish, so I couldn't read it. I had someone from the nursing home down here translate it for me. My grandmother's mother, Esme Jacobs, says that her daughter, Rebeccah, had left Maida, my mother, with her for the day."

"Rebeccah? Was Rebeccah your grandmother's name?"

"Yes."

"I'm sorry I interrupted; please continue."

"My mother, Maida, was left with her grandmother, Esme, who wrote that Rebeccah, her daughter and Maida's mother, had asked her to take Maida for the day because she had to do something to help a friend. My great-grandmother Esme wrote in her diary that Rebeccah was always helping others. Listen to her words, Elizabeth; they moved me so. The date of the entry is March 25, 1911. 'Rebeccah brought little Maida to my home. It was my joy to have my beautiful granddaughter Maida for the day. I asked Rebeccah who she was going to help. She just said it was a friend who needed her. I am proud of my Rebeccah. She cares for all people.' Then on March 26 she writes, 'I will go mad. Rebeccah never came home last night. There was a great fire at Triangle. I ran to the building and saw it burning. There were young girls lying on the sidewalk. They had jumped from the windows. I went home and prayed and prayed. But Rebeccah never came home. She never came home. I fear she is dead.'"

Elizabeth tried to sip her coffee to get the dryness from her mouth, but her hands were shaking too hard and she had to put the cup down.

"Then on March 28th, 'I went to the morgue on 26th Street. I looked at all the bodies. They were lined up in coffins in rows against the walls. There was one. Oh, God, there was one who was surely Rebeccah. She was burned. Her beautiful face was burned. But she seemed so like my Rebeccah. If I identify her, she would really be dead. She is dead though, I know it. A mother knows.'

"March 29th, 'I went back to the morgue. No one had identified the body I think is my girl. The clothes are charred and unrecognizable. She lies there unclaimed. A kind policeman told me it couldn't be Rebeccah if she didn't even work there. He must be right.' There are only two more entries, April 5th and April 6th; on April 5th she wrote, 'Today they are burying the girls who were unidentified. Is Rebeccah among them? Walk through that door, Rebeccah. Come home now and end this nightmare.'"

"It is almost unbearable to listen to this even knowing that it happened over ninety years ago," Elizabeth whispered.

"I know, but here is the last one from the 6th, 'What have I done? I allowed my child to be buried in a mass grave with the other nameless girls. I must go to the rabbi and tell him what I have done. I must tell Maida that her mother is dead. Of course it was Rebeccah, so small and thin. I will say Kaddish. I cannot bear to go on living.'"

Mrs. Levin was silent for a long moment, and Elizabeth was too.

"The diary was ripped here, and the cover is missing. There is no more."

"What happened to Maida? Where was Maida's father? Did they find out for sure where Rebeccah was that day and what had happened to her?"

"Maida grew up, married, and had me. Her own father, my grandfather, died before the fire when he was a young man. I don't remember my mother talking much about her childhood although

I always believed that it was an unhappy one. Has any of this helped you, Elizabeth?"

"I'm not sure. I wish I could have talked to her, to Maida, your mother, I mean. It would have given me some understanding of the hallucinations."

"Why, my dear," a triumphant note sounding now in Mrs. Levin's voice, "you *can* talk to her. She is right here in Florida, living in a nursing home."

Chapter Twenty-Five

Elizabeth began interviewing housekeepers in anticipation of Millie leaving the nursing facility soon. She interviewed at least six and was beginning to feel discouraged about finding someone she could trust. Then a neighbor told her about Mrs. Ahern. The neighbor was moving and would no longer need Mrs. Ahern, her housekeeper for seven years. Elizabeth was acquainted with Mrs. Ahern and found her to be just what she wanted for Millie-responsible and mature, cheerful, upbeat, and warm. She had excellent references. She would start immediately, even though Millie was not yet home. It wouldn't be long though, since Millie's improvement was dramatic. She had begun intensive physical therapy and was stronger each day.

Preparing for the trip to Miami to meet Mrs. Levin's mother was tinged with guilt and worry about leaving Millie. Mark said that he would visit with Millie daily. And even though she'd already returned to Pennsylvania, Ellen was coming back with Moss to stay in Elizabeth's apartment and be with Millie all day while Elizabeth was away. Dom, Marty, Doris, even Al and Joe and Mrs. Margolis would stop by too, she knew.

The policemen were no longer on duty around the clock because of the cost to the taxpayers so Elizabeth hired private security guards to take their place. The fear of King was never far away despite the fact that he seemed to have stopped stalking Elizabeth.

Mark drove Elizabeth to the airport. He used his badge as an officer of the court to get passed security and right up to the gate where he stayed with Elizabeth until the last moment. They kissed long and hard before it was time to board the United Airlines flight at J.F.K. Airport. She turned one last time. They looked at each other wistfully before Elizabeth stepped into the jetway.

She took her seat in business class and reflected on her father's death. This was the first time she was on a plane since the crash that took her father's life. She was grateful that she did not fear flying even now. She wondered about her father's death. Why did it happen? How did he feel at the end? She willed herself to stop thinking these painful thoughts and to remember the peace she had felt in Martine's in New Hope, peace because he was with her in some way she didn't understand.

The flight attendant came down the aisle and offered her a choice of beverages. Sipping the tea she had ordered, she turned her thoughts to Millie. Millie had shown so much courage when she came out of the coma that she was an inspiration to all the people who came in contact with her. She chatted merrily and was friendly to everyone who came to see her, even when it was a doctor or nurse to poke and prod her.

She couldn't wait until her slightly blurry vision would clear up completely so she could read on her own again. That was the only thing she did complain about, but Elizabeth was indulgent with her whining. She knew how important reading was to Millie.

Her physical therapy was intense and painful but Millie worked so hard at it, almost without complaint, that everyone knew her muscle tone and complete physical ability would return.

She would have a happy life when she got out of the hospital. Elizabeth was going to see to that. She would go home with Elizabeth to the apartment. They would decorate her room together. The school was nearby, but was New York City any place to raise a child? She herself had been raised there, and the cultural benefits were enormous. The weekends in Pennsylvania would be the needed respite from the hustle and bustle of city life. Elizabeth imagined Millie's delight at seeing all the museums in Manhattan and the theater too. She couldn't wait to take Millie to a Broadway show.

She made a mental list of all the things she'd like to do with Millie and Mark too. Mark would be a part of it. She couldn't imagine her life without Mark. He had been a wonderful friend to her, and her love for him had been growing steadily. She thought about his desire to get away from city life and the rat race. Perhaps they could plan a future, a future away from the stresses of city life, away from . . . Her thoughts stopped short with a jolt. King . . . no matter where they went, they would always feel the threat of this evil. She knew King was more than a criminal. He was insane and lusted for revenge against Elizabeth. Jane's brutal murder had shown that.

The flight attendant brought her a light meal that she just picked at. She dozed until the plane was on approach to Miami International Airport.

Mrs. Levin beamed at Elizabeth as she entered the baggage claim area. Elizabeth was happy to see that Mrs. Levin was tanned and looked healthy. Maybe she was past the first wave of her grief.

"Larry's outside with the car, Elizabeth. He'll take us home, and we'll go to the nursing home tomorrow. Mother is much more alert early in the morning."

Larry and Elizabeth exchanged warm greetings and they talked all the way to the house, catching up on the last weeks—Millie's recovery, life in Miami, how they were coping.

Elizabeth admired their new house. It was open, spacious and smelled of fresh sea air.

"Very different from Brooklyn, isn't it?" Mrs. Levin said.

Elizabeth nodded seeing the sadness deep in Jane's mother's eyes. They hugged, and Mrs. Levin immediately resumed her cheerful demeanor.

"Why don't you get settled in your room and I'll fix us a cold drink and something to eat."

Elizabeth was stunned by the heat the next morning as she stepped from the air conditioned house to the driveway. The sun, though low in the sky, burned brightly. She was blinded momentarily by the reflection of it on the windshield of the car. Points of brilliant light in a circle with colors sparkling and moving in perfect symmetry mesmerized her, and she began to feel the start of a hallucination.

The child was in that same apartment Elizabeth had seen before, but this time Catherine wasn't there. The child was seated in the large room. She was completely focused on Elizabeth as she pointed, pointed at something out of Elizabeth's view. You'll find it, you'll see it, the child's eyes seemed to say, but Elizabeth's view of the room only included the child seated on an enormous chair and the furnishings of part of the room.

A massive sofa was flanked by dark wooden tables with lamps crowned with ornate lampshades. Over the sofa hung an enormous painting. A gold rope made a perfect triangle on top of the painting which attached it to a nail on the wall. The painting depicted a rural scene with wide open space, blue skies and farm animals, a far cry from the dark apartment that was probably in New York. Framed photographs crammed every surface in the living room.

Elizabeth looked at the child. She was wearing black lisle stockings and heavy leather shoes. Her skirt was a coarse dark material, maybe serge, and she had on a white blouse. Her hair was a rich brown and was braided in a single plait which hung down her back. She was pale and had delicate features. Her eyes showed sorrow, but strength and intelligence flowed from them as well. She pointed to the corner where Elizabeth could not see. Elizabeth tried to speak to her, but she faded from Elizabeth's view. She met the worried eyes of Mrs. Levin.

"Are you all right, dear?"

"Another one. I had another hallucination. The child, the same child, was in an apartment. She was pointing to something, just as Catherine had been when I wouldn't look. What do they want me to see?"

"Do you want to go back to the house and lie down? You're so pale."

"No, please. I'm getting used to this." She smiled and attempted to brush the incident aside. "I want to meet your mother, really; I'm okay," she said to a distressed Mrs. Levin. "What does your mother know about Jane?"

"The truth. We told her the truth. She cried but she accepted it. Old people are more accepting than we are, I think."

"What's her name?"

"Her name is Maida Sternberg. She is ninety-five now but she is usually alert and remembers the past more easily than she remembers the present."

The day room of the Miami Jewish Home for the Elderly was large and sunny. It was freshly painted and cheerfully decorated with colorful paintings and artwork done by the residents. Elizabeth welcomed the cool but not cold air conditioning which kept the staff comfortable while catering to the elderly residents, many of whom wore sweaters to keep the chill from their waif-like frames.

Elizabeth noticed how the residents, most of them in wheelchairs, kept to themselves, not clustering in groups, not talking to one another. Maybe they had lost their hearing and so they couldn't participate in conversations. A woman was holding a baby doll wrapped in a blanket in her arms. Her eyes were sad and empty. Elizabeth smiled at her. She smiled at some of the other women too, and found that only a few returned her smile. She had an eerie feeling that most of them were robots or people who were already dead. Over and over she looked into lifeless and vacant eyes. She and Mrs. Levin made their way to the corner of the large day room.

They approached a wheelchair whose occupant was turned away from them. Elizabeth saw the long white hair drawn tightly into a luxurious bun at the nape of her neck, a sharp contrast to most of the other women whose hair was sparse and wispy. Walking slowly around the wheelchair, making a wide arc so she wouldn't startle her mother, Mrs. Levin called softly, "Mother, good morning. It's me, Francine." Elizabeth stepped in front of the old woman in time to see her face move from repose into a brilliant smile.

"My darling, Lovey," she said to Mrs. Levin.

As Mrs. Levin turned to Elizabeth, her mother followed her gaze and stared at her. Elizabeth felt a sharp bolt of recognition as she looked into Mrs. Sternberg's eyes, eyes that she felt she had seen before.

"Bridget Mary, Bridie, how have you come back to me?"

Mrs. Levin looked alarmed. "Mother, this is Elizabeth Charles, Jane's friend from New York. Elizabeth, this is my mother, Maida Sternberg."

"Sit down, child," the old woman said, her face composed now. "Please forgive me. I am getting senile. You look so much like someone I once knew. She had hair the exact color of yours. It was wild and unruly like yours too."

"Yes, it's hard to control this hair," Elizabeth stammered. The earlier hallucination, the recognition she thought she had when she saw Mrs. Sternberg, and then being addressed as Bridget had shaken her.

"Who was Bridget, Mother?"

"It was so long ago, dear. It is a long story, too." It didn't seem as though Mrs. Sternberg wished to continue the conversation. Mrs. Levin looked at Elizabeth. Her frustration was obvious. She shrugged as if to say, "What can I lose?"

"Mother, Elizabeth is very interested in the fire at the Triangle Shirtwaist factory. I know your mother was killed in that fire. Do you remember anything about it?"

A soft flush suffused the elderly woman's papery cheeks. "I wish I could say that it no longer hurts to think of my mother. But even now when I am so close to being with her again finally, I feel that pain of her loss. It was so great I never spoke of it, not to your father, not to you, Francine. I cannot speak of it now either."

"Mrs. Sternberg, I don't wish to upset you. I'm not asking you out of idle curiosity. I've been troubled by this fire in dreams or hallucinations of some sort. I don't know what they are, and I don't understand them. I was hoping you could help me."

Mrs. Sternberg reached for Elizabeth's hands. Elizabeth noticed how long and graceful her fingers were when her cool dry hands clasped both of Elizabeth's.

"I can see you are indeed troubled. I don't know what I can do. I have spent my life avoiding memories of my childhood, and I cannot go back there now as much as I would like to help you. I was a small child at the time of the fire. My grandmother told me that my mother was killed in the fire. That is all I know."

Elizabeth tried to hide the disappointment from her face, but Mrs. Sternberg saw it. "You are beautiful and good. You have your life before you, a life which you will live in great peace. Put these things out of your mind." Mrs. Sternberg reached for Elizabeth's hair and stroked it for a moment. A single tear fell from each of her eyes and made their way down her cheeks. She wiped them away quickly.

"I know I will see you again. I am quite tired now, Francine, my dear." Mrs. Levin looked miserable as she got behind the wheelchair and rolled it gently toward the bedrooms in the back of the building. Elizabeth stared at the beautiful bun at the back of Mrs. Sternberg's neck as Mrs. Levin wheeled her from the room.

Chapter Twenty-Six

Mrs. Levin was hopeful as she said her farewells to Elizabeth. Just before Elizabeth slipped through the magnetometer prior to walking to the gate, Mrs. Levin said, "I'll keep talking to her, Elizabeth. I'll try to persuade her to tell me more. I'll write everything down."

"Don't distress her. Obviously she was deeply upset by remembering. It's unlikely that she would know anything anyway. She was only a small child when it happened."

Later in the seat of the plane she closed her eyes and drifted off to sleep.

Mrs. Sternberg was calling her from her wheelchair, "Elizabeth, Bridget, Elizabeth," she cried over and over. Elizabeth could see her eyes in the dream, the eyes that were hauntingly familiar.

She awoke suddenly and felt ill at ease. Upsetting an elderly woman was not something to feel good about.

Soon she was on the ground and in Mark's arms as she stepped off the jetway. They planned to go to Antonio's for dinner immediately after the airport. Ellen and Marty were with Millie.

"I know you want to skip Antonio's and go straight to the nursing facility to see Millie. Believe me, she's just fine and having a ball with Ellen and Marty. Let's have a nice dinner, brief but relaxing, and then I'll whisk you off to see our girl."

Elizabeth was touched by his words, "our girl." As anxious as she was to see Millie, the thought of sharing a delicious meal with Mark was appealing. Antonio made a big fuss over them. Mark excused himself and went to Antonio's private office. He returned in a moment. "There's a call for you," he told Elizabeth as he handed her his cell phone which had been behind his back.

"Elizabeth, where are you?" Millie's voice sounded so strong and joyful that it brought tears to Elizabeth's eyes.

"I'm at Antonio's with Mark. We're going to have dinner here. We'll be there to see you right after we finish dinner."

"Take your time and have fun. Give Mark a big kiss for me." Millie was giggling. Elizabeth felt lighthearted as she snapped the phone shut and kissed Mark gently on the cheek. "That's from Millie. Thanks for placing that call; I feel relaxed now."

After Antonio came over and filled their wine glasses, Elizabeth related her experiences in Miami and her fascinating, if disappointing meeting with Mrs. Sternberg.

"It was a lead that didn't pan out, but we're not going to give up." Mark wasn't one to give up. Of that Elizabeth was quite certain.

"Is there anything new with King? I've only been gone two days, but it seems like forever since he was released with no news."

"Let's not talk about King right now, other than to say that there is nothing new." He reached for her hand and played with her fingers. "I'm in the mood for some plans. Meeting you and falling in love with you . . ." She tightened her fingers on his hand, her face softened. "Yes, I'm in love with you. Nothing has changed since I told you so on the night of your dinner party."

"I love you too, Mark."

"I can hear a 'but' coming."

"It's King. It's the hallucinations. I feel that I can't plan anything."

"Life is never simple; there are always difficulties, impediments . . ." He saw the distress on her face. "Maybe the impediments are not as bad as a murderer on the loose and trips into the past," he said and smiled to lighten the moment, "but life will throw us equally serious curves, more ordinary perhaps, but equally serious . . ."

"I know, and I know we can handle them together, as partners. I want that."

Their dinner arrived and the serious conversation ended. As always, Antonio's dinner was delicious, and despite the heavy conversation of moments ago they enjoyed it thoroughly.

Mark suggested that they stop at Elizabeth's apartment to drop off the bags before going to see Millie. Elizabeth put her key in the door and was surprised to see Ellen and Marty who she thought were at the nursing facility. As they stepped back into the foyer, Elizabeth could see Millie standing in the doorway to the den. She walked slowly to Elizabeth and Mark.

"Surprise!" Millie shouted, all child now, with no trace of the serious old-before-her-time kid she had become because of the hardships in her young life. Millie's delight at the surprised Elizabeth could not be concealed. Elizabeth was speechless and could only hug Millie and croak out murmurs of wonder at seeing Millie home and walking.

Finally she said, "Look at you! I can't believe my eyes."

They all sat in the den as Elizabeth had imagined only weeks ago, everyone grateful for Millie's recovery. Millie excitedly told Elizabeth about her release from the nursing facility, her thrill at coming home, and about the new book she had started, *David Copperfield.*

When Millie was tucked in for the night, Ellen brought Elizabeth up to date on the details of her release from the nursing facility. "Doctor Piscali came from Downtown Hospital to the nursing home for his daily examination and pronounced her fit to go home where he believed she'd recover more rapidly." They went over the instructions for Millie's home care and the schedule for her continued physical therapy.

"Elizabeth, Millie is truly an exceptionally gifted child. You'll need to find a special program or special school for her," Ellen said.

"I know. We'll start with a tutor until she is fully recovered. Meanwhile I'll research the schools."

The phone rang. It was Francine Levin. "Elizabeth, dear." Elizabeth's heart started to race. "The nursing home called me shortly after you left today. They took my mother to the hospital because she suddenly had difficulty breathing. When I got there, she told me I must tell you something. She made me promise to tell you. She said, 'Tell Elizabeth to keep looking. Tell her I will see her again.' She was peaceful then. She died only moments later. She's with Jane now," Mrs. Levin sobbed.

Chapter Twenty-Seven

"Where should I keep looking, Doris? Mrs. Sternberg's message to me was to keep looking."

"Some of your episodes are baffling, Elizabeth. When you were on St. James Place, in Downtown Hospital, in Washington Square Park, I believed you were in a time slip. But Jane's desk, Francine Levin's driveway in Florida . . . I don't know how you could go into the past in that way. There are so many things we do not understand. But I am still certain, absolutely certain, that this is real. There are no coincidences in this, Elizabeth."

"You mean Sherlock being my grandmother's name, someone at Triangle named Sherlock, Jane's great-grandmother dying in the fire, her grandmother telling me to keep looking?"

"Yes. You have been so busy with Millie, your father's business, and the worry over Chet King that you haven't found the opportunity to go back to your home in Pennsylvania and look in the attic for something related to your family history. Do you think you can squeeze in the time?"

"I guess I need to make it a priority. It's time for Millie to see her country home anyway."

"How's the adoption going?"

"It takes a full year to finalize, but it's going fine. I have custody of Millie."

That night Elizabeth asked Millie if she was up to the two-hour car ride to Lumberville, Pennsylvania.

"Yeah!"

Elizabeth scrutinized Millie and thought there might be some more weight on her. Her cheeks didn't seem quite as hollow.

"Can Mark come with us?"

"I'll ask him, but he may have trouble getting away."

As Elizabeth suspected, Mark was unable to join them because he was in the middle of preparing for an upcoming trial.

When Dom called and heard they were going, he was full of protective admonitions and advice.

"Bodyguard or no bodyguard, keep all the doors and windows locked. I know how it is in the country. No one locks their front doors. Stupid not to."

Marie must have grabbed the phone from him. "Don't let the old grump scare you, Elizabeth. You and Millie need lots of fresh air. Enjoy."

A call from Mark followed. "I wish I were going with you. I'm going to miss you both and worry too. Please be careful. No sign of King. We have no leads. I'm glad you have a bodyguard going with you. I thought he was a gem when he was guarding Millie in the nursing facility. I'm glad he agreed to go with you." He had said "I love you" to Elizabeth and later to Millie before hanging up. They said it back to him.

She left the office early on Friday and arrived home to find Millie all ready to go.

"I couldn't get her to rest at all today, Elizabeth. She was so excited," Mrs. Ahern said.

They double-checked their overnight bags. Satisfied that they had everything, Elizabeth and Millie went downstairs to the lobby to meet the bodyguard who was picking up the rental car and would do the driving to Lumberville. He arrived shortly, and Elizabeth and Millie climbed into the back seat together.

As usual, Elizabeth began to relax as soon as they left New York. She told Millie about her childhood and how the house they were going to in Lumberville was really home to her. She told Millie that her mother had died when she was only three.

"I know how you feel when your mother dies because my mother died too."

Elizabeth nodded, and Millie poured out her feelings of love and sadness about her mother. Elizabeth listened quietly, nodding or murmuring sympathetically. They squeezed hands, cried, and talked some more.

Elizabeth marveled at Millie who had survived a bleak abusive home where she was neglected. Yet, Millie was a phenomenon, one of an exceptional group of indomitable survivors, intact emotionally, and able to move on with her life. Most children in her situation would be broken and scarred forever.

"I'm glad you told me about your mother. Now I know we have something important in common," Millie said solemnly.

Millie was almost speechless as they crossed the Delaware from Stockton and saw the gleaming river sparkling in the near dusk. Until now she'd only been outside of Manhattan in her imagination.

The driveway was in semi-darkness from the trees and the rapidly approaching evening, but as they approached the house they saw that it was all lit up. An aura of welcome surrounded it.

A dog barked, and in a flash Moss was beside them furiously wagging his tail. His effusive greeting included jumping, licking, and nuzzling both of them. He was suspicious of the bodyguard at first, but soon warmed up to him too.

"You can see he wouldn't be much protection for us. Moss loves everyone," Ellen said with her hand extended to the bodyguard.

"This is Mohammed," Millie said to Ellen before Elizabeth had a chance to introduce them. "He's real quiet, and all our talking drives him crazy. And I oughta know since he was watching me at the nursing home. We've stopped trying to get him to talk to us. You didn't say one word in the car all the way here, did you, Mohammed?"

Mohammed's face twitched in a smile as he shook Ellen's hand. "How could I get a word in edgewise with you two chattering like a couple of bluejays," Mohammed said.

Inside Ellen had placed a tray of cheese and crackers and chips and dip on the coffee table.

"You're so thoughtful, El." Elizabeth turned to Millie. "How about a tour of the house first? Then we'll get into our nightgowns and enjoy the snacks Ellen made?" Millie nodded enthusiastically, but Elizabeth couldn't help but notice that the trip had worn her out. Millie was pale and limp somehow. The dark semi-circles under her eyes had returned.

"You may have my old room; I hope you like it. And Mohammed, I'll show you your room too."

"I do like it," Millie said as she stood on the threshold of Elizabeth's room a moment later. She entered the room slowly and fingered the books in the bookcase reverently. She turned to Elizabeth who gave her instant permission to read them.

"They are yours now, every one of them."

Elizabeth had left the room this way when she went away to college, never transforming it from that of her childhood to a room for an adult. The canopy bed with its eyelet dust ruffle, the floral comforter, with matching dressing table skirt and curtains, and her desk and bookcase were all the same. She thought of Jane's room in Brooklyn. It had not been changed either. Had they both been afraid to grow up?

Millie sighed with pleasure when Elizabeth left her to change into her nightgown.

Elizabeth put her own bag on her father's bed. "I'm moving in here now, Dad," she prayed silently. "Now I'm the grownup with a child."

Mohammed had the guest room. "Don't worry, Elizabeth, I sleep so lightly; I'll wake up if a mouse sneezes."

Elizabeth woke slowly the next morning, luxuriating in the comfortable bed. She had purposely left the shades up in her room so the East facing windows would display for her the glorious Delaware in the morning sun, a beautiful sight at any time of year.

A small knock on her bedroom door was a pleasant surprise. "Come in," she called and Millie was standing on the threshold as she had last night on the threshold of Elizabeth's old room.

"Mohammed's up and checking around the house already. I hope I didn't wake you. I know you get up early. Usually," she added.

"Of course not. Come snuggle up." Millie got into the queen sized bed. "Well, you certainly missed a great party last night. Your hot chocolate got cold, your cheese and crackers and your chips would have been in danger of getting soggy, so Ellen, Mohammed, and I did the only noble thing-we ate them for you. Not to mention that you weren't exactly the most scintillating company."

Millie giggled. "I guess I was too tired to stay awake."

"I'll say. You sat down on the couch, and the next thing we knew, you were asleep. Moss was at your feet in the same condition. We couldn't even rouse you, so Mohammed had to carry you upstairs." Elizabeth noted with pleasure that the circles under Millie's eyes were gone, and she looked well rested, even sporting a little pink in her cheeks.

They had a leisurely breakfast, but not before Millie thoroughly explored the house, confessing she had been too tired to take it all in last night.

Finally they went upstairs to get dressed. Elizabeth was thrilled to put on her "country" clothes of jeans, a soft cotton tee shirt and comfortable Bass shoes, the suits and high heels of her city life far from her mind. Millie was a country girl too, wearing the same outfit of jeans and a tee shirt. They had to buy a belt for her jeans. Her tiny waist was impossible to fit with jeans that were long enough for her fifty inches of height.

Moss's familiar bark called them downstairs. He was standing on the patio outside the French doors from the kitchen, his tail wagging furiously. Ellen was a few feet behind him strolling down the well-worn path from her house to theirs.

"How about you and I going exploring today, Millie? I'd like to show you the countryside, and maybe we could have a picnic on the Delaware."

Millie looked at Elizabeth who nodded at once. "I'll be going through papers and boxes in the attic today. I'll leave out the interesting things for you to look at when you come back."

"Can I leave Moss here with you?" Ellen said.

"Sure, I'd love the company. Mohammed will go with you. Moss will stay with me."

Elizabeth headed for the attic soon after they left, locking the doors behind them at Mohammed's insistence. She was tempted to stall by pouring herself another cup of coffee but she resisted the desire to procrastinate. She tugged at the rope that dangled from the ceiling of the second floor landing and pulled down the attic stairs.

She felt some trepidation as she climbed the old steps, groping for the string to pull on the light. She listened, but there was no sound. Would there be mice up here? When she reached the top of the stairs she saw that her neat, organized father kept the attic as he had everything else-in order. The attic was about forty feet by thirty feet. Elizabeth could stand up easily in the middle but had to stoop under the eaves. It didn't look too promising for hidden treasures. There were no dusty old trunks, no old rocking horse from her childhood, not even a seamstress's model. It was instead a storage room lined with cardboard boxes, all of which were neatly labeled with black magic marker. There were a couple of pieces of old furniture and a wooden wardrobe.

She glanced at the North wall and decided to tackle the boxes there first. "Business files 1961, etc." lined the wall. These ended in 1968 when Michael's business really took off and his files were kept in the corporate offices he leased in Manhattan. The sight of these boxes made Elizabeth realize how hard her father had worked to develop his business to the extent he had. She felt the awesome responsibility of continuing it.

She decided to dig in. The first box contained cancelled checks for expenditures related to establishing the new business, lists written by her father of things he needed to do, an appointment calendar detailing his meetings and activities that year, receipts for tax purposes, and much miscellaneous paper.

She moved to the West wall next and found items from Michael's past and present. Copies of medical bills for her mother's illness, mortgage, insurance, and tax documents spanning twenty years were contained in several large boxes. Baseball cards her father must have collected as a child were in another. Several gifts, still in their original boxes, unwanted and never used, were next. There was a box of clothes too. A suit lay on top in a classic style that was never out of fashion. Why did he put it away? Maybe a few extra pounds got in the way. No, Michael Charles was conscious about his weight and fitness for as long as she could remember. She lifted the suit completely out of the box; a piece of paper slipped out. "Worn on our wedding day, April 27, 1972." She held the fabric up to her face and fancied that she could smell her father. The suit felt as though it were new, the quality of it making it endure almost thirty years. Under the suit was a layer of tissue. She lifted it and saw her mother's wedding suit. It was a lightweight navy blue wool with a lined slim skirt and a simple jacket. The white silk blouse she had worn was also in the box. She quickly put away the clothes, knowing that the nostalgia sweeping over her would impede her search for clues to help her understand the episodes into the past.

The South wall had Elizabeth's things. Some of her baby clothes and toys that her mother must have wanted to save were carefully packed away. School projects, awards, report cards and some treasured items Elizabeth herself could not bear to throw out were stored there too. Her college textbooks and college memorabilia spilled into the South wall and took up all of the boxes there.

Her stomach growled and she felt hot and sweaty. Maybe she'd go down and have lunch before she tackled the East wall. She started to read the labeling on the boxes when the light attracted her to the oiel de boeuf on the East wall. She struggled with the old handle on the circular window. She was finally able to crank the window out and was treated to the familiar view of the Delaware moving languidly along in the summer sun. She wondered if Ellen, Millie, and Mohammed were sitting on its bank this very moment having their lunch.

With no warning, the attic faded and Elizabeth was back in that apartment. The child was seated on the overstuffed couch. Her beautiful dark brown braid was hanging down her left shoulder. She had on similar clothes to those Elizabeth had seen her in before, black lisle stockings, a dark skirt, and a white blouse. Catherine walked into the room and embraced the child. Elizabeth saw two men carrying a plain wooden box, a coffin, into the room. Catherine pointed to a doorway. Elizabeth "followed" the men.

They entered a dimly lit bedroom. The furniture was dark, heavy, and solid. On the bed lay an old woman. She was very still. The men lowered the box onto the floor.

Elizabeth was shaking, her hand still on the attic window, her eyes slowly focusing on the Delaware sparkling below.

She lowered herself to the floor, afraid her shaking legs would not support her. Moss came over to her and licked her hand. His ears were back, and he was whining softly. She petted him and tried to reassure him, but the shaking continued. She pulled her knees up to her chest and wrapped her arms around them, willing them to stop shaking.

Who was the old woman who had died? An episode about an old woman dying so soon after Mrs. Sternberg's death. Was it a coincidence? Doris had said they weren't to think of these things as coincidences any longer. She felt grief over Mrs. Sternberg's passing and now this episode. She took deep breaths to calm herself and stood up. How long would she have to live with these painful episodes? She was being drawn into the past, drawn into the lives of these people. They were real people. She was sure of that.

Her only hope was to live in this moment, to focus on the present and do the best she could in the now of her life. She had Millie and Mark to love and the promise of a wonderful future with them. Dom and Marty would get King somehow too. The episodes would end. She'd get to the bottom of them, and they would end. In the here and now she had to look for clues to the mystery of the episodes. She got up and looked around the attic. What had she accomplished? The North, West and South walls were done. All that remained was the East wall and the wooden wardrobe. Since opening the attic window on the East wall triggered the episode, she wasn't anxious to tackle the boxes there just yet.

She looked at her watch. It was almost three o'clock. The day had flown. She realized she was no longer hungry. A box marked, "Mother" lay at her feet. She opened it carefully and found a manila envelope on top. Inside was a letter.

March 31, 1933

Dearest Daughter,

I know I don't deserve to call you that, but nevertheless you are my daughter.

It is now the end of my life, too late to make amends in any meaningful way. I will go to my grave with the sorrow of this and with unmitigated remorse for the wrong I have done to you and to your mother.

I do not now ask you for your forgiveness.

I understand that you turned out to be a fine young woman. You put yourself through college with a straight A average and excelled in everything you did. More importantly, you became a good person, something you probably would not have become had I been there to raise you.

So I leave you now, never having known you. I try to touch you over the years by giving you this house which has been in our family for many years. I also leave you the sum of over two million dollars.

May God forgive me.

Your father,
Austin Fennell

What was this? The paper was brittle and yellowed. She put the letter back in its manila envelope, shaken yet again, this time by the powerful emotions expressed in the letter. She put the envelope in the box and slowly carried it down the stairs. Moss followed quietly behind.

Chapter Twenty-Eight

The country air agreed with Millie. She returned from her excursion with Ellen with rosy cheeks and sparkling eyes. Her walk had a bounce that belied the serious injury she had sustained at the hands of King.

"This lady wore me out," Ellen sighed as she dropped into the rocking chair by the kitchen fireplace. "She fell in love with the Delaware and she seemed to want to get acquainted with the whole river in one day. I think even Mohammed was worn out." The enigmatic Mohammed made no comment, though Elizabeth thought she detected a twinkle in his eye.

Millie laughed at Ellen sprawled out on the chair. She was still bouncing around the kitchen recounting the impressions and experiences she'd had along the river which included sighting a deer. Despite the fatigue of the three adults, they caught her enthusiasm and saw the countryside anew through the eyes of a child who had never seen such wonders before.

"It's beautiful here," Millie said finally and yawned. "I think I'll take a nap now."

She kissed them and started for the stairs, Moss following. Millie looked at Ellen.

"Oh, he's big on putting people to bed. When he sees you get in bed, he'll come back down."

This delighted Millie. "Come on, Moss, I'm going to bed." They watched Millie and Moss leave the room.

"Excuse me, too, Ladies. I'm going to scout around outside," Mohammed said.

Ellen turned to Elizabeth. "How'd it go today?"

"I found a letter that'll blow your socks off and one box that may hold some promise. And I had an episode." Concern filled

Ellen's face. Elizabeth told Ellen about being in the apartment with Catherine and the child, an old woman dead in one of the bedrooms.

"Do you think that the old woman was Catherine's mother or the child's mother?"

"She was too old to be the child's mother, but somehow I didn't think she was Catherine's mother either. Catherine was upset but she seemed to be comforting the child."

"Why don't you call Doris. Maybe this bit of information will help her."

"You're right." Elizabeth made the call and filled Doris in on the latest episode.

She was encouraging. "We're getting closer, Elizabeth. Keep looking in that attic. The answers may be there."

They heard the click of Moss's nails on the hardwood floor as he headed through the dining room into the kitchen.

"Is Millie sleeping, old boy?" Moss settled down with a thud at Ellen's feet. "Want some help tackling the rest of the attic?"

"No, thanks, El. You've had enough today trying to keep up with Millie. I'll go up there now and go through the rest of it. How about dinner at Martine's tonight?"

"Great idea. I'll come by and get you at 6:30."

Elizabeth headed upstairs. She surveyed the attic and summarized the contents so far, North wall, business documents; personal documents relating to marriage, homes, taxes, some boxes of clothes; West and South walls, Elizabeth's school projects, report cards, clothes and toys from childhood, Elizabeth's college books, souvenirs and mementos.

Still wary about the East wall because of the episode earlier in the day, she decided to do the wardrobe first. It contained her mother's clothes. Her mother's taste in clothes was eclectic. She was a young adult during the sixties. She had some long flowing skirts, a black wool maxi coat, and mini dresses, as well as conservative business suits. Elizabeth ached with longing to know her mother as she fingered the clothes. The picture her father kept of her on his dresser came into mind. Her mother had been young

144 P<small>ATRICIA</small> R<small>ILEY</small> L<small>EYDEN</small>

and smiling in that moment frozen in time, long unruly red hair framing her lovely face. She remembered her mother only vaguely as safe and warm and soft. She guessed Michael could not bear to throw out all of her clothes.

The wooden wardrobe also contained some of her father's clothes. She reached for the hatbox on the shelf and lifted the lid to find a gray felt halt with a grosgrain band. She didn't remember when men wore hats like this.

The urge to go downstairs and check on Millie and maybe have a cup of tea came over her, but she knew it was the desire to procrastinate because of her dread of the East wall.

She sat on the floor and opened the next box on the East wall. It was marked with her mother's name, "Eleanor," and contained memorabilia from Eleanor and Michael's romance: theater tickets and "Playbill" from *Butterflies Are Free, Promises, Promises, Prisoner of Second Avenue,* and *The Importance of Being Earnest* at City Center, matchbooks from restaurants in New York and Paris and Rome. There were many photographs of the young couple on their honeymoon in the box also.

Elizabeth went through these things which were precious to her mother. She could picture her mother happily preserving the memorabilia from good times. The next box contained love letters and other papers. Elizabeth thumbed through them and decided to take the whole box downstairs to peruse later.

When she got downstairs Ellen was in the kitchen. "You're still here," Elizabeth said.

Ellen looked as though she might have taken a nap too, in the rocking chair in the kitchen. "That's a big box. Do you want some help going through it?"

"No, thanks, Ellen. Most of it will go back to the city with me. I'll go through it there at my leisure."

"You look tired. It must be a strain on you looking through old memories."

"It is." The phone rang. It was Dom checking up on them for the fourth time this weekend. She reassured him that they were all right and hung up. Elizabeth pulled out the "Dearest Daughter" letter and handed it to Ellen.

Ellen read it quickly. She whistled softly. "Do you have any idea . . ."

"No, I can't imagine who that is, but I hope I find something else in the box that ties into this. Even if I do, it doesn't mean that it'll have anything at all to do with the present circumstances, with the hallucinations, or episodes, I mean."

"You haven't told Millie about the hallucinations?"

"No, she's mature for her age, but after all she has been through, I don't think she needs to worry about her new mother having trips back to 1911."

"Her new mother? I guess that is what you are. How does it feel to be responsible for another life?"

"I love Millie, and I love to be with her, so it's easy. I feel honored to be entrusted with her life for now. Of course her life is her own."

"I'd be scared, I think," Ellen said. "But when I'm with Millie I feel strong maternal instincts I never knew I had. I even think about Marty, getting married, having a family of my own." Ellen paused.

Ellen was twisting her hands. Elizabeth smiled at her friend.

"He's been calling me, and we talk for hours on the phone."

"I'm not surprised; I had a feeling about you two as soon as you met."

"It's too soon to say. A New York City cop and a country girl . . . I don't know. The thought of living there is not appealing to me, and I don't know if he'd come here."

Elizabeth thought of Mark and his desire to leave the rat race. "Maybe Marty would like to get away from the city."

"But what would he do here? He's very independent and I think he loves his work. His work defines him in some ways. I don't think he understands about me."

Ellen was referring to her life which did not include a job. She had an inheritance from her deceased parents that she lived on, which, in addition to stocks, bonds and a trust fund, also included patents and copyrights on a game invented by her mother. She did volunteer work at Doylestown Hospital, she'd written four children's books which had been published, and she was an industrious and prodigious maker of country crafts which were sold by some of the local merchants in New Hope to the tourists.

"If he likes you, he will understand. Marty is someone who knows what he wants and goes after it, I think. You are too . . ."

"Two hardheads, you mean." She sighed. "I think I'm falling in love with him, but I've never felt this way, so I'm not sure."

"Give it time. It will be okay."

Ellen reread the letter that Elizabeth had handed her at the beginning of their conversation. Elizabeth knew she wanted to change the subject from herself and Marty to the matter at hand.

"This letter speaks to us from the past of a great family tragedy. The question is, whose family tragedy? It must be your family, Elizabeth, or why would it be among your parents' papers?"

"Maybe it belonged to a client," Elizabeth said lamely. She didn't know why but she felt saddened by the letter and didn't want this sorrow to be part of anyone's history much less her own family's. Her own family that she knew almost nothing about . . .

"When we find Austin Fennell, or rather who he was, the rest should be fairly simple to figure out."

"It may not be easy to figure out who 'my dearest daughter' is. I hope we get lucky," Elizabeth said.

"I'll check the records in Doylestown to see if there is any record of an Austin Fennell. I go there anyway to work in the hospital," Ellen said.

"Thanks, that's a start." Elizabeth didn't get into Doylestown, the county seat of Bucks County, very often. She knew that birth and death records were kept there though.

"You know, I don't even know how long this house has been in my family. Would you check that too, if possible?"

"Sure, I'd be glad to do some investigating, like a cop. It will be fun. Wait till I tell Marty."

Moss looked up from his position at Ellen's feet and started to wag his tail signaling the arrival of Millie after her much needed rest. Elizabeth hugged the yawning Millie as she entered the kitchen.

Ellen said, "Let's forget Martine's and have a real country dinner at my place tonight. It's your last night, and I want you to sample my great cooking."

Both women saw the look of excitement on Millie's face which always appeared whenever she was about to experience something new.

Ellen gave the letter back to Elizabeth who put it in its box, the box that was marked, "Mother." They forgot about it. They had forgotten about King too.

Chapter Twenty-Nine

Millie adjusted to the change from Pennsylvania to Manhattan with ease. Elizabeth watched with pleasure as Millie showed Mrs. Ahern, their new housekeeper, all the things that she had brought back from Lumberville, several rocks and leaves from the shore of the Delaware, and a tee shirt purchased at the Lumberville General Store.

"The mail is on the hall table, Elizabeth," Mrs. Ahern said after she oohed and aahed over Millie's treasures.

A buff colored envelope of high quality paper with an unfamiliar handwriting caught Elizabeth's attention. She heard Millie excitedly telling Mrs. Ahern all about the deer she'd seen as she opened the envelope. A business card floated to the floor as she unfolded the letter. She stooped to pick it up and began to read:

> Dear Elizabeth,
>
> Please forgive me for addressing you by your first name, but your father spoke of you so often that I feel that I know you.
>
> Your father was staying with me, at my home in the Bahamas, just before he died. I flew out of the Bahamas on my way to Europe on the day he left. In fact, we went to the airport together. I hadn't heard and was unaware that there had been a plane crash until the next day. Even then, I didn't realize it was Michael's flight.
>
> I only became aware of your father's death when I returned to the United States from Europe and called him at his office. The secretary told me what happened and asked if I wanted to speak to you.

I'm afraid that I was shocked and overwhelmed with grief and therefore was unable to talk to you.

Business associates told me the details, about the crash, the funeral, your taking over the business. I am an international accountant and your father and I knew many of the same people in the financial planning and accounting businesses.

Elizabeth, I am sorry I have not contacted you sooner to offer my condolences and my comfort to you at this unbearable loss, but I needed time to get over the first raw stages of grief myself. I loved your father very much. From the beginning he loved me too, but in his own way. I believe he was unable to make a commitment because of his fear of loss again. Your mother's death was always with him.

I was not one much for commitment myself, so it was okay. But eventually things began to change. We fell more deeply in love. We began to recognize how wrapped up in our work we had been, how our involvement with work was draining us. We decided to change our priorities regarding work and make a fulfilling personal life for ourselves. We were both so business oriented that we thought that it would be hard to change. Instead it was glorious after so many years to discover love again and to share our lives with one another.

Your father was to bring you to the Bahamas that weekend, if you could get away. Since you couldn't, we planned to get together as soon as possible to tell you about our love. Your father was so anxious for us to meet and to like one another.

This news must be very shocking to you. Your father only kept it from you because it happened so gradually that he didn't realize how committed we were until quite recently. We'd been very discreet; you would have been the first to know. And like a kid, he wanted to surprise you as he had no doubts about your happiness for him.

I would so like to meet you, Elizabeth. If you would like to arrange a meeting, please call me. My business card is enclosed.

Sincerely,
Regina Jordan

Elizabeth walked slowly up the stairs to her father's room. Her knees were shaking; she gripped the banister tightly for support. Millie must not see her this way. She closed the bedroom door behind her and sat on the bed. The letter rested on her lap as she tried to collect her thoughts. Her father had been in love. She remembered their last conversation. How many times since his death had she recalled that last evening they had shared together, savoring the memory of his face, his voice, his laugh. That was why he was going to retire. Regina Jordan's letter. Of course he had no doubt that Elizabeth would be happy for him. How long she had waited for the day when he would have some love in his life!

The tears came then, tears that her father's chance at love had been taken away from him with his life.

There was a soft knock on the door. She hastily wiped away the tears. "Come in." Millie hesitated at the doorway and then entered. She sat on the bed and Elizabeth put her arm around her.

"You've been crying. Will you tell me what's wrong? I am your friend. Will you tell me, Elizabeth?"

Elizabeth handed Millie the letter. Millie's eyes darted rapidly over the paper. Comprehension shone in her eyes. Then she stood up and faced Elizabeth and hugged her with all the strength in her little body. "You are sad because your father missed having this lady to love."

Elizabeth nodded, not daring to speak. "You must not be sad, Elizabeth. Your father wouldn't want you to be sad. You told me that he taught you to accept things that couldn't be changed. You told me that you are able to be happy partly because he taught you that."

The words of this eight-year old child, who had suffered more in those short years than many do in a lifetime, were a comfort to her. They gave her the grace she needed to deal with the knowledge that her father had lost his future in a way she had not been aware of until today.

She looked at Millie with renewed admiration. How lucky she was that Millie had come into her life.

She smiled then. "You are a brave girl and you've shown me that I must be brave too."

"You are always brave," Millie said seriously. They talked about calling Regina Jordan and meeting her. Elizabeth gently moved on to other things, afraid Millie was too burdened with grown-up issues.

"Do you still like Mrs. Acevedo?" Mrs. Acevedo was the tutor who came in each day to help Millie with her schoolwork. Elizabeth was careful to hire someone who spoke Spanish so Millie wouldn't lose her knowledge of her second language and her Hispanic heritage. Mrs. Acevedo told Elizabeth that Millie was way beyond third grade in most areas and would personalize the instruction to challenge Millie academically. When she was fully recovered she'd begin school, something Elizabeth dreaded in a way. She was glad Millie was being tutored at home during her recovery period. It minimized the danger from King.

"Oh, yes," Millie said. "She is very smart, and she is very funny."

The phone rang. It was Dom. He still called daily, always full of admonitions. Elizabeth could hear Marty in the background yelling out reassurances. But although Marty tried to make light of it by joking, even he had warnings when he and Dom came to visit one evening. "You can never leave her alone for a minute, you know, not until we get him," Marty had said.

The buzzer sounded. "Mr. Lewis, Miss Charles."

"Send him up, Bruce," Elizabeth said. She turned to Millie whose joyful expression reflected her own. She didn't realize how much she'd missed Mark over the weekend they were away.

"I have tickets to a revival of *The Sound of Music* for the three of us," he said. "One of the other lawyers had tickets but can't make it tonight."

Mrs. Ahern frowned in disapproval when they told her they were going out to dinner.

"I know you are teaching Millie to enjoy nutritious foods, Mrs. Ahern. Look how she is thriving with your good cooking."

Mrs. Ahern was somewhat mollified, but said, "Don't let her be tempted by junk food or you'll undo the good I've tried to do. I am glad she's going to see that wonderful show, though," she added.

The play was a huge success. Millie was enraptured from the first note until the last. The excitement was too much for her though, and she fell sound asleep in the cab on the ride home.

Mark carried her into the building and upstairs to her room. Mrs. Ahern had waited up and helped undress Millie. Elizabeth lingered a moment staring at this lovely child in her warm bed. She was breathing softly. She left the door ajar and turned for one last look before joining Mark in the den for a cognac.

"Thank you for a delightful evening," Mark said as he handed her a crystal snifter with one finger of Remy Martin.

"Thank *you*. She really did enjoy the play, didn't she?" Elizabeth sipped her cognac, the thick liquid warming her instantly.

"I hate to bring this up, but I have to know. How do you feel about King? Have you been nervous?"

"Not really. With Mohammed there, I wasn't afraid to take Millie to Pennsylvania, far from our high security apartment building. Actually I felt completely safe there even with Dom's warnings and phone calls." They laughed.

"I wish I could have Mohammed all the time, but he has a full time job during the week. Dom knows him from somewhere. Mohammed only did this weekend job as a favor to Dom. He was moonlighting in the nursing facility, too, when the regular NYPD were called off. Dom trusts him and says he's good at what he does. He's the strong silent type, but I suspect he's crazy about Millie."

"I'm sure of it, and I've barely met the guy," Mark said. "How could he not be crazy about Millie?"

"I think you're a little prejudiced here, Mark."

"I love Millie and I want her to be safe forever from King."

Elizabeth looked Mark hard in the eye. "It may never be wrapped up, Mark. Isn't that true?"

ST. JAMES PLACE 153

"If King commits another crime, we'll get him. We may have a long wait. It worries me too." Mark put his hands on Elizabeth's shoulders. "His release on a technicality was a setback, but he's not going to get away with what he did to Millie, with Millie's mother's murder, and Jane's murder. His fingerprints were at the scene. There's plenty of forensic evidence there. We've just got to find him."

"Dom's retirement is resting on this, too. I know how anxious he and Marie are to get to North Carolina when this is over."

"We'll get him. We will," Mark said.

"Let's change the subject for a moment. I have something to tell you."

Elizabeth told him about the letter from Regina Jordan. He listened intently then put his arms around Elizabeth. "I can only imagine how this feels, Elizabeth." She melted into his arms.

"I want some closure, at least of one of these crazy things-the episodes into the past, or King, but with both of these things hanging over my head, I feel like I can't stand it, and I feel like yelling at God, 'Give me a break,'" Elizabeth said.

"It's only human to feel that way."

"I forget about all the love in my life, living in a free country, being so comfortable financially, a million things to be grateful for. I rail against the threat of King, of not understanding the episodes. I want to be free of this tension. I want to be free to be joyful and at peace," Elizabeth said.

"Then we are going to have to make that happen. We have the best of New York's Finest working on King. We have to work harder on 1911."

"Let me show you the letter from 1933 that I told you about." Elizabeth left the den and returned with the box containing the letter. She handed it to him and watched his handsome face as he absorbed each line. His forehead creased as he concentrated intensely on the contents of the letter. He finally looked up in amazement, speechless.

"Ellen is researching this in Pennsylvania to find out who Austin Fennell is. Doris is checking in New York."

"I hope you hear from them soon. In the meantime let's look through the rest of this box."

But it was late, and they were tired. They drank some more cognac and did some relaxed kissing. They finally said goodnight, the contents of the box forgotten yet again.

Chapter Thirty

"Regina, this is Elizabeth," Elizabeth said on the phone. She heard Regina Jordan's quick intake of breath and realized that this contact was as highly charged for Regina as it was for her.

"I'm so glad you called, Elizabeth. Can we meet somewhere, perhaps today, for lunch?" They arranged to meet at The Russian Tea Room at noon. Elizabeth arrived at the table to find Regina already there.

Regina Jordan was a beautiful woman. She was about five feet four inches tall, not weighing more than one hundred and ten pounds. Her hair was light brown which she kept in a soft natural style to her jaw bone. Elizabeth guessed her to be about fifty-two years old. The beige silk suit she was wearing was a classic style, beautifully tailored to her trim figure. Timeless beauty and grace was Elizabeth's immediate impression of Regina Jordan.

"I am so pleased to finally meet you, Elizabeth." Intelligence shone from Regina's green eyes. She had a strong handshake.

Elizabeth fought with her emotions. She wanted to show this woman how welcome she would have been into their little family, but her father was gone. It was strange and sad. A lump formed in her throat and she couldn't speak. Instead she reached for Regina's hands. Tear spilled down both her cheeks.

"Oh, my dear. This is so hard for you. I'm sorry to have distressed you so much."

Elizabeth willed her composure to return. "I know you understand my reaction to meeting you, Regina. My father must have been so happy and in love. I'd hoped for that for him for as long as I can remember."

"He told me you did. Of course I understand."

Elizabeth fumbled in her purse for a tissue. "I'm so glad that you contacted me and that we have met. It's a comfort to know that my father had personal happiness and love in his life."

The waiter unobtrusively appeared at the table and asked them if they would like something to drink. They ordered white wine.

They began to question one another at the same time, then apologized and attempted to get the other one to continue. It was awkward because they were so assiduously polite. At the third attempt they laughed finally, breaking the ice and Regina said, "I guess you must be especially anxious to hear about your father's last days, our plans. Suppose I fill you in and answer your questions. I'll be patient to hear about you, though it will be hard, as I have heard that you are adopting a child, and I'm bursting with curiosity."

Regina told Elizabeth how their friendship turned into love. She told her how excited Michael was as he planned telling Elizabeth that he and Regina were going to marry, how it had taken him all these years to be able to put his first marriage behind him.

"Your father told me about his marriage to your mother. He loved her so much and her death was unbearable to him. You were his reason to live, and you gave him the strength to be happy again because he found happiness through you. He filled the gaps by being devoted to his business too."

"He never spoke of my mother. It was something that hurt me because when I mentioned her, I could see that he didn't want to talk about her."

"It was so painful for him."

"Her picture was always on his dresser and one of her with me as a baby was on mine. Sometimes he'd say I looked like her. But there were no stories, no anecdotes of their history. I wanted so much to hear all about her."

"Elizabeth, your father regretted that. He knew it was wrong even as he was doing it. He was human and this was the one thing he couldn't face, the pain of remembering."

"He was a wonderful father. I knew it was strange that he didn't speak of my mother. As I grew older I knew intuitively the reason why he did not. But I'm glad you have told me. It affirms my belief."

"It all would have changed," Regina said sadly. "He told me how he met your mother and it disturbed him that he never told you about that first meeting which he said was love at first sight."

"How did they meet?" Elizabeth asked breathlessly.

"Michael had just started his own Certified Public Accounting/ financial planning business. He'd rented a small office in lower Manhattan. He couldn't yet afford the midtown rents. Your mother just walked into his office one day. She had seen the newly painted sign on his door announcing that he was a financial planner. He told me how young and lovely she was. He was completely flustered when she appeared in his office."

"It sounds romantic," Elizabeth said, thrilled to be hearing at last, about her mother and father together. The irony that she was hearing it from a stranger who may have become her father's second wife was not lost on her, and yet she felt comfortable.

"Eleanor sat down in front of your father's desk and grilled him for a half hour. Your father said he felt she was interviewing him to find out if he knew what he was doing. Apparently she was finally satisfied because she hired him as her financial planner."

"My mother needed a financial planner at the age of, what could she have been, just in her twenties?"

"She sure did, Elizabeth. You see, your mother had well over two million dollars to be invested."

Astounded, Elizabeth barely croaked out, "How did she get that much money at that age?" And why is that sum familiar, she wondered.

"It was given to her by her own mother, your grandmother."

"I wish I could remember for sure what my grandmother's name was." The words were barely out when Elizabeth felt a strange sensation of numbness begin to come over her.

"I know it," Regina said. "I wouldn't forget it because I thought of the detective and because the first name was so lyrical. It was Sherlock, Bridget Mary Sherlock."

Mrs. Sternberg's face flashed before her, "Bridget Mary, my Bridie," she had said, "how is it you have come back to me?"

Chapter Thirty-One

They raced to Doris's office in a cab leaving the Russian Tea Room waiter with a big tip and two barely touched lunches to clear away.

Doris had been having lunch at her desk when her receptionist announced that Elizabeth and Regina were in her waiting room.

Elizabeth quickly introduced Regina.

"No coincidences, finding connections. Doris, listen to what Regina just told me."

"Go ahead, Elizabeth."

"The woman I have been seeing in my 'episodes' is named Catherine. A Catherine Sherlock died in the Triangle Shirtwaist fire. I thought my grandmother's name was Sherlock. I went to Florida and Jane's grandmother thought she knew me. She called me Bridget Mary. Regina told me today that my grandmother's name was Bridget Mary Sherlock." She was out of breath when she was finished.

Regina was sitting on the edge of the other leather chair next to Elizabeth. She was stunned by the story Elizabeth had told her. She would never forget how Elizabeth had paled when she said the grandmother's full name. The whole story had then come tumbling out. She wanted to help Elizabeth. She missed Michael and prayed to him now to help Elizabeth.

Doris appeared calm, but Elizabeth knew she was excited by the news.

"I have no doubt that there are connections between these people."

"Ellen was going to research the letter I found in the attic. Mark and I never finished going through the box. That letter will tell us something about my father's or my mother's family."

"Your mother's, I think," Doris said.

"I agree. Your father told me that he had been raised in foster families and orphanages. He had no one really," Regina said.

"I guess that was why he was such a good father to me. He was deprived as a child, and he wanted to make sure it didn't happen again to his own child."

"It was another thing that made your mother's death so painful—that the family he created, one he had not had as a child himself, a real family, was lost with your mother's death, and that you, too, would grow up without a mother," Regina said.

"So he became both mother and father to me. He spent his whole life trying to make up for his losses and mine."

"Yes, but he was happy all along and mostly at peace with himself. He knew what choices he was making always."

"How wonderful that you came into his life," Elizabeth said. They looked at one another recognizing how bittersweet the love had become with Michael's death.

Doris was listening, her kind eyes taking in the emotions passing between the two women. They remembered she was there, and Elizabeth told her how her parents had met.

"This is a great clue for us too. The money your mother had. We will have to follow up on that. Let's call Ellen and see if she has come up with anything." Doris dialed the number that Elizabeth dictated, but the answering machine picked up. She left a message.

"How about hypnosis today, Elizabeth?"

"Yes, I'm ready."

"Should I leave the room?"

"You're welcome to stay, if Elizabeth doesn't mind." Regina looked to Elizabeth.

"You can stay of course. I want you to stay." She positioned herself on the chair as before. She felt the tension leave her body. She felt very relaxed.

The last thing she saw was Doris's smile and her long, pale fingers. She went under as easily as before.

She was in the apartment again. No, maybe it was a different apartment. She was in a very bright kitchen with sunlight streaming through the window onto the yellow linoleum. Catherine and the child were seated at the kitchen table. Catherine looked tired but was smiling at the child. The child seemed sadder and more withdrawn. The little girl got up and walked into the living room. Now Elizabeth knew that this was the same apartment that she had seen before. The living room shades were drawn, and the room was in shadows. The dark, heavy furniture, the ornate decorations, and the clutter of pictures crowding every available space made the room seem oppressive and suffocating. Elizabeth groaned. Doris's gentle questions received breathless answers from Elizabeth. "She's looking at me. I can feel that she knows I'm there."

"Where is Catherine?" Doris asked softly.

"She is following too. I'm afraid. I don't want to look."

"Follow the child."

The child stopped suddenly in the dark corner of the room. She was standing in the shadows. She stepped aside and turned so the object in the corner was clearly visible to Elizabeth.

Elizabeth gasped and almost jumped from the leather chair. Doris quickly brought her out of the hypnotic state.

"What was it that you saw, Elizabeth?"

Elizabeth looked at Regina who was clearly upset and then at Doris whose hands were gently wrapped around hers.

Elizabeth suddenly felt calm, relieved somehow. "It was Jane's desk. In the corner of the room was Jane's mahogany desk."

Chapter Thirty-Two

The grungy squad room matched Dom's mood. He wasn't glad to be there this morning. Marty was already in. He'd made coffee which he began to pour from the permanently stained glass pot which was cleaned daily with only a quick rinse under the men's room faucet. Dom gratefully accepted the steaming mug Marty handed him. He sipped it even as the hot liquid burned his lips.

Marty was bursting with frustration. "How much longer can this go on? We can't find King."

"Yeah, no stalking, no phone calls. Doesn't go near Elizabeth or Millie. Not the usual pattern of a stalker."

"It's only a matter of time. He's a hype. He'll go back to the stuff and crime sooner or later."

"But he's playing us, Pardner. He's hiding out thinking we'll give up sooner or later."

"We've been looking for him for weeks now. He's gotta be bad, man."

"I know, and he will. I just feel that it'll be over soon."

"But Elizabeth and Millie are in danger now."

"Yes. We know what King is. Elizabeth is aware that King is out there so she's very cautious."

"I know. But he's street smart. He's crazy. We can't predict what he'll do." The squad phone rang.

"Gentilli."

"Dom, it's Mark. How are you?"

"Good, Mark, what's up?" Mark heard the concern in Dom's voice.

"Nothing new. Worried about King as usual. Is there anything new on your end?"

"Nothin. I'm sorry."

"Dom, Elizabeth is holding up well but I know how relieved she would be if he were behind bars."

"We all would, and that's what we're counting on happening soon, Mark."

"You'll let me know."

"The minute anything happens, of course." Dom hung up and looked at Marty.

"I see what's on your mind, Dom."

"Yeah, let's get some paper work done on our other cases and then let's get outta here."

Soon they were headed for the streets of the Lower East Side.

Ellen's finger slid slowly down the register page as she sat stiffly in the uncomfortable chair in the library in the historical society building. Her eyes carefully read each line entry in search of the name Fennell. She started with the year 1870. If the '"dearest daughter" letter was written in 1933 to a child who was born to him, she decided that Austen Fennell was probably under seventy at the time. It was an educated guess. It was somewhere to start.

She rubbed her eyes around 1891. The intense concentrating on the old handwritten script was beginning to strain her eyes. At 1924, her lethargy disappeared. A Robert William Fennell was born on July 24th, son of Austin and Alice Fennell. She took some notes and continued reading. She stopped again when she found the record of the same child's death in 1932. There were no other Fennell births or deaths in Bucks County between 1880 and 1935.

"No luck?" the young librarian asked as Ellen reluctantly handed her back the register.

"Some, actually, I think. Now I need to look at the history of the houses."

"What town?"

"Lumberville."

"What do you want to know?"

"Who purchased or built the house, you know, the original owners. And all the subsequent owners," she added hastily.

"Here's what you have to do."

They met the plainclothes cop assigned to watch the apartment building on the corner of St. James Place and Oliver Street, in front of the project where Millie had lived with her mother and King. Dom knew the cop to be a good one despite his phlegmatic appearance. His droopy eyelids and the heavy folds of excess skin on his face made him look like Sleepy of the Seven Dwarfs.

"He hasn't come near the place, you guys." He picked up the log from the front seat of the unmarked Ford and handed it to Marty. The log chronicled the entries of each cop assigned to this duty. Nothing of interest. They hung around for a little longer and finally left.

Doris walked along Worth Street, her logical mind grappling with what she had learned. Inside 125 Worth Street, where she had a connection who was willing to help her, and where New York City housed its birth and death records, Doris had found the record of Austin Fennell's birth on January 3, 1878, making him fifty-five at the time he wrote the "dearest daughter" letter on March 31, 1933. She searched the death records from March 31st forward and found that Austin Fennell had died on April 18, 1933.

There was no connection so far between the letter written on March 31, 1933 and Elizabeth's episodes. The Triangle Fire had happened in 1911. Yet Doris felt that there would be a connection. It didn't trouble her that there was no logical reason to believe that. She sensed these leads would not turn out to be a dead end. She was sure that it was not a whimsical idea that the episodes were related to the old letter found in Elizabeth's family home in Pennsylvania. She hailed a cab and headed uptown to her office with the photocopies of the birth and death records. She pulled her cell phone from her purse to call Elizabeth.

Chapter Thirty-Three

Elizabeth stared at the papers on her desk in the office. Concentration was getting harder and harder. As much as she enjoyed this business, she felt herself thinking about other things to such a degree that her productivity at the office was not up to her own high standard. She was fortunate that the staff of professionals was highly motivated and committed to their clients and to the company.

She had to admit that there were good reasons she had trouble concentrating. Millie, loving Mark, King, the episodes, Michael's death, Jane's death all whirled around in her mind.

Being a new mother to a child who had been greatly traumatized was an enormous responsibility, albeit a wonderful new dimension to her life. Millie needed a safe and loving environment in the wake of losing her mother and the life threatening beating she'd received from King.

King. Not one to dwell on the negative, Elizabeth nevertheless felt a gut wrenching punch of fear whenever she thought of him. She recalled the phone calls, the early morning stalking, his face in the courtroom. If only the threat from King would end. That would be a relief she'd welcome. She worried about Millie and she feared for herself as well.

But the fear was almost immediately replaced by anger as she thought of Millie's mother, Jane's murdered body on the floor of her apartment, and Millie on the respirator at Downtown Hospital.

Dom and Marty would get him. She had to have absolute faith that they would. It was only a matter of time, and she'd stick it out; they all would.

Mark's face popped into her mind and the love she felt for him washed away both the fear and anger about King for a moment. A future together, surely they would have that. But stalkers often killed their victims. That's what she was afraid of. Danger to Millie and danger to herself. No. It could not end like that. They would prevail over King. It had to be over. Then they could joyfully make their plans, free from fear of King.

She thought of Millie now. They were getting so close. She had told Millie about the adoption and asked her if it was all right with her.

"You were still unconscious when I petitioned the court to adopt you. I couldn't ask you," Elizabeth had told her.

"Why did you do it?"

"I wanted to help you and take care of you because I have grown to love you. You are a special person."

"I would like to stay with you, Elizabeth," she had said simply.

The phone's soft ring interrupted Elizabeth's thoughts. "Your house," began Ellen without even saying hello, "it was originally owned by the Fennell family, built by them in 1809. It remained in the Fennell family until 1933 when it was signed over to a Bridget Mary Sherlock." Ellen also told her about the eight year old son who had died.

Elizabeth had been gripping the phone tightly, sitting at the very edge of the leather desk chair as Ellen began to speak. The tension was released at the name Sherlock, and Elizabeth collapsed back into the chair, surprised in some way, but not really, at the connection between Bridget Mary Sherlock and her house. Bridget Mary Sherlock, who was her grandmother.

She hung up with Ellen and was running to the closet in her office when Doris's call came through.

They quickly exchanged information. Elizabeth jotted down the dates of birth and death of Austin Fennell. "I was just going home to finally look through the box I brought back from Pennsylvania."

"I'll meet you there."

Millie was lively and curious when Elizabeth came home in the middle of the day. Mrs. Acevedo, her teacher, was gone and Doris had not yet arrived. Elizabeth decided to tell her about the episodes.

Having lived much of her life in imaginary flights of fantasy through literature, Millie was unfazed by Elizabeth's account of her episodes. She accepted everything Elizabeth told her.

"I'll help you in any way I can," Millie said when Elizabeth finally finished. The bell rang and Mrs. Ahern let Doris in.

"Millie knows all about this now, and she's going to help us."

Doris squeezed Millie's shoulder. "I'm glad you're going to help." They opened the box and divided the contents among the three of them. They decided to move to the dining room table where they could spread the papers out and make piles.

Millie found the first clue. It was a letter. The letterhead identified the law firm of Adams, Edwards, and Royance. It read,

April 30, 1933

Dear Miss Sherlock,

     This is to inform you that you are a party in interest in the estate of the late Austin Fennell.

     Please contact me at your earliest convenience so that this matter may be adjudicated.

Sincerely,
Cyril J. Adams, Esq.

"It looks like Austin Fennell was a very wealthy man. We know from the 'dearest daughter' letter that he left a house and money to a daughter he had somehow wronged; apparently Bridget Mary Sherlock was that daughter."

"And my grandmother. The box marked 'Mother' must have referred to my mother's mother, who was Bridget Mary Sherlock," Elizabeth said.

"So it would seem. But the names are different. Fennell and Sherlock might be father and daughter if Bridget had married and assumed the name Sherlock with marriage, but then there is Catherine Sherlock, possibly Bridget Mary's mother?" Doris said.

"Yes, because my Catherine, who is possibly Catherine Sherlock from the accounts you read, Doris, *didn't* die in the fire. On the day I was supposed to meet Jane at NYU, I had an episode. I saw

Catherine marching in the demonstration protesting the unsafe conditions in the sweatshops two days after the fire," Elizabeth reminded her.

"Yes. How likely is it that there is no connection between Bridget Mary Sherlock and Catherine Sherlock?" Doris said.

"Right, so let's just keep looking until we find it," Elizabeth said.

"Do you think Bridget Mary is Catherine's daughter? The child you see with Catherine in the apartment?"

"I don't know why, but for some reason, I don't think that the child is Catherine's daughter," Elizabeth said.

They were all so engrossed in their task that they didn't hear Mrs. Ahern announce that Detectives Gentilli and Martinez were at the door.

"Please invite them in," Elizabeth said. A strong familiar aroma preceded them as they entered the dining room. Marty looked sheepish as he put two large McDonalds' bags on the table.

"We know Mrs. Ahern hates it for Millie to have this stuff, but we know she loves it so we drop by with it once a week," Dom said.

Elizabeth saw Millie beaming with pleasure. She had heard Mrs. Ahern's complaints about this weekly ritual but thought it was a great treat for Millie and heartily approved of it. The two detectives loved Millie, and the visit was good for all of them.

Elizabeth kissed them both as did Millie, and they shook hands with Doris. Dom looked at all the papers on the table. "What are you guys doin'?"

"I think it's time we called in the NYPD. What do you think, Doris, Millie?" Doris nodded and so did Millie.

Then, for the second time that day, she told the whole story, this time to the astonished detectives, beginning with the first episode on St. James Place a few short months ago.

Chapter Thirty-Four

King paced through the filthy rooms he'd rented in downtown Flushing, Queens. He'd gotten a one-bedroom apartment above a Korean market in a pre-World War II building that needed a lot of work. Not that he couldn't afford something better. He could. His drug dealings were lucrative, thanks to his supplier on St. James Place. Someday he would live in a nice place. He'd never lived in a nice place before. It was time. It was his turn.

But for now he'd have to lay low. He went to the window and pulled back the stiff, yellowing curtain. There were no cops on the busy street below his window. But why would there be; at least why would there be cops looking for him here? They didn't know he was in Queens. He was smart. They didn't have a clue where he was.

But how would he stay away from St. James Place? That's where his business was based. He needed to go back there. He missed it even now. There was no place on earth like the Lower East Side. The excitement and the noise, the music, the people. He was born there. It was his home.

His latest woman came into his mind. Late was the operative word. He wouldn't ever let a woman go, only if he was tired of her, and he did tire of them. And he hadn't ever killed one before either. But he never, ever let one go if *she* was the one who wanted to.

He remembered the first time he met her, Sonia Ruiz. He was on his way down the hall to do some business. She was coming out of her apartment with her kid. She lowered her eyes when he passed her. He was sure she was attracted to him. She was pretty. Slim, with strong arms, brown skin, thick curly dark hair that framed her face. He wondered how his pale white skin would look next to her rich brown skin. He wondered then what she'd look like when she smiled. But he rarely saw her smile after they started living together. Only at the kid sometimes, and even that stopped after a while.

She was a liar too. She'd say anything to keep him from hitting her, all of it lies-what she thought he wanted to hear. Too bad she was always wrong about what that was. He'd had to beat her a lot to teach her, but she never seemed to learn.

But the kid. The kid knew stuff. He didn't know how or what. He could see it in those big brown eyes. They followed him around the apartment when he was there. She didn't tell any lies. She wasn't afraid of him and never whimpered when he smacked her or hit her with his belt. The only way he could get to her was by hitting the mother. She tried not to show it, but she was scared then.

The last time she interfered in a fight he had with her mother, he'd had to beat her instead. He put her in the hospital too. She almost died. He had to kill her mother anyway. That woman would never learn, and she got what she deserved.

Now he had other things to deal with. That red head. What a bitch she was. She got him in trouble when she took the kid out of the apartment and put her in a group home. No one goes into his home and calls the shots except him. How dare she? He'd hated her ever since.

And he almost got her, after a few tries. First, there was the night she got out of the cab in front of her apartment in Brooklyn. He wasn't sure he was ready to try that night anyway; someone might have come down the street. No, he had to plan it. He could tell she was scared though. He loved that. He could almost smell her fear. She kept looking around, and she dropped her keys. Then there was the time he chased her when she was going to the fancy office building. How he loved to scare her. And oh, the phone calls. He remembered how he felt when he called her and told her to mind her own business. Then finally he got into her apartment.

When the key turned and he could see from his hiding place that it was not she who came in, he'd been really mad. That woman came into the apartment in Brooklyn and calmly told him she wasn't afraid of him. Ha, she must have regretted saying that when he stuck the knife into her.

It would soon be time to end it, to get revenge for the things the red headed bitch had done to him.

Chapter Thirty-Five

Elizabeth was excited that Regina was coming to visit. She opened the door to let her in to the apartment and was alarmed when Regina's eyes filled with tears. She's been here many times before, Elizabeth realized. It was hard for her to come back with Michael gone.

"It makes it real," she told Elizabeth as she composed herself. Elizabeth put her arm around Regina's back and squeezed her shoulder gently as she walked her into the den. Mark rose at once and shook Regina's hand.

"I've heard so much about you from Elizabeth and I'm very pleased to meet you," Mark said.

Regina responded warmly and seated herself on the loveseat.

"I'll call Millie. She's anxious to meet you too. She made toll house cookies in honor of your visit."

Elizabeth left the den and headed towards the stairs as Millie was racing down. They embraced, giggling.

"I heard the door so I know Mrs. Jordan is here." They stood in the doorway to the den.

"Regina, I'd like you to meet Milagros Ruiz. Millie, I'd like you to meet Mrs. Jordan."

Regina rose. They had been studying each other intently as Elizabeth went through the formal introduction.

Regina spoke first, "Please call me Regina."

"Please call me Millie."

Smiles broke on both their faces.

"How about the cookies? I smelled them before I heard that you had made them, and my mouth has been watering ever since."

Mark got up. "Let's go get them." He and Millie headed for the kitchen.

"She's a beautiful child. I can't wait to get to know her."

"I can see you'll be great friends."

Regina's eyes hit the desk suddenly. "It's exquisite, Elizabeth. The mahogany looks alive. It amazes me that it's in such good condition."

"It was obviously cherished by everyone who owned it in Jane's family, including Jane."

They approached the desk and like everyone else, Regina was unable to resist touching the gleaming wood.

Elizabeth turned the key with trepidation, fearing another episode, but it did not come. She gently opened the slant top and laid it down. She watched as Regina took in each detail of the gallery inside. "Do you mind?"

"No, of course not, open the little door and the drawers. They're beautifully made."

"Wasn't it marvelous the way they made these 'secret compartments'?" she asked Elizabeth as she deftly pulled on one, then the other of two sections of the gallery, one on either side of the tiny center door.

Elizabeth gasped. "What is it, dear?" Regina asked. "Didn't you know these were here?"

"No, Regina. Mrs. Levin, Jane's mother, never mentioned them. I'm sure she didn't know about them."

Elizabeth pulled the left one all the way out. The carving on its facade was like a Doric column. She peered inside the hollow space but it was empty. The compartment was about six inches tall and one and a half inches wide.

"This is a reproduction of a Governor Winthrop desk. This reproduction was made around 1905."

"You are an antique lover."

"Yes, I was even getting your father interested. I've always spent weekends combing antique shops all over the Northeast as a hobby."

Elizabeth removed the right compartment fully. "There's something in here." Wedged down inside the right section they could see folded sheets of paper. Elizabeth turned the wooden section of the gallery upside down but the papers didn't budge as she shook the compartment.

"What are you guys doing?" Mark was carrying a tray of mugs with hot cocoa for Millie and coffee for the adults. Millie was right behind him, a plate of cookies and napkins in her hands.

"Regina recognized this desk, the style of the gallery. She's an antique lover. She knew that this type of desk had secret compartments." Elizabeth's face was flushed with excitement.

Mark and Millie put their mugs and cookies on the coffee table. Elizabeth showed them the compartments with the pages wedged inside the hollow section of the right compartment.

Millie ran out of the room and returned seconds later carrying kitchen tongs.

"The paper may be old and brittle. It may be better to dismantle the compartment," Mark suggested. Regina looked disturbed at that idea.

"We should have it done by a craftsman. This is a beautiful and valuable piece of furniture."

Millie took the compartment from Elizabeth and put her tiny hand into the narrow space. They watched her intense little face as she worked the wedged papers slowly up and gently pulled them free. She handed the papers to Elizabeth.

Elizabeth sat down in the wing chair. She gently unfolded the first sheet.

She lifted her head and made eye contact with each of them. Finally she said, "I think it's in Yiddish. I'll bet it is the rest of Esme Jacobs' diary. It starts where Mrs. Levin's copy left off. The first entry is dated, April 7, 1911, thirteen days after the Triangle Fire in which her daughter Rebeccah died."

"I can get it translated," Regina said. Elizabeth handed her the diary which she tucked into her purse.

Mark broke the somber silence. "I guess we should drink our summertime hot cocoa and eat the delicious cookies," he said.

"He's teasing Millie as he sometimes teases me, Regina. Millie likes hot cocoa even in this heat and, as you can see, I still put a fire in the fireplace in the summer."

"In this air conditioned apartment, it works. You'd never know it was eighty degrees outside," Regina said.

"You're just defending them, Regina. No one has a fire and hot chocolate in New York in the summer."

"Well, they should then," Regina said. Everyone laughed, the horror of the death of Esme's daughter Rebeccah and so many others temporarily forgotten.

The fire in the fireplace burned benignly.

Chapter Thirty-Six

Marty left Dom at the stationhouse. He smiled as he remembered Dom hunched over his desk, frenetically punching numbers into his computer.

He drove to Varrick Street to the New York City Fire Museum. An old friend from the FDNY had promised to meet him there and show him some archived records on The Triangle Fire that were not available to the general public.

He entered the museum and asked for his friend George. The young fireman on duty picked up the phone while Marty waited. He resisted the temptation to browse through the museum. The excitement he had felt as a boy in the projects at the sight of the big red engines came back to him now. He reluctantly passed some highly polished fire engines of times past as he followed the directions he had been given to an office in the rear of the museum.

"How have you been, and what brings you here asking about the Triangle?" George asked as he vigorously pumped Marty's hand.

"It's too bizarre to explain, George, but it involves a murder case my partner and I are working on."

"A fire in 1911 has something to do with a murder case you and your partner are working on?"

Marty shrugged and smiled. "It's really a matter involving a victim in a murder investigation."

"Well, I guess you're going to let me die of curiosity. Let me show you what I've got." George removed a large folder from his desk. "I got this from the archives the day after you called. You can sit at my desk and look through it. We have a photocopy machine here if you want to copy anything."

Marty felt guilty that he was holding out on George in view of all he had done to help him, but he couldn't tell him the true reason he was looking at this stuff. George would have him committed.

"I really appreciate this, George. It means a lot to me."

"I could tell that it did when I spoke to you on the phone. You're so intense, Marty. I remember when we were kids on the street. You were always looking out for the little kids and fighting the bullies. Everyone knew you'd be a cop."

"And everyone knew you'd be a fireman. Your father was the hero fireman, and you wanted to be just like him."

They laughed together and Marty knew George had no hard feelings about the secrecy.

"I'll go out and get us a couple a sandwiches and coffee. Hey, you still a coffee lover?"

"Yeah, thanks."

Marty sat behind the desk and opened the folder. Photographs lay on top. The first showed two young women lying on the sidewalk side by side. They were dead. The next photo was of the Asch Building, smoke pouring from its windows. A firetruck was alongside the building, its ladder sadly extended to its fullest length which was two floors below the fire. The photos of the temporary morgue affected Marty the most deeply. The coffins were lined up in rows, the dead on display to be identified by heartbroken loved ones. He saw the anguish on the faces of the relatives in the photos and felt the pain of their loss.

"It's all over now," he murmured. Their grief and pain were gone, as were they. It was highly unlikely that any of these people could still be living today. Next, there were photos of the protest by the workers and there were photos of the public funeral for those victims who had never been identified.

Marty was especially interested in the women who went to their grave unidentified. He read through the police reports.

Coffin numbers 46, 50, 61, 95, 103, 115, and 127 had been unnamed and unclaimed. Were their lives so valueless in the teeming masses of the Lower East Side of New York that no one even knew they were missing? One hundred and forty-six dead. Catherine Sherlock was listed among the dead but her name was crossed out. What could that mean?

Marty's mind went over the story Elizabeth had told. Catherine, the little girl, the old woman. There were addresses in the police file, addresses of the victims, both dead and surviving as well as eyewitnesses to the tragedy. His instincts as a cop made him pull out his notepad to start copying them down. He put his notepad down as he came back into the present with a start.

"It's all over," he repeated to himself. Most of these buildings would be gone as would the people. One of the addresses jumped out at him though. It was on New Bowery Street. Was that the original name for St. James Place? He wasn't sure, but he thought Elizabeth had said her first episode was on New Bowery Street. He copied it down.

The newspaper clippings were next. A man named William Shepherd, a United Press reporter was present during the fire, apparently the only reporter who was an eyewitness. He personally counted sixty-two bodies falling from the burning Asch Building. Marty read part of Shepherd's account about a man in the window.

"He brought another girl to the window. I saw her put her arms around him and kiss him. Then he held her into space-and dropped her. Quick as a flash, he was on the window sill himself. His coat fluttered upwards-the air filled his trouser legs as he came down. I could see his tan shoes. Together they went into eternity. Later I saw his face. You could see he was a real man. He had done his best. We found later that in the room in which he stood, many girls were burning to death. He chose the easiest way and was brave enough to help the girl he loved to an easier death."

Shepherd also wrote, ". . . they were jammed into the windows. They were burning to death in the windows. One by one the window jams broke. Down came the bodies in a shower, burning, smoking, flaming bodies . . ."

Marty's hand shook as he put the article down. The lump that had formed in his throat gradually diminished. He read through each of the other documents in the file, making a small pile of the ones he wanted to photocopy. He came across two survivors named Sarah, Sarah Cammerstein and Sarah Friedman. One of the dead was named Sara Saricino.

There were heart wrenching newspaper accounts of some of the funerals. Two of the girls, best friends who lived in neighboring houses, jumped from the ninth floor of the Asch Building with their arms around each other. Marty was unable to find their names but wondered if they could be Catherine and Sarah. It was a possible lead. He'd try to check it out.

The unidentified workers were buried on April 5 at Evergreen Cemetery in the East New York section of Brooklyn. This was the last funeral and Marty read how it poured that day. An enormous demonstration took place that day with the marchers ending up in Washington Square Park. Marty remembered Elizabeth's episode in the rain in Washington Square Park, the day Jane was murdered by King.

She had seen Catherine in the crowd that day. Catherine survived the fire. He looked thorough the list of the dead again, the list with Catherine Sherlock's name scratched out.

George came in with the sandwiches and coffee. "How'd you do?"

"I got a lot. Need to make copies."

"Let's eat first and I'll help you. There are some more photos on exhibit in the museum too if you want to take a look. We are redoing the museum area to show the terrorist attack on the World Trade Center," George said.

"Your guys were so brave that day," Marty said. "And everyday," he added.

"You guys too," George said.

"When I was looking at the photos of the people jumping out of the Asch Building, I was thinking of the World Trade Center. This tragedy of 1911 is long over, but in some ways the effects of it are like those of the terrorist attacks on September 11[th.] They will remain with the survivors and the families for our lifetimes and longer," Marty said.

They ate their sandwiches and talked about the old neighborhood, but Marty's mind was also back in 1911, trying to connect Catherine Sherlock with someone named Sarah.

Marty's cell phone rang and brought him sharply back into the present. George wordlessly handed him a pad and paper, a small piece of pastrami and mustard hanging from the corner of his mouth.

"Martinez."

"Marty, meet me at Elizabeth's," Dom's gruff voice commanded. "King has attacked Millie again."

Chapter Thirty-Seven

The scene at the East 72nd Street apartment was chaotic. Detectives and patrolmen were everywhere performing their assigned tasks. Marty found Dom in the foyer.

Mrs. Ahern was sobbing at the kitchen table, a police officer trying to console her. Marty knew that someone was needed to give Mrs. Ahern the "it wasn't your fault" treatment but he couldn't do it himself now.

Dr. Piscali came downstairs and recognized Dom and Marty immediately from the vigil they had kept at Millie's bedside when she was in a coma at Downtown Hospital.

"How is she, Doc?" Dom was trying to be calm.

"Her injuries are superficial. She managed to fend off blows to her head completely with her arms."

Their faces reflected the astonishment that an image of Millie's slender arms fighting off King' blows created. Marty groaned.

"Mrs. Ahern fought like a tiger, too. I'm going to look at her injuries now."

"How'd he get in?" Dom asked.

"He rang the bell, and Mrs. Ahern looked through the peephole and saw a guy with a floral arrangement. Something like that. Anyway, you two can go in and see Millie. She's in a mild state of shock, but I'm sure it will be good for her to see both of you. Elizabeth is in with her. I've got to see to Mrs. Ahern."

As anxious as they were to see Millie, their cop minds were racing toward the crime and getting King.

"First things first," Dom said quoting an AA axiom.

"Yeah, and then we'll get him, for good this time," Marty said.

They knocked on Millie's door. Elizabeth opened it and stared at them through hollow eyes.

"It's okay, Honey." Dom took her hands and entered the room. Marty followed and closed the door softly. She led them to the bed. Marty sat on one side; Dom on the other. Ellen and Regina were there too. Millie stared up at them. A flicker of recognition moved across her face and was gone.

"How's our little girl?" Millie didn't smile. Dom patted her hand and stood up facing Elizabeth.

"The doc said her injuries were superficial. I see bruises and small cuts. Why is she so still?"

"She's terrified." Elizabeth's voice was flat.

"You're both in shock over this. It's our fault. We didn't lock him up for good and didn't protect you when he got out." Dom's anguish was palpable.

The door opened again, and Mark came in. The fear and rage left him as he grabbed Elizabeth in his arms and flew to the bed. Mark bent down and tenderly picked Millie up in his arms. She went to him without protest and nestled in his arms. Elizabeth had her arm through his and on Millie.

He spoke softly to Millie, "You're going to be okay, Millie. Dr. Piscali said you were okay." The room was filled as Mrs. Ahern, Dr. Piscali and Doris entered completing the group. Elizabeth looked around the room.

"Look, Millie." Her voice was strong. "Look at everyone here who loves you—Mark, Ellen, Dom, Marty, Regina, Mrs. Ahern, Doris, Dr. Piscali. We have all the love with *us*, Millie. That's why we've beaten King so far, and that is why he'll never get us."

Millie started to cry. It was a relief to all of them to see the animation return to her face and form. Except for Mrs. Ahern and Regina, everyone in the room had seen Millie in a coma. The stillness they observed only moments earlier had reminded them of the terrible stillness of her coma.

Mark cradled her like a baby and murmured in her ear. Elizabeth held on to them both.

Finally, Mark asked everyone to leave the room except Doris. "Millie needs some rest." He held her as each of her friends said some words of love and encouragement and kissed her before leaving.

"I'm sorry this happened, Millie. We're going to try harder to make sure it doesn't happen again. We love you so much." Mark looked at Elizabeth and then at Millie. This time there was a little smile on Millie's face. That was enough for Mark. He hugged her again, put her gently on the bed and left the room leaving Doris to help Elizabeth and Millie.

Chapter Thirty-Eight

He was gone. There were no signs of King. The hapless rookie who didn't see him enter the building was subjected to a tirade from Dom that he wouldn't forget if he lived to be Commissioner one day. Usually gruff but kind Dom didn't get any satisfaction out of the trouncing of the young cop. Guilt at directing his frustration at the officer and the reality that King was still at large and couldn't be found put him in a state he could hardly bear.

At the precinct, Dom and Marty went over the sequence of events as described by Millie, Mrs. Ahern, Bruce, the doorman, and Mrs. Acevedo, Millie's tutor, in their statements.

The tutor worked with Millie each morning from 8:30 to 11:30. The attack, which occurred at approximately 11:45 a.m., happened just after she'd left for the day. She didn't leave through the lobby of the apartment building. The doorman reported that he let her in each day through the lobby doors but she always exited at the back of the building, through the service entrance door which was locked on the outside but could be opened from the inside. The tutor explained that the rear door provided her quicker access to the subway she took to her next student. In fact, she'd said, cutting through the rear door took almost a whole block off her walk. Did she notice anything when she was leaving the building the day of the attack?

No, she didn't. Oh, no, yes, maybe she did. As she was leaving, a man was coming in carrying flowers. Had she ever seen him before? No. She didn't think so. Had she opened the door to let him in? No. Yes, maybe she had. She had opened the door to exit and he was standing right there with the flowers. She almost collided with him. No, she didn't let him in. No, she didn't hold the door for him. Did she see his face? No. Did she see a truck? Yes, no, she wasn't sure.

She had been thinking that she would call Miss Charles and

suggest that Millie meet children her own age. She had been startled out of these thoughts when she opened the door and saw the man with the flowers.

Had she spoken to the man with the flowers? Yes, she'd made some inane remark about someone being lucky to get those flowers. No, he didn't answer her.

Dom and Marty looked at each other. What was this woman holding back?

Mrs. Acevedo started to cry. They waited.

"He was so handsome. He was always there when I came out of the building. He walked me to the subway every day for a week. He asked me to dinner. No one has paid attention to me since my husband left me last year. I talked about Millie and Elizabeth. Oh, God, I talked about their lives with this man. I invited him to my home. He was so sweet and gentle. I let him . . ." Mrs. Acevedo put her head in her hands and sobbed.

Dom looked at Marty. "It wasn't your fault," he said to Mrs. Acevedo before he started the questioning again.

What did this phony florist deliveryman look like, he asked Elise Acevedo. Around thirty-five years old, about five foot ten inches tall, approximately one hundred and seventy pounds, mustache, fair complexion, dirty blonde hair, she'd said.

King.

Then they went to Mrs. Ahern. She told them what happened.

When the bell rang, Mrs. Ahern was in the kitchen preparing lunch for Millie. Mrs. Ahern assumed it was a neighbor at the door, since people from outside are announced by the doorman calling on the intercom from the lobby before being allowed into the building. But when she looked out of the peephole and saw the flowers, she didn't think twice, and she opened the door, admitting King.

Millie was upstairs in her room when Mrs. Ahern opened the door. King threw the flowers down and sent Mrs. Ahern crashing to the marble floor with a blow to the face. Mrs. Ahern had a black eye and a mild concussion as a result. Mrs. Ahern fought for her consciousness, rang for Bruce, and called 911.

Millie was struggling with King when she heard Mrs. Ahern running up the stairs screaming that the police were coming and so was the doorman. King panicked, ran past her, and out of the apartment.

King had staked out the apartment building. He knew the tutor's schedule and that she left through the rear door. He undoubtedly left the same way.

Later, the phone rang in the squad room. "Gentilli."

"Detective Gentilli, this is Jake, the night doorman at The Arms."

"It's Elizabeth's night doorman," Dom whispered to Marty.

"I thought you'd wanna know. We found a card from Dugan's Florist in the elevator."

Dom and Marty raced to Elizabeth's building to meet with Jake. He handed them a white envelope. "I tried to be careful handling it when I saw what it was," Jake said.

"Maybe we'll get some prints," Marty said.

"Dugan's Florist on E. 78th Street."

Dugan's verified that a floral arrangement had been stolen from their truck which was parked on E. 72th Street while the driver was delivering another arrangement nearby. Did the driver notice anything unusual that day, they asked the store's owner.

"Sure, one order of flowers was stolen. And, the delivery to E. 72th Street where my driver was while my truck was being robbed, was bogus. The person who received the flowers, a Ms. Rowan, didn't know the sender, no name on the card," Mr. Dugan said.

"How do you know that? She didn't refuse the flowers at the time of delivery, did she?" Marty asked.

"Oh, no. She called later to ask us who ordered the flowers. We looked it up and told her it was a telephone order paid by American Express card."

"What was the name on the card?"

Dugan flipped through a pile of yellow receipts. "Mr. Joseph Pacheco. I'll write the address and phone number down for you. The woman, Ms. Rowan, said she didn't know anyone by that name. She asked me if we wanted the flowers back." He laughed. "I told her to keep them as she was definitely the one the flowers were to be delivered to according to Mr. Pacheco's orders. He even specified a time, paying extra for delivery at precisely 11:40 a.m."

"Is there any chance the American Express card was stolen? Do you remember the call, when the order was placed?"

"No, my wife took the call. It wasn't a stolen card though. We checked. We always check." He showed them the electronic box next to the phone that verifies the cards. "We use this when we have the card physically. We call on the other line when we get a phone order."

"Can you check again?"

Dugan looked puzzled. "Sure." He dialed and punched in the American Express card number that was on the yellow receipt. "Damn, it *is* a stolen card. My wife notated the receipt showing that she called but I guess the card was reported stolen after she did the verification."

Marty and Dom looked at one another. Some victims don't discover their card is stolen until after the thief has made charges against it. By the time this victim reported his American Express card stolen, the flowers had already been charged.

"What did the guy on the phone want written on the card that went with the flowers?"

"Look at this order," Dugan exclaimed. He didn't include the first name of the recipient. He gave the last name only with no Mr. or Ms."

"He got the name and apartment number off a mailbox, I'll bet," Dom said.

"Anyway, the card said, 'Thanks for giving me a chance.' There was no signature."

They headed for the E. 72nd Street apartment building next to Elizabeth's building.

There was no doorman and the outer door led into a small lobby with mailboxes lining the wall. They scanned the names and found a Rowan. No first name or initial appeared next to the surname which was neatly typed in the little square above the apartment number, 8B.

There was a locked door between this area and the main lobby where the elevators were located. Entrance to the main lobby was only possible by using a key or being buzzed in by a resident.

They rang the buzzer under the mailbox marked, "Rowan."

"Who's there?" The voice from the intercom speaker was squeaky.

"Detectives Martinez and Gentilli from the New York City Police Department, Ms. Rowan. We'd like to talk to you about the flowers you received." They were buzzed in immediately.

Margaret Rowan invited the detectives in after viewing their credentials through her peephole. Her apartment was spotless.

"Please sit down, gentlemen." She pointed to her couch.

They could see that Margaret Rowan was a no nonsense person, so they got right to the point.

"Ms. Rowan, we are investigating a homicide and stalking. We're here to find out if you know who sent you the flowers that were delivered earlier today by Dugan's Florist."

She pointed to the table near the living room window on which sat the lovely and tasteful flower arrangement.

"No. I do not know who sent them. The florist told me that they were charged by a man named Joseph Pacheco. I know no one by that name."

"Try to think, Ms. Rowan. Is there any chance that you have forgotten some person who may have that name?"

"No, young man," she said sharply to Marty. "There is absolutely no chance that I have forgotten that I know someone. My memory is precise, far superior to your own, I am quite certain. I can recite the entire Gettysburg Address and hundreds of poems from memory which I am sure is much more than you can do. I taught school for over forty years, and I remember the names of every single student I ever taught."

She didn't have to say, "So there," but Dom and Marty heard the silent exclamation. They had no doubt she was right.

"Can we see the card that came with the flowers, Ma'am?"

She handed Dom the card and they studied the words, "Thank you for giving me a chance." It was King. The delivery of these flowers by the authentic deliveryman, ordered by King over the phone using a stolen American Express Card, gave King the chance to steal other flowers from the Dugan Florist delivery truck and get into Elizabeth's building next door. But how did he know there would be another order of flowers in the truck for him to steal? How did he know the truck would be unlocked?

They went back to Dugan's and posed these questions. "That's easy," Mr. Dugan said. The luxury building around the corner is a customer of ours. They want an arrangement of fresh flowers for their lobby each week. We deliver an arrangement every Monday at around 12. And the truck wasn't unlocked. The guy broke into it, a professional job."

Marty and Dom looked at each other. They had a clever adversary in King.

Chapter Thirty-Nine

The child continued to amaze everyone who knew her. Even after the terrible shock of King invading the place where she thought she was safe, and his attempt to harm her further, she was again cheerful and optimistic, at least on the surface.

"We're going to stay in Lumberville until this is over. Dom and Marty think we'll be safe there. Mark agrees," Elizabeth said to Millie a few days after the attack.

"How do we know Chet will not go to Pennsylvania, follow us there?"

Elizabeth had never heard Millie refer to King by his first name. It made it real that she had lived with this monster and had suffered so many times at his hands. Elizabeth hugged Millie tightly.

"Dom and Marty have a plan to get us there safely. He won't follow us."

Millie stepped back from Elizabeth's embrace, "Maybe he already knows about Pennsylvania." Her fear was masked with the stiff facade of courage she was so good at affecting.

But Elizabeth knew the truth. Millie did have courage, real courage, but she was a grieving child too. After so many nights of hearing Millie cry out in her sleep for her dead mother or waking from a nightmare about King, Elizabeth certainly knew about the vulnerability underneath that courage. She had spent many hours in Millie's room at night comforting her after one of these occurrences. The look on Millie's face moved Elizabeth now because her eyes reflected the fear, pain, hurt, and loss she had endured in her young life. All the politeness, the humor, the reason, the intellectual prowess that had been learned from her reading were real, a part of her, but she was still a very young child, one who had been gravely injured emotionally and physically most of her short life.

But Elizabeth knew that Millie's fear that King may already know about the home in Pennsylvania was valid. It is a stalker's business to know these things, and King had already shown his attention to detail when he planned the flower delivery. King was so smart. Maybe he would have no need to follow them because he already knew about the house in Lumberville. She felt chilled at that thought. Yet she had to reassure Millie.

"It's possible, Honey. It is. But we don't think so. When we went to Lumberville the last time, we had Mohammed with us. He was certain we weren't followed. If he didn't follow us that time, how would he know about the house in Pennsylvania?"

Elizabeth saw hope in Millie's eyes. Incredibly she could trust in these adults yet again even after being attacked in what was supposed to be a secure Manhattan apartment building.

Elizabeth shuddered as she remembered Mrs. Ahern's account of that day.

"I thought it might be Rita from down the hall ringing the bell. Sometimes she brings something for Millie that she baked. When I saw the flowers and he said, 'Dugan's,' I thought Bruce forgot to buzz us." Of course Mrs. Ahern had no way of knowing that the man standing on the other side of the door had come through the back door with the help of Millie's tutor. The doorman had never seen him enter the building. Neither had the cop assigned to look out for him.

She had opened the door.

"He struck me so hard. I fell backwards and heard my head crack against the marble. I must have lost consciousness. But I heard Millie screaming somewhere in my mind and I knew I had to get help."

King must have raced up the stairs leaving the bleeding, unconscious Mrs. Ahern in the foyer as he searched for Millie.

Millie had been working on the homework assignments given by Mrs. Acevedo.

Millie told them how King had rushed into her room, grabbed her by the arms, and pulled her from the desk chair. He held her tightly with one arm as he swept the desk, dresser, and night tables with his other arm, sending all her things crashing to the floor. King was in a blind rage.

"I thought I was having a nightmare. It was all so familiar. Chet always gets like that. First he starts by pinching my arms and that's what he did." Millie described the absolute rage in this man, a rage she had seen so many times before. He had cursed her then and told her that this would be her final beating.

Elizabeth thought gratefully how it had not been a beating at all, never having gotten past the nasty pinches, thanks to Mrs. Ahern who had come to almost immediately, summoned the doorman Bruce, and dialed 911. She was running to Millie and screaming that help was on the way. King was long gone when the police arrived only moments later.

Elizabeth still marveled at Mrs. Ahern's courage and physical strength. If she had waited for the police to come without telling King she had called, King might have had time to kill Millie. Mrs. Ahern had risked her own life to save Millie. Millie escaped with the memory of terror and badly bruised arms.

Elizabeth knew she had to answer Millie now. "Nothing is sure in this life, but Millie, I believe we will be safe at home in Lumberville. Ellen is overseeing an electronic security system being installed right now."

Millie's face brightened. "I can't wait to see Ellen and Moss again." She was an eight-year-old once more. "Ellen came to see me after Chet tried to hurt me."

"Yes, she drove from Lumberville right away because she loves you," Elizabeth said. "We are lucky girls to have so many people who care about us in our lives."

"Mrs. Ahern, are sure you'll be all right?" Elizabeth had tried to convince Mrs. Ahern to join them in Lumberville or to go anywhere she wanted to, to recover, but Mrs. Ahern wanted to stay in the apartment. She minimized her physical injuries when Elizabeth brought her to her own doctor, Dr. Ellis. Dr. Piscali had suggested that Mrs. Ahern go to the hospital after the attack. Mrs. Ahern refused but agreed to follow up with a doctor. Dr. Ellis was shocked that Mrs. Ahern didn't go to the hospital after a head injury that caused her to lose consciousness. A brain scan showed no damage, however.

"Yes, Elizabeth, I'll be all right. I've recovered from the concussion. I'll keep the house clean and ready for your return. I'll miss you both so much."

Elizabeth knew the extent of Mrs. Ahern's attachment to them when she didn't give notice after the terrifying attack by King. The fifty-nine-year-old childless widow who had made a life out of caring for affluent New Yorkers, their homes and families, had endured the injury stoically. She was indignant when she finally learned the whole story of Chet King and what he was doing to Elizabeth and Millie.

"Are you sure you don't want to come with us to Lumberville?"

"No, Elizabeth, I'm a city girl. I couldn't bear to be away from New York."

"Do you feel safe here, Mrs. Ahern?"

"Of course, don't worry so. I feel perfectly safe. No one tricks Kay Ahern twice. It's you and Millie I'm worried about."

They got the rest of their things packed in two overnight bags.

"Don't forget the snack bag," Mrs. Ahern said. She'd packed food and drinks for them to eat along the way.

They giggled when they opened the bag of snacks. "Mrs. Ahern must think Lumberville is at the end of the earth," Elizabeth said. The abundance of fruit and juice packs couldn't be consumed by the two of them on the two-hour drive. Not that it would really be a two-hour drive. The "detour" would make it longer.

The car service pulled up in front of the apartment building and the driver loaded in the bags.

"Beautiful summer day for a drive," Elizabeth said to the driver. She and Millie had agreed that they would not look around nervously when they were outside.

"He's just one man, Millie. He can't watch us twenty-four hours a day. We just have to act normally, like two people going away."

The driver took them to LaGuardia Airport. They carried their bags inside and headed up the escalator to the gate area. They presented "tickets" to the airline representative at the gate and walked down the jetway. Dom and Marty were at the end of the jetway where they escorted Elizabeth and Millie down the stairs to the tarmac. An unmarked NYPD van with tinted windows stood waiting for them out of the view of the terminal windows. Dom and Marty watched as the van drove away from the aircraft on the beginning of its journey to Lumberville, Pennsylvania.

They were on the last leg of the journey.

Their stomachs were growling now and they were glad to have Mrs. Ahern's bag. They sipped from the juice boxes and munched on the fruit and other snacks.

The policeman drove carefully. He made several small detours. He assured them that they hadn't been tailed as he pulled into the driveway of the big old house that had been left to Bridget Mary Sherlock by someone named Austin Fennell in 1933. Mohammed was standing in the driveway.

Chapter Forty

The solid old walls of the house welcomed them warmly and so did Ellen and Moss who were standing in the driveway, too, as they got out of the car. Elizabeth knew it was the right thing to come here. She felt immediately at ease and could tell that Millie did also. She wrapped her arm around Millie's shoulder and gave her a quick squeeze. Mohammed greeted them formally, but Millie's enthusiastic attempt to hug him, his great height and girth making that difficult, elicited the hint of a smile that was the best they could ever get from him.

Moss was next. Millie stroked his massive head as he ran back and forth between Millie and Elizabeth, jumping and whining with pleasure at their reunion.

"I have some stuff to show you inside." Both Elizabeth and Millie stared at Ellen.

"You found out more about the house?"

"Yes, and Doris and I have been on the phone. We think we've put together some of the pieces of the puzzle.

Let's drop your things off in your kitchen. Then we'll go to my house. Everything's in my house. I have some food for you too."

They both groaned. "We just ate compliments of Mrs. Ahern," Elizabeth said.

"It won't be long before the country air gets to you and you'll be hungry again. Wait and see."

They carried their bags around to the back of the house, to the French doors from the patio to the kitchen. Elizabeth slipped her key into the gleaming door and opened it. The screech of the alarm scared all of them, even Moss, who started to bark furiously.

"I forgot, the alarm was installed and I forgot all about it."

Ellen ran inside and they watched as she quickly punched a code into a keypad on the wall. The alarm stopped.

"Will the police come?" Millie asked.

Elizabeth thought she sounded anxious.

"No, there's a special code I used which tells them it was a false alarm. I'll explain how it works when we come back here later tonight."

"I'll check the house out, Elizabeth," Mohammed said.

"Then come up to my house for some refreshment, Mohammed," Ellen said.

They walked rapidly up the short path to Ellen's house, Moss running happily beside them.

"Look at the river," Millie said.

Elizabeth and Ellen looked at the majestic Delaware, its waters gleaming and churning in the late day sun. "Remember how we played on its banks every summer of our childhood?"

"I remember," Elizabeth said. The sight of the river seemed to have the same effect on Millie that it had on her. It gave her strength. It filled her with peace. These things were on Millie's face now.

Ellen's house was an eclectic mixture of furnishings consisting of the things her parents had from the early days of their marriage, a few fine antiques Ellen had collected, and some pieces Ellen had purchased from local shops, including artifacts from the sixties and seventies.

The three of them settled down on the old comfortable sofa with glasses of iced tea for them, but hot cocoa for Millie who didn't care if it was summer. Once she had discovered hot cocoa, she never wanted anything else.

Ellen handed Elizabeth a folder. "As you know, Austin Fennell died in New York. I didn't find any record of his birth or death here in Bucks County, but Doris found the record of both his birth and his death in New York. I did find the records on your house though." Ellen paused to sip her iced tea.

"Your house has been in the Fennell family since it was built in 1809. Much of the original building was replaced or restored over the years. The stone exterior is original. The entire interior as we know it now was renovated in 1972. The kitchen and dining rooms were added then, and so they're not part of the original structure."

"I remember my father telling me that the kitchen and dining room were added on. He was so proud of the fireplace in the kitchen. He designed the kitchen himself when he and my mother moved in here."

"Anyway, Austin Fennell was very wealthy. He was the only son of an old moneyed family. He had a gift for investing, and his financial wizardry really made the dollar amount of his assets astronomical. He quadrupled the family fortune by the time he was twenty-five. He married and bought a home on Fifth Avenue in Manhattan. He had one son who died at the age of eight. The family had always spent their summers here in Bucks County but closed up the house when their son died."

Elizabeth and Millie were at the edge of the sofa, waiting. But Ellen couldn't go much further.

"The son probably died here in Pennsylvania because he is buried in Doylestown. We can try to find the grave if you want. Apparently, Austin and his wife returned to New York and never visited Bucks County again because your house wasn't opened up until after Fennell's death when it was taken over by Bridget Mary Sherlock in 1933."

"And Bridget Mary, my grandmother, who was she and where did she come from?"

"I don't know anything about her before 1933. I only found out that she married Kevin Nolan in 1941 and gave birth to Eleanor in 1942."

"My mother, Eleanor Nolan."

"Yes. Now we know. Bridget Mary was married here in Bucks County, and your mother was born here. The birth and marriage and death certificates tell us that much anyway."

Chapter Forty-One

The next few days were restful. They slept in, ate leisurely country breakfasts, and explored the area. Mark called several times each day, as did Dom or Marty. Doris called every morning at nine sharp and Regina called daily too. And there was no sign of King. Mohammed's huge and mostly silent presence reassured Elizabeth.

"Let's try to find the grave of Austin Fennell's son today," Millie said on the fourth day. Elizabeth was pleased. Only a few days ago, when Elizabeth had suggested this, Millie was afraid of venturing too far from the house, of being exposed to King.

"Today's my day to volunteer at Doylestown Hospital, so I'll drive you to the cemetery. In the early days of this community, it was known as the 'graveyard.' It's next to the Presbyterian church."

"I'll follow in my car," Mohammed said.

"How far is it from here?" Millie asked.

"About a twenty minute drive. The graveyard is the oldest cemetery in Doylestown. It was here even before the church was built. There was an epidemic of typhoid or cholera, I forget which, so they had an urgent need for a cemetery."

Millie's eyes were glued to the bucolic scenery as they drove from Lumberville to Doylestown. Elizabeth and Ellen looked at one another and grinned. Millie was getting a lot of new information to add to her knowledge of the world outside the pages of books.

"I'll pick you up here at four o'clock. This is a great walking town and you'll find lots of places to choose from to have lunch."

They watched her drive away and then turned toward the cemetery. They looked at each other and then smiled. "I'll bet we're thinking the same thing," Elizabeth said.

"Yeah," Millie said. "It's a good thing it's daylight."

"That's it, all right."

They wandered through the old graveyard.

"Look at this one, Elizabeth," Millie said. "Here's a man who died in 1815."

"The dates seem to be in the nineteenth-century. I wonder if there are any in the twentieth. Maybe this isn't the right cemetery."

"Wait, here's one dated 1924, Joseph Brunner. He was born in 1840."

"Good job, Millie. Let's see if we can get some information in the church office."

They walked past more gravestones and headed for the church building.

"I like the light brown stone on the church," Millie said.

"Me too. It's beautiful. And the graveyard doesn't seem scary any more. I don't think I'd be scared even at night. It's just a lovely resting place."

"Yeah, it's special; these people, don't you think they were just like us, Elizabeth?"

"Yes, I do," Elizabeth said.

They reached the entrance and stared up at the majestic spire towering above the old church. A smiling young woman approached them.

"Can I help you?" she asked.

"We are looking for a particular grave. Can you tell us where we might find out where it's located?" Elizabeth asked.

"The church office is located in the modern building across the street behind the church. It's on the second floor. I'm sure they can help you in there."

An attractive woman in early middle age, who turned out to be no less than a pastor of the church, was willing to give them her time.

"We're looking for the grave of a child. His name was Robert William Fennell. He died in 1932."

"I have to get the record book from the safe in the archive room. It will take a moment."

She was back within five minutes with a large dusty ledger book. "Do you know the date of interment?"

"No, I'm sorry, we don't."

"That will make it only slightly more difficult since back in those days the ledger was kept by date of interment. Today we can cross check names and dates of weddings, births, and so on using the computer, but these old graves were never entered into the computer."

"I see," Elizabeth said. "Do you have any suggestions?"

"You can make yourselves comfortable here and we can look through the ledger." It did not take them long to find Robert W. Fennell's name. The child was born in 1924 and died in 1932. He was the child of Austin Fennell and Alice Campbell Fennell, of Lumberville, Pennsylvania.

"Is there any way we can find out what he died of?" Elizabeth asked.

"You can try the library on Pine Street. They have the newspaper on microfilm. Maybe there's an obituary for the child. There are a lot of prominent families from the early community buried here. Maybe the Fennells were such a family and would have an obituary published for their son," she said. "I'm sure you'll want to see the grave itself first, though. Here is a map of the cemetery. I'll mark off the location for you."

They returned to the cemetery and found Robert W. Fennell's grave in a sunny spot at the edge of the graveyard bordering the unromantically named Mechanics Street.

> Robert W. Fennell
> Beloved Son of Austin and Alice Fennell
> July 24, 1924-March 31, 1932
> Rest in Peace with the Angels Sweet Boy

Elizabeth and Millie stood silently in front of the child's grave. The stone was worn with seventy years of wind and weather but was nevertheless one of the newer ones in the graveyard.

"Let's say a prayer for him," Millie said. Elizabeth reached for Millie's hand and they recited the Our Father.

"He would be seventy-eight next month if he were still alive," Elizabeth said.

The library on Pine Street was their next stop. They asked directions of a pedestrian and learned that it was a short walk from the Presbyterian Church. The quiet streets of historic Doylestown boasted fine old homes along the way. Most of these homes were marked with a plaque that documented the year they were built.

"The people here are so friendly," Millie said after the reference librarian sent them to the Bucks County Historical Society across the street from the library where they found the obituary.

> Boy Accident Victim
> Funeral services were held yesterday for Robert William Fennell, beloved son of Austin Fennell and his wife, Alice. The child was fatally injured in a motor accident in Lumberville. Robert, who was the only child of the Fennells, was pronounced dead at the accident sight. Interment was at the Doylestown Presbyterian Church immediately after the services.

"How sad and how awful," Elizabeth said.

Millie nodded. "And his mother; she must have been so sad too."

"But, you know something? We haven't added a piece to the puzzle with this information. What does this, that happened in 1932, have to do with Catherine and Sarah in 1911?"

"Catherine's name was Sherlock," Millie reminded Elizabeth.

"Yes, and my grandmother's name was Bridget Mary Sherlock and Austin Fennell left his house, now our house, to Bridget Mary Sherlock. But we can't connect Bridget Mary with Catherine. And we still know nothing of Sarah."

They put these thoughts out of their heads while they had a delicious lunch at Maxwell's on Court Street. Mohammed joined them. They were unaware that before long the clues would come, fast and furiously.

Chapter Forty-Two

The flashing red lights in the driveway, the squawking of the radio from the police car, and Moss's frantic barking from Ellen's house next door could mean only one thing-they'd had a visit from King while they were out. A glance at Millie's frightened face told Elizabeth that she couldn't let the child see her own fear; she couldn't let her pick up the sinking feeling of despair that they'd never escape this stalking murderer. Ellen's car crunched the gravel in the driveway and screeched to a stop as she jammed on the brakes behind the police car.

Veins bulged from Mohammed's thick neck, his skin now a dull red with anger and frustration as he jumped from his Chevy Blazer and stomped up the driveway. Elizabeth got out of the car, helped Millie out, and held her hand tightly as they approached the old stone house.

A familiar face greeted her, Officer Matt Gerard, a local cop who'd been on the job since Elizabeth was a little girl.

"We got the alarm at two-thirty this afternoon and we were here in no time, Elizabeth. He didn't have time to do much damage, but," the officer's face twisted into a grimace, "but," he repeated, "what he did is . . ."

"Millie, you wait here with Ellen. I'm going inside with Officer Gerard. I'll be right back."

Ellen took Millie's hand. "Let's go to my house, Honey. Moss is real upset."

Elizabeth watched them walk toward the path to Ellen's home.

As they headed up the driveway to the house, Officer Gerard said, "I'm so sorry about your father, Elizabeth. You know that we all thought highly of Mr. Charles here."

"Thank you, Matt. Do you know who did this?"

"We didn't catch him. I'm sorry. I got a call from a detective in New York, Gentilli, his name was. He called me when you were on your way down here earlier this week. He told me about Chet King. We've been patrolling here more than usual. Nothing, nothing, until today." Officer Gerard shook his head.

The living room and kitchen looked fine when they first entered. A shudder raced up Elizabeth's spine though when Officer Gerard pointed to the circular cut in the slider above the lock. Mohammed cursed under his breath.

"He used a professional tool to cut the glass and then just opened the door from the inside. He must have seen the sticker advising of the security system and ignored it, ignored the alarm which is deafening, and just went about his business as quickly as possible. Stalkers think they're invincible. The problem is upstairs. I hate for you to see it," Gerard said.

They went into Elizabeth's bedroom. The curtain rods were ripped out of the wall and the curtains were on the floor. There was fresh, bright red paint like a blanket covering her comforter. "Your blood," he had written on the mirror over the dresser, also in red paint. A sob rose in Elizabeth's throat. Where can we go, where can we go, she heard herself ask over and over in her head. She stared at the police officer, no longer able to take any of it in.

"Nothing has been disturbed anywhere else in the house, except the glass on the slider downstairs," Matt Gerard told her. Elizabeth nodded, returning to the moment. At least Millie's room was unmolested. Mohammed put his arm around Elizabeth. She fell against his hard chest and sobbed.

It was Friday, the day after the break-in, and everyone assembled at the home in Lumberville. Mark and Doris came together, the first to arrive, followed by Dom and Marty, and Regina.

"How could you stand to sleep here?" Doris asked.

"Ellen and Moss stayed over, and we all slept on the living room floor, close together in sleeping bags. Moss preferred the couch, though." Elizabeth smiled when she said this. "We refused to leave, even to go to Ellen's. We didn't want to give King the satisfaction. Mohammed was in the next room, and I imagine he barely slept. I heard him wandering around the house all night."

"Mohammed, did you find anything outside?" Dom asked.

"Yeah, I found footprints in the dirt. The cops found King's fingerprints in the house. He's a stalker, and he's not even trying to hide who he is," Mohammed said.

"It isn't safe here anymore. I have to take Millie back to New York. What am I talking about? She wasn't safe there either," Elizabeth said.

"He's after *you*, Elizabeth. You are his primary target. It may be that you'll have to send Millie away so we can set a trap for him," Marty said.

"No, Elizabeth isn't going to be used as bait," Mark said.

"No, of course not. We can't take any chances with her. We have to keep her safe," Marty said.

Dom sat next to his partner, misery stamped on every feature of his face.

Elizabeth threw her shoulders back and straightened up in the chair. There was no fear on her face. She looked at Millie and then around the circle, at the rest of them.

"I want it all to be over; I wish I could be a part of bringing King down. I'll never be free of this unless I do," Elizabeth said.

Mark recognized Elizabeth's new demeanor because he'd seen it before. He remembered witnessing the same strength on the day after Jane's murder.

Chapter Forty-Three

Mark cleaned up Elizabeth's room when the police were finished.

"We'll get you a new comforter and new curtains," he said. "I threw the curtains and rods away because he had touched them."

"I'm glad. I wouldn't want to see them again." Elizabeth smiled when she saw how meticulously he had removed any trace of King. The room was sparkling from its cleanliness, and from the sun reflecting off the Delaware through the curtainless windows.

"You'd never know," she said. She would not allow herself to think of this room as it had been after King's handiwork. She would think of it as she always had, a beautiful place to rest and relax, the room her mother and father had shared, and later, just her father as she was growing up. Her own room now. She suddenly wondered. Had this been Bridget Mary's room too?

"You'd never know," he agreed, interrupting this thought.

"Thank you, Mark." She put her arms around his neck. He held her close and kissed her.

"It's going to be our turn soon, Elizabeth. We have that to hold onto. Going back to New York now is temporary."

"I know it is," she said, but she knew that the fear that pricked at her could pierce her happiness at any time if she thought of what lay ahead. "I called Mrs. Ahern. She's expecting us. She sounded happy that we're coming home."

"I'm glad you're not going home to an empty house," Mark said. "If you change your mind and you and Millie want to stay at my place, we can get you there today."

"No, I have to be home, make it normal for Millie. Dom said we'll just have to take more precautions."

Regina popped her head in the door to the bedroom. "Ellen is helping Millie pack; I thought I'd help you."

"Packing's not my strong suit, so I'll leave you ladies to it," Mark said. "I need to talk to Dom and Marty about these precautions that have to be taken, anyway." Elizabeth felt cold as he took his arms away and left the room.

"How are you doing, Elizabeth?" Regina asked.

"I think of him watching us, knowing our every move, as he must have ever since he was released. And all the while, we were oblivious, thinking we were safe because we saw no sign of him. But he was only lying low. Waiting. And what will be next?"

"Let's take it one step at a time. Today we'll go back to New York and take it from there. We don't have to think ahead to anything else but that," Regina said.

"You're right," Elizabeth said. "We don't have to think ahead to anything else but that."

They finished packing and went downstairs. Doris was sitting at the kitchen table.

"I just spoke to Officer Gerard. He said he'd have officers check out the house on each shift," she said.

"I'll be here too," Ellen said.

"Don't come near the house, Ellen," Mohammed said. "It's too dangerous."

"He's right," Marty said. His forehead was furrowed and his dark eyes bored into Ellen's. His message was unmistakable.

"Promise us, Ellen, that you won't come near this house while we are gone," Elizabeth said.

"I promise," Ellen finally said.

"Don't forget that now, little girl," Dom said in his gruffest voice.

The entourage left Bucks County with heavy hearts. A place they thought was safe was not. Only Millie refused to be somber and chatted non-stop all the way from Lumberville to Manhattan. Elizabeth and Mark smiled at each other during Millie's discourse on the disparities between county and city life.

Mrs. Ahern greeted everyone warmly. She wouldn't allow them to fuss over her injuries from the King attack; she only wanted to hear about what happened in Pennsylvania.

A buffet of cold cuts, rolls, salads of every description, and delectable desserts covered the large dining room table. The aroma of freshly brewed French Roast coming from the coffee urn called to the weary travelers from its place on the buffet server across from the huge china cabinet. Elizabeth saw Millie eye the desserts longingly.

"After a salad and a turkey sandwich," Elizabeth said.

"I know," Millie said pouting.

Mohammed was next to Millie, telling her the joys of being fit through proper nutrition. Elizabeth was beginning to relax when a cell phone rang. It turned out to be Regina's. Elizabeth saw Regina's eyebrows lift as she said, "Oh, okay." She slapped the flip phone closed.

"Elizabeth, my friend from the library has completed the translation of Esme Jacobs' diary. We can pick it up today."

Chapter Forty-Four

Only Mark and Doris remained when Regina returned with the translated diary. Dom and Marty had gone home; Millie and Mrs. Ahern were in bed.

Regina handed the original diary and its translation to Elizabeth. Mohammed excused himself and headed for the guest room.

"This will take our minds off King," Elizabeth said.

Regina grimaced. Mark and Doris nodded.

"May I?" Doris asked.

"Of course," Elizabeth said. She handed the diary to Doris.

Doris took a deep breath and resettled herself in the wing chair. She began to read. Elizabeth closed her eyes and pictured Esme Jacobs writing these words.

> 7 April 1911
> The child stares at me. She is so unhappy. I will tell her today that her mother is dead.

> 8 April 1911
> We were so happy when we came to this country. The triumph we felt when we passed through Ellis Island without an X chalked onto our backs by the officials, unlike some of our unfortunate countrymen who were sent back to Russia. It didn't matter that the streets here were crowded and dirty, not paved in gold like everyone said. I never believed that anyway and neither did my Seymour. It didn't matter that the rooms to rent were so small and dirty. I cleaned up the apartment we found and made it home for Seymour and me. We had a secret too. We had smuggled diamonds from

Russia. We'd wait. When we figured out what it was like here, maybe we could get another apartment, nicer. We knew that and it made it easier to bear the awful place we lived in. We told ourselves that it couldn't be worse than all we'd been through before, and anyway, we wouldn't have to stay here for long. It took a long time for Seymour to find someone he trusted to sell the diamonds to. I always thought he was cheated since we did not get a fortune for them. But we were desperate when Rebeccah was on the way and we wanted to move from the tenement to nicer rooms. And that's what we did. I almost died giving birth to her and Seymour made sure there would be no more. But we had this nice apartment and I was happy. America was a good place just like everyone said. Seymour and me worked very hard and we saved and we worked and we raised our girl. Then he died. My Seymour died. He got so sick and there was nothing we could do. He couldn't breathe and he was gone.

9 April 1911
Rebeccah was only fourteen when Seymour died. I had to send her to the factories to work. She worked so hard, and she thought she was an American. She had an Italian girlfriend at Triangle and she stopped liking the old ways. She said her name was too old-fashioned and long. She wanted a short name like her friend, a modern name. Then the Italian friend got married and left the factory for a while. Her Italian friend was named Sara and she wanted to be Sara too. I told her that her name was Rebeccah and she couldn't change it. She defied me and said she could and she would. She told all her friends that she wanted to be known as Sara. I asked her to at least put the h on the end and she said she would.

Mark stood up. The excitement on Regina's face was the antithesis of the shock on Elizabeth's. Doris had dropped the pages in her lap.

"Have we found Sarah?" Doris said. "Somehow I think we have."

"We found Sarah in Jane's desk in a diary written by Esme Jacobs, who, as we know was Mrs. Levin's great-grandmother." Elizabeth said. "Mrs. Levin had the first half of this diary; she read from it to me when I was in the office one day."

"Shall I go on?" Doris said.

The three listeners nodded silently. Mark did not resume his seat but instead began pacing. Regina's fists were clenched and her shoulders hunched. Elizabeth silently prayed that this would be understood now, finally, and that some sense could be made of it.

> I still called her Rebeccah, of course. The "R" was for Seymour's mother whose name was Rachel. It's not that Sarah is a bad name. I had an aunt named Sarah. It is a name from the Bible, but it is not her name. I don't understand young people. But she worked hard. We both did and we got to keep this nice apartment even after Seymour died. She had many friends at Triangle and in the neighborhoods around our apartment. She was friends with everyone, Irish, Italians, Germans and our own kind too. Rebeccah was always helping others. That's why Sol Mendelsohn fell in love with her and married her. And because she is pretty, too, so pretty. Sol was smart and good. He made good money and my Rebeccah didn't have to work anymore after she told him she was going to have a baby. He took care of her and he took care of me too. When Maida was born . . .

Doris stopped reading.

Maida is Sarah's child! Maida is Mrs. Sternberg, Mrs. Levin's mother whom I met in the nursing home in Miami, . . . Jane's grandmother," Elizabeth said. "Esme is Jane's great-great grandmother."

Chapter Forty-Five

"In Miami, Mrs. Sternberg said to me, 'Bridget Mary, Bridie, how have you come back to me?' Mrs. Sternberg thought I was someone else, Bridget Mary, when she saw me," Elizabeth said. "Bridget Mary is my grandmother's name. Can it be that Jane's grandmother knew my grandmother? That is ridiculous and impossible."

"We cannot think of these things as coincidences," Doris said, "that's even more impossible."

Elizabeth looked up at Mark who had stopped pacing and come to her side. He was stunned or baffled, she thought as she studied his face and felt the tension in his arm that was wrapped around her. She looked at Regina, still hunched over in the chair, hugging herself. Regina was probably thinking that she wished Michael were here, just as she herself was. She focused back on Doris. Calm and thoughtful, untroubled, but with a hint of excitement in her eyes, Doris was determined to figure this out. She would follow her lead.

"Shall I go on?" Doris asked.

No one answered as Doris picked up the pages on her lap and began reading again, this time to bring Catherine to them.

> 10 April 1911
>
> An Irish girl, Catherine, came to see me today. It was she who asked my Rebeccah to help her that day. My girl wouldn't have been at Triangle on March 25th if she hadn't tried to help that girl. She kept saying she was sorry Sarah had died in her place. She said she wished it had been her. God forgive me, I wish it too. Catherine is a young person with no children. My Rebeccah left Maida behind. My

poor Maida. She will never know what a wonderful mother and father she had. Why did Sol have to die too? If only she still had her father. How will I raise her alone? My Seymour survived Russia only to die young here anyway. But our Rebeccah was born here. Sol was born here and yet they are both gone, Rebeccah and Sol, so young. Sol's accident at work would have killed Rebeccah but she had to go on for Maida. Now I have to go on for Maida. I am rambling, all my lost ones jumbled together. I must rest. I must not think.

Doris looked up.

"We know now about the episode I had where Catherine and Sarah were deep in conversation – Catherine was asking Sarah to help her. She asked Sarah to take her place at Triangle that day, March 25, 1911, when the fire destroyed Triangle. But why? And why, in the first episode I had, when I was on St. James Place, did Catherine seem to be asking me for help? What does she want from me?" Elizabeth said.

"That is surely an important question," Doris said. "Maida and Catherine tried to show you the desk in two of the episodes. Clearly they wanted you to find the diary in the present. Catherine asking you for help has some great significance."

"But Mrs. Sternberg is Maida. She was alive when the little Maida tried to show Elizabeth the desk," Mark said.

"She told Elizabeth she'd see her again," Regina added. "Is it possible that the living, elderly Mrs. Sternberg knew that her younger self was appearing to Elizabeth in these episodes?"

"I doubt that," Doris said. "She may have known on a spiritual level. She was so close to death, only hours away, maybe she had some kind of intuition. But I doubt she had any real knowledge of any of what Elizabeth had seen in these episodes."

"We will probably never know the answer to that question," Elizabeth said.

"Not here, anyway," Doris said.

Did she really believe this stuff, Elizabeth asked herself again.

How could any of this be true? Maybe the frightening world of Chet King was saner than any one piece of this craziness of going back to 1911, meeting people who were long dead, getting messages from them.

Instead of sharing these feelings, Elizabeth said, "Let's finish Esme's diary. I assume she is the old woman who dies in one of the other episodes I had, the death that caused Maida such sorrow."

"Yes, and when Esme died, Catherine was there to comfort Maida," Doris said.

"Once the diary is finished, we may reach a dead end. How will we find out what happened to Catherine and Maida after that?" Regina said.

"I don't know," Doris said, "but I do think it will come to us somehow, just as everything else has."

Chapter Forty-Six

Mohammed had an uneasy feeling. The July morning could not have been sunnier, but he sensed a darkness somewhere that made him more alert than usual. He considered it a warning and would trust in Allah to help him to do his job, to protect the young woman Elizabeth, and the bright spirit of little Millie.

He shrugged off the dark feeling and began his morning routine which included starting a pot of coffee for the family, though he didn't drink it himself. He could hear the shower running; Elizabeth would grab a cup before leaving for the office. Mrs. Ahern would be up soon too, and so would Millie who always got ready very early, eager for Mrs. Acevedo to come and teach her. He closed and locked the apartment door behind him quietly and went to the lobby to get the night doorman's report. Jake's note said that nothing unusual had happened during the night. Bruce, the morning doorman, said his patrol of the premises had been routine. Mohammed double-checked every entrance to the building and found them all locked, nothing unusual. He marched to the elevators.

He saw the bouquet as soon as he got off the elevator on Elizabeth's floor. Pink and yellow flowers and an awkward stalk of gladiolas wrapped in silver cellophane rested on the doormat in front of Elizabeth's apartment. Mohammed picked it up and read the card, "Welcome Home, see you soon. Love, Chet."

Dom and Marty arrived within the half hour. So did Mark.

"Stalkers play games like this, you know, like with the flowers. King isn't an ordinary murderer. He's a stalker too. We can't forget that. His games will be his downfall," Dom said.

No one asked why, if this were so, they still didn't have him.

Suppose he'd had a way to get into the apartment when he was downstairs, Mohammed asked himself silently.

We brought Elizabeth and Millie back here and he knew it, Mohammed thought. Is it possible that we can't protect them, that we can't get this guy?

"Where is Elizabeth now?" Mark asked Mrs. Ahern.

"She left for Dr. Fisher's office soon after Mohammed went downstairs. I was up and dressing when I heard Mohammed leave. Elizabeth knocked at my door and told me she was going to Dr. Fisher's, instead of to the office as usual."

They all groaned. King would have been in the hall with the flowers sometime after Mohammed left the apartment.

"It must have been pure luck that she missed him," Marty said.

But did she miss him? They all had the same thought at the same time.

Mark punched in Doris's number. "He wouldn't have left the bouquet there, on the doormat outside the apartment, if he'd gotten her. He wouldn't have. There would be no point."

"Of course not, Buddy," Dom said, his voice huskier than usual.

"Is Elizabeth there?" Mark shouted into the phone to Doris's receptionist.

"Who is this?" the indignant young woman answered.

"I'm sorry, Patsy. This is Mark Lewis. I'm worried sick about Elizabeth. Is she with Doris?"

"Yes, Mark. She's here now, and she's fine. Do you want to talk to her?"

"Yes," Mark said after apologizing again to Patsy. "I'd like to talk to her."

Mrs. Ahern allowed herself to fall into the nearest chair when she heard Mark's words. The others were smiling, grimly though, relieved at the news that Elizabeth was safe, but frustrated and helpless at being unable to protect Elizabeth and Millie from this madman. Mohammed calmly left the room, heading for the study where Millie would be waiting for Mrs. Acevedo. Dom and Marty left the apartment and soon Mark followed.

There was work to be done and they knew they had to do it.

Chapter Forty-Seven

Elizabeth saw a cab coming down Gramercy Park South as she stepped out of Doris's house. The tree-lined block and the park across the street seemed to call, and she let the cab pass. It was too far to walk all the way home, but the day was beautiful and she wanted to think about her visit with Doris.

She crossed the street and gazed into the quiet retreat for Gramercy Park residents. It looked inviting, but Elizabeth knew she couldn't go in because the park was locked. As a resident, Doris would have a key. Elizabeth wondered if Doris ever went into the park, or to the famous restaurant around the corner, Pete's Tavern, where O. Henry supposedly had penned some of his famous short stories. The statue of Edwin Booth that was imprisoned behind the tall black cast iron fence with its pointed lancers that enclosed the park stood majestically among the trees, shrubs, and benches as Elizabeth passed by.

This would be a great place to live, Elizabeth thought. The homes that surrounded the park were from the nineteenth century. Most of them were townhouses and most were brick with brass doorknobs and lampposts now gleaming in the morning sun. She reluctantly left the quiet neighborhood and headed for Third Avenue to walk uptown. She'd get a cab when she got tired.

Third Avenue was a polyglot of interesting shops that distracted Elizabeth from thinking about her visit with Doris. She went into a bookstore and bought *Anne of Green Gables* for Millie. Sunshine warmed her as she stepped back onto the street from the bookstore. At the corner of Twenty-Third Street, her feet would no longer take her on the walk uptown, though, and she knew she had to head west on Lexington Avenue. The sight of the subway entrance stopped her like an invisible barrier. She stared at the subway sign for a second and knew she had to go down the steps. She took her Metrocard from her wallet and entered the station, not hesitating for a moment as she stepped onto the number 6 downtown train that had just pulled up to the platform. It pulled away from the station with Elizabeth holding tightly to a pole. She watched the Uptown sign blur and disappear as the train roared into the blackness of the tunnel.

She got off at Canal Street and walked the rest of the way to the projects. Her projects. She missed working here. But her life had taken a turn and started on a new path she had to follow, just as she had to follow her instincts and step on the downtown train to St. James Place instead of the uptown train to her intended destination, her father's apartment.

And then it was in front of her, the apartment building on St. James Place, Millie's former home. It loomed seventeen stories into the sky above Elizabeth. With her hand shielding her eyes, she watched white cumulous clouds floating over the building in benign harmony with the universe. She knew that when she looked down, the bustling world of the projects would be gone, and the world of 1911 would be before her, and so it was.

Catherine and Maida were walking down the street at twilight. Was Catherine pregnant under her bulky clothes? Yes, and she was enormous, surely at term. She looked tired with dark circles beneath her eyes. Her glorious red hair was pulled tightly into a bun at the nape of her neck.

"When I get big, I'm going to work, Catherine," Maida said.

"No, you and my baby are going to go to school. You're going to get out of this place. I will not condemn you to the life I've had by sending you to work. I know your mother wanted you to be free, to be somebody. You'll both be educated, you and the baby, you know, smart, like the ones we met after the fire, those rich ones, the women who came to help us."

"I'm hungry," Maida said.

"I know. We can't go on like this much longer," Catherine said.

"I want to go home. I'm tired," Maida said.

"We're going home now. We'll get something to eat when we get there."

Catherine picked up the pace as much as she could in her condition and the two of them began to hurry on their way.

They passed a garment factory. "I'll never let you go into the sweatshops. Never. I swore to your mother and your grandmother that I will never let that happen."

"How could you swear to them if they are dead?" the child asked.

"I know they can hear me. I talk to them every day," Elizabeth said.

"But you said they were in heaven and they couldn't come back, even though they miss me," Maida said.

Catherine stopped. She bent down awkwardly cradling her huge belly before taking Maida by the shoulders. "They *are* in heaven. They're with the angels. I don't know if they believe in angels in your religion," Catherine said, "but every religion believes that we are here on earth for a time and then we go back to where we came from. In my religion, we call it heaven. That's where your mother and grandmother are. And they can see you here and they can watch over you and protect you, like the angels do too. We're not alone here, Maida. We're going to be okay." Catherine hugged Maida tightly before she struggled to her feet, swaying unsteadily with the weight of the unborn child before they began to walk again.

How much could a child who appeared to be about six years old understand of this conversation, Elizabeth wondered, but however much she understood, Maida seemed less agitated. Maybe she was comforted. And after all she'd been through, like Millie, she was probably much older emotionally than we would imagine a contemporary six-year-old to be, Elizabeth thought. Elizabeth wanted to reach out to the thin, pale little girl with her black lisle stockings who hurried down the street next to her unlikely protector.

Elizabeth followed them to a tenement on St. James Place, or was it New Bowery Street? Where was the beautiful apartment that Esme had lived in? They must have lost it when she died. The squalor in the hall was stunning. Garbage and dirt filled every corner of the darkness they stumbled through until they got to their door. The tears she frantically wiped at were spilling from Catherine's eyes too fast for her to keep up with, and Maida saw them.

Now the child comforted Catherine. "It's okay, Catherine. We are going to be okay." Catherine smiled then, and they went into the unexpectedly light filled apartment. Elizabeth looked around. It was scrubbed clean and a few pieces of Esme's furniture, including the mahogany desk, were there.

Catherine quickly spread something on a piece of bread and gave it to Maida who ate it in a flash. She prepared another slice for the child who sighed in satisfaction after finishing it just as quickly as the first. Then Elizabeth saw Catherine stop dead still and watched as her face paled and she looked down. Elizabeth looked with her at the spreading puddle of water beneath her long skirt.

"Maida, the baby is coming," she said.

Chapter Forty-Eight

Elizabeth looked into Catherine's eyes and heard her thoughts. "I can't send her for the midwife. It's three blocks away. Too dangerous. I can't go myself. The pain is worse than I thought. We don't know anyone in this building, and we don't want to. We'll have to manage on our own."

Elizabeth didn't know how many hours passed in 1911 as she watched Catherine go through an excruciating labor. She saw Catherine conceal her pain from Maida as she walked around the small space they rented during each contraction. She finally put Maida to bed in the back room of the two-room apartment.

Sweat poured down her face and she clenched her teeth as the contractions became more intense. Elizabeth tried to touch her, but there was nothing to touch. Catherine was unaware of Elizabeth this time.

Elizabeth winced as she saw the young woman's ribs protruding below her neck and collarbone, just like the waif models of the present, as Catherine undressed herself and put on a voluminous white cotton nightgown. Would the baby be all right, Elizabeth wondered, if Catherine had not gotten the proper nutrition during her pregnancy?

Catherine carefully spread a clean comforter on the floor and covered it with a sheet. She brought a bowl and string and scissors to the comforter when a violent contraction hit her, causing her to double over and scream. Maida ran from the back room and cried out when she saw Catherine.

"Lie down, Catherine; I'll take care of you," Maida said.

"I can't lie down, Honey. My back hurts so much. I can't get down."

Elizabeth felt herself crying as Maida's pale face crumbled into tears of fear and distress.

"It's okay, Catherine; the angels are here with us. They will bring the baby safely. You'll see. The baby will come soon and be okay," Maida said as the tears poured down her face.

"I know, darling girl, I know." Catherine then bent over a small table in the living room, held on to it with one hand, and reached under her nightgown. "I feel the baby's head. I've got to lie down."

A piercing scream escaped from Catherine's throat. This has already happened, Elizabeth kept telling herself, when she felt her own tears pouring down her face. This has already happened. She's not in pain anymore; there is nothing I can do to help.

A knock on the door of the apartment startled them. "My name is Mrs. O'Rourke, are ya needin help in there now, Missus?"

Maida ran to the door to open it, but Catherine whispered, "No. Let her go away."

The knocking continued, but neither Catherine nor Maida made a sound. They heard the front door slam as Mrs. O'Rourke left the building.

"Can you help me to lie down, Maida?" Catherine asked between contractions.

Maida approached her and took her hand when the front door of the tenement building slammed open. Heavy footsteps in the hall and finally pounding on their door accompanied a booming voice with a trace of a brogue.

"Open the door. Police. If you can't open the door, I'll break it down, I'm here to help you."

Elizabeth could see that Catherine and Maida were frightened, but Catherine gave Maida a sign to open the door. Catherine's shoulders slumped as she stood still bent over the low table with her hands tightly gripping its edges. Elizabeth thought she'd given up.

A huge and handsome young cop roared into the room. His face was red from the cold. Intelligent green eyes scanned the room. "You were right, Mrs. O'Rourke, a girl about to deliver."

Catherine started sobbing then. "The baby's coming, and I can't lie down."

"Missus, can I be taking your little girl to my place for some tea?" Mrs. O'Rourke asked.

"No, Catherine, I can't leave you. Please let me stay," Maida said.

"Go with this nice lady, Maida. When you come back, the baby will be here."

Maida left, and Catherine remained with the cop. "I'll get the midwife; will you be all right until I get back?" the cop asked.

Catherine screamed as the urge to push came over her. She didn't answer.

"Put your hands on my shoulders," he ordered, pulling off his cap and exposing thick, wavy blue-black hair. He knelt down in front of Catherine. "Put all your weight on me. I know this is hard, but let me help you." He lifted the nightgown and Catherine cried out in humiliation and pain.

"It's too late to go for the midwife. Can I help you lie down?"

"No, I can't lie down. I can't."

"It's okay, it's okay. You can have the baby this way." The cop took Catherine's hands off his shoulders and put them back on the table, gently squeezing them tightly around the edges, as they had been when he first got there. He stood up and ripped off his uniform coat. A newspaper that was tightly rolled protruded from his rear pants pocket. He pulled it out and kneeled down beside Catherine again. "My hands aren't clean, not that they are dirty, really," he stumbled, "but I don't want to touch you."

Catherine nodded miserably.

"Swing around a little and put your hands back on my shoulders. Push down as hard as you want to."

He unfolded the newspaper with his fingers as close to the edge as they could be and then he lifted her nightgown again.

"You've got to start pushing as hard as you can," he said.

The next contraction came and Catherine pushed. With each contraction, the big cop murmured encouragement. Finally the head was born and Elizabeth saw a change in Catherine. She lifted

her head from its bent, defeated pose and turned her face to the
ceiling. The anguish was gone, replaced by a spark of joy.

"The worst is over," the cop said. "The baby's face was the
wrong way; that's why you had such back pain. A few more pushes
and you'll have your baby in your arms."

Elizabeth watched in awe as the cop delivered the tiny baby
into the newspaper without touching it or Catherine. But then he
reluctantly put his finger into the baby's mouth to clear out the
mucus. The baby started to cry vigorously and he whispered
soothing nothings to it as he wrapped it up carefully, so that only
its small round face peered out from the newsprint. Slowly and
tenderly he placed the infant onto the comforter on the floor. Then
he picked up the string and tied it around the cord in two places.
He cut it in the middle.

"Do you think I can lie you down now, Miss?" he asked. "If
you start to feed, you know," he stumbled, "the afterbirth will
come sooner."

Catherine nodded. The enormous man scooped Catherine into
his arms and had her on the comforter with the baby at her breast
in a moment.

"She has flaming red hair," he said. "Like my mother, like you,
too," he said and laughed.

"She?" Catherine said.

"She," the cop said. "You have a tiny baby girl and she sure is
pretty. By the way, I'm Officer George McGlinchy."

"And what's your mother's name, Officer McGlinchy?"
Elizabeth could barely hear Catherine. Her voice was a whisper.

"It's Bridget, Bridget Mary," he said.

"And I'm Catherine Sherlock," she said, her voice picking up
strength, "and this is my daughter Bridget Mary. Since she can't
be named after you, and since she has your mother's flaming red
hair."

Chapter Forty-Nine

The first thing she remembered was that she hadn't thought about her visit with Doris. Was that visit early this very morning? Where was she now? She was cold even though the sun, shining brightly in a now cloudless blue sky, was warm and bright on her face. The present returned in a rush as she realized that she was sitting on a bench in front of Millie's apartment building, and Chet King was sitting beside her.

"You on drugs? You were really tripping out here," he said. "Funny, I never would have pegged you for the kind that uses drugs."

Elizabeth got up and began to run away from the bench and toward the lobby of the building.

"I don't think so," Chet King sang in a nursery rhyme voice.

He was at Elizabeth's side in an instant. In the same instant he had her left arm pulled up tightly behind her back and his own arm around her in a vice like grip. He pushed her into the vestibule of the building toward the elevators. Elizabeth thought fleetingly of movies and TV shows she'd seen where the heroine doesn't scream or try to save herself, but rather seems to cooperate with her tormentor. She immediately began to scream and struggle to get away. Her screams died unheard in the noisy environs of the apartment building on the Lower East Side as her arm snapped, the bone pierced the skin, and she fainted.

Sometime later Elizabeth heard King's voice, "I didn't want to break your arm, Elizabeth." She opened her eyes. "It's your fault, though, you know."

She saw she was in the Ruiz apartment. Fear was absent, Elizabeth realized, inside this cocoon of pain that radiated from her arm.

"I got drugs, or I will in a few minutes, but I never give away my junk. I don't even use it myself, though everyone assumes I do. You'll have to deal with your arm," he said. "And the other stuff that must hurt like hell too. I had to half kick you into the elevator, and dragging you by one arm to the apartment couldn't have done wonders for your shoulder or your back either. I thought it was nice of me not to pull you by the broken arm too. Bad luck for you, no one was around to see. And even if someone had been," he added, "they wouldn't have tried to help you." He was laughing at her.

Elizabeth looked King directly in the eye and her pain stopped. She didn't speak, as she looked him over. His dirty blond hair rested in disarray on top of his head and around his gaunt face which needed a shave.

"How'd'yah like the flowers I brought you this morning?" King asked her.

What flowers, Elizabeth wondered, but she didn't answer.

"You better start answering me," King said. His eyes were gray steel inside his ghastly pale face.

"I didn't get any flowers from you," Elizabeth said. She marveled at how her calm matched King's.

"Oh, so you didn't know about my little visit to your place today."

Millie, oh God, please don't let him have Millie. She looked around the apartment immediately, raising herself up on her good arm. The effort and the pain that shot through her when she disturbed the broken arm with the movement exhausted her, and she fell back down on her back on the filthy floor.

"She's not here," King said bitterly. "She's not here because you interfered in my life. Her mother is dead because of you, too. She started giving me so much crap over that kid. I couldn't help myself because she was asking for it. She was always asking for it."

"How did you get into this apartment?" Elizabeth asked.

"I still have the key and they haven't rented it yet. I'm always in this building for what you might call 'business.' I know what's going on."

"What happened at my apartment building this morning?" Elizabeth asked.

"Oh, I gave them a run for their money," King said. His mouth twisted up in a wry smile as he remembered how easily he got into the luxury apartment building and had everyone looking for him. "That big guy you got working for you. He's good, but not as good as me. And the Jewish guy, your *boyfriend*, he didn't even see me."

"Did you hurt anyone?" Elizabeth's heart was racing as she asked him about Mohammed and Mark. She remembered that she had to keep calm. She'd done it so far; she could continue to do it. She willed the pain to stop again, and it did.

"Just his big head, your thug, that is," King said. "I didn't get near the lawyer."

"What do you want with me?" Elizabeth asked.

"What do I want with you? Are you kidding me? You came here to me. What do you want with me?"

"I want to leave now," Elizabeth said.

King ignored this. He seemed to be talking to himself as he continued.

"You were like a wrapped up present when I saw you standing in front of the building staring at the sky. Yo, I couldn't believe it. The heat's off here, no cops looking for me anymore. I came here to get my merchandise and there you were. When you looked down from your sky gazing, I could see you were high on something. I was surprised, but I knew you came here to be with me."

Elizabeth saw sweat break out on King's forehead and upper lip.

"We got business to conduct, you and me, lady, and I'm gonna love taking care of that business." He touched Elizabeth's face in a mock caress, then he picked up her purse and took the money out of her wallet and put her cell phone in his pocket. "But now I got other business. I never did get my stuff. I know you'll miss me, but I'll be right back."

He got up and walked into the kitchen. Elizabeth looked around for anything she might use as a weapon. There was nothing and her broken arm would make any real defense almost impossible.

King came back with a wad of dirty paper towels in his right hand. She realized with horror and fear that he was going to put the paper towels into her mouth.

In his left hand was a roll of duct tape.

Chapter Fifty

"I might be able to catch her at Doris's office," Dom said to Marty.

"Okay, drop me off at the precinct and go to Doris's. I'll talk to the lieutenant about our next move."

"She left here about ten minutes ago," Patsy said when Dom got to Gramercy Park. "I assumed she was going home."

Doris came out of her office.

"I gotta find Elizabeth, Doc. Any ideas?"

"Our visit was the usual; we talked about the episodes, or time slips she's been having, putting pieces together," Doris said. "She was excited; maybe she wanted to walk to collect her thoughts."

"Maybe . . . I'll call the apartment and see if Mrs. Ahern or Millie have heard from her."

Millie told Dom that Elizabeth had just called from her cell phone inside a bookstore where she'd bought Millie a copy of *Anne of Green Gables*.

Dom jumped in the unmarked car and headed for Third Avenue. He saw Elizabeth turning west onto Twenty-Third Street which was blocked off for construction. He circled the block frantically and spotted her again as she was heading down the steps of the subway at Lexington and Twenty-Third. He looked around for a uniformed patrolman to leave the car with and soon found one. He leaped out of the police car and told the surprised young officer to take care of the car until he came back. Just as he reached the platform, the doors closed on the downtown train. He could see Elizabeth through the windows as it pulled out of the station.

Dom cursed and pounded his fist against the steel beam nearest him on the platform. Why was she going downtown? Her office and her apartment were uptown. He ran upstairs and called Doris.

"Maybe she went to the projects. Maybe she thought she'd have another episode there and unravel this thing more."

"But where? I don't know where to look for her."

"Maybe Elizabeth went to the place where she had the first episode. As I remember, the first episode happened on the way to a routine call on a child who was being adopted by his aunt," Doris said.

"We don't have time, we don't have time. I have a bad feeling about this, Doc."

Dom didn't know it, but Doris had a bad feeling about it too. She wished she could tell him that Elizabeth was probably going downtown for a particular reason that had nothing to do with the projects, the year 1911, or Chet King. But Doris was sure this wasn't so.

"I'm going to the Ruiz apartment. It's on St. James Place too. I was there quite a few times after Millie's mother was murdered."

"Dom, I don't' know why, but I think that's a good place to start," Doris said.

"I hope with all my heart she didn't go there, Doc, but I've got to check it out."

Chapter Fifty-One

She wouldn't allow herself to feel humiliation as she remembered King stuffing the dirty paper towels in her mouth and duct taping over it, then duct taping her ankles together. And she wouldn't feel the pain from her broken arm, or the weakness from the blood loss where her bone was sticking grotesquely through the skin on her arm. She wouldn't give in completely to all the rage she felt against King either; she'd only let enough of that in to give her the adrenaline necessary to save herself.

She breathed in and out of her nose as she had learned in a series of Yoga classes she'd taken a few years ago while she quickly assessed her options. Resisting the urge to gag on the dirty paper towels in her mouth was the only one that came immediately to mind. The Yoga would take care of that. She could try to get to the door and hope it was unlocked. She'd figure out how to open it when she got there. She began to inch her way across the floor on her back. Although King had taped her ankles together, he had left her hands free. He had assumed the useless broken arm would immobilize her, but it didn't. She wouldn't let it.

The dirty floor offered resistance which jolted her injured arm with every move. She didn't feel any pain; she must be in shock. If her journey to the door didn't get her out of this apartment, her only chance would be when King came back and untied her. Maybe she could somehow escape then. She believed he would untie her because he said he had unfinished business with her. She shuddered at the thought of the unfinished business.

Her only hope was to stay calm and think clearly. Would being in shock make that impossible? She didn't know; she only knew that she couldn't panic. If she didn't survive, who would care for Millie? She knew Mark would. Ellen. Regina. Okay. But if she didn't survive, it would be her own fault. She had placed herself in this situation. King even said it; she was like a wrapped present. She had handed herself over to him by coming here.

No. She was meant to come here. She still wasn't sure why, but she was. This thing has to play itself all the way out. She would not give up for a second. She would go back to Millie and Mark, to all her friends. She and Mark would love each other always. They'd raise Millie who would be a fine young woman. They'd adopt other kids-maybe she could find Johnny Jackson, the little boy she'd brought to the shelter the last time she'd seen her father. Thoughts of Johnny had never been far from her mind since that night. She'd eat Mrs. Margolis's chocolate chip cookies again. She'd see Ellen and Marty in love. Moss would nuzzle his big head under hand again. Al and Joe would bring Thunderball over to play with Millie. Regina would be a surrogate grandmother to Millie. They all would always remember this time and be bonded forever. Mrs. Levin would be part of their lives too, and Dr. Piscali, Nancy Caballo, Mohammed, people who had been kind to Millie, to her; they would be their circle of friends, hers, Millie's, and Mark's.

Mark-she loved him so much. They'd had little time together lately. She'd been so involved with Millie and the past of 1911. But he never complained. He knew she loved him, and his own love was so strong that he was always there for her and Millie whether it involved King, or the episodes into the past. She wanted to be there for him too. She knew he'd been stressed trying to get King, but neither that nor all the other pressures of his very demanding caseload had changed his warm and loving nature. Tears stung her eyes when she thought of them in Antonio's. To be back there with Mark, that was her wish for later. It was something to hang on to as all these thoughts were.

She was making faster progress across the floor now. She had a rhythm going and it was working. Mark, how I wish you were here. She thought suddenly of the people who had passed from her life, her mother, her father, Jane. Were they with her now? What about Bridget Mary, her grandmother-was she here with her now too? From nowhere she was jolted by the thought that it was her fault Jane was dead. "Just like it was my fault that Sarah died . . ." Where did that thought come from? She remembered seeing Catherine and Maida in the tenement room, seeing Catherine giving birth. Giving birth to Bridget Mary, her grandmother. She remembered what Doris said about these episodes being time slips that existed in another dimension outside of time and space as they knew it.

She couldn't think about any of that now. She had to survive in the present. The door. It loomed before her as she inched her way across the floor, listening for footsteps in the hall. She reached it; it was time to sit up and turn the knob.

Dom approached the building with his hand on his Glock 45. Why did he think Elizabeth had come here? All he knew was that she was going downtown. She could have been going anywhere. He didn't know why he thought she was here, but it was more than a hunch. Something was telling him she was here. He got into the elevator and pressed the button for the tenth floor.

Elizabeth struggled to reach the doorknob. She could touch it and almost turn it from the lying down position, but not quite. She did some Yoga breathing then and allowed all the crunches she'd done in her life to help her to sit up without the help of her left arm. Her hand was soon around the knob.

Chapter Fifty-Two

Mark paced the faded Aubusson carpet in front of Doris's desk while he questioned her as he would a witness on the stand.

"Where did she go, Doris? Why didn't she take a cab? She knows King is a stalker; why would she take a chance like that?"

"I don't know, Mark. I think it was after she left here that she decided not to go straight home. She certainly didn't tell me she was going elsewhere before she left here."

"What did you talk about? Was it anything that may have sent her somewhere other than home? Was she upset when she left here?"

"We talked about the episodes in 1911. We talked about the right brain and 'memories' that can appear there. This pleased her. No, she wasn't upset, quite the contrary."

Mark stopped pacing and spun around to face Doris. "What? Memories? I thought these were 'time slips.'"

"Yes, they are time slips, but some of them took place in Florida, in Elizabeth's father's apartment, not in the places where the events from the past actually occurred. It has to do with the right temporal lobe of the brain, as we know. There are things we can't explain with our left brain that we disregard. Our left brain tells us these things are impossible. We reject them as absurd based on that left brain input. We feel foolish for considering them. Seeing events that took place in 1911 would certainly fit into that category. The right brain, however, has abilities that modern peoples have disregarded to the point where the right brain has become less functional than it could be."

"Doris, please talk to me in language I can understand about this."

Doris laughed. "Cut to the chase, huh? Well, simply put, Elizabeth has inadvertently tapped into her right brain enabling her to access memories that are not stored in her brain at all, but are outside her consciousness. The right brain is the conduit to these universal memories, if you will. Her right temporal lobe somehow found these memories on St. James Place."

"Why her, why then and why there?"

"I don't know the answer to that, Mark, but if I were to guess, I'd say it had something to do with her connection to Jane and the mahogany desk. Since Mrs. Sternberg, the child of a victim of the fire, appears in the, let us say now, 'memories,' I feel more confident that the connection is there."

"It sounds like hocus pocus to me, Doris, but so did everything you ever told me. I always learned you were right later."

Patsy walked in. "Detective Gentilli is on the phone for you, Dr. Fisher," she said.

Doris went into her office to take Dom's call. When she came out, she said, "Mark, Dom found Elizabeth on Third Avenue when he left here. He saw her turn onto Twenty-Third Street heading west. He watched as she went down into the subway at Lexington Avenue. He saw her on board the downtown number 6 train. He wasn't in time to get on the train himself. He thinks she may be heading for St. James Place."

Chapter Fifty-Three

She pulled herself upright with her good hand on the doorknob. It took all her strength, but she turned the doorknob. She'd gotten Millie out of this filthy apartment with its aura of abuse and death. Now she'd get herself out. But how would she be able to move with her ankles taped together? The tape around her mouth, that had to go. She tried to pull it off with her one good hand, but she couldn't do it. She could hop but what would that do to the broken arm? It didn't matter. She had her eyes and ears and one good hand; she could produce a muffled grunt through the gag in her mouth. These would have to be enough.

She heard footsteps in the hall. They were soft and stealthy. No, no, she'd almost gotten out and now King was back. She hopped backwards, ignoring the pain from her arm, so that when he opened the door she'd be behind it. Could she get out before he realized she wasn't in the living room where he'd gagged and taped her ankles? No, one glance would tell him that. Would he search the two bedrooms and bath before coming back to the front door? It didn't matter. She couldn't get out; he'd hear her. She couldn't move quickly with her ankles taped. She was just as trapped as if she had never moved from the spot where he had left her. The footsteps were coming closer. Maybe it was a resident of one of the apartments, someone who would help her. No, no one would walk like that to his or her apartment, so slowly, trying to be silent. She closed her eyes and held her breath; he had reached the door.

The door slammed back violently against her. "Police," Dom shouted, his gun extended before him. She managed the grunts she'd practiced until Dom heard her.

"Oh, Honey, oh, Honey," he said over and over as he pulled out his pen knife and started cutting the duct tape that was over her mouth and around her head.

He saw her arm and winced. "I guess he thought you'd never get this gag off with only one good hand."

"He was right," Elizabeth answered silently as Dom continued to work on the duct tape, apologizing as he pulled her hair trying to get it off. Finally, she was able to pull out the paper towels. She began to wretch. Dom groped through his pockets and came up with a roll of peppermint Lifesavers. She gratefully put one in her mouth. He had just sliced through the duct tape between her ankles when King walked into the apartment.

Dom jumped to his feet, his gun drawn and pointed at King. "Call for some back up, Elizabeth," he said. "Go down in the elevator now and call on your cell phone."

"No, I won't leave you until you have him cuffed. I'll help you."

Dom never took his eyes off King as he said, "I'll never ask you to obey me again, but this is an order with no room for discussion. Go downstairs now and do as I told you. Please don't question me, just do it."

Elizabeth looked at King. Contempt, hatred, and finally, amusement crossed his face in turn. But he looked empty, like there was nothing inside his head, nothing behind his eyes. He had no conscience, Elizabeth realized.

"Okay, Dom." Elizabeth backed out of the apartment and realized that King had her cell phone. She turned toward the elevator. She wanted to run but all the pain she did not allow herself to feel before now took her breath away. It radiated from her arm in relentless waves. Her muscles were sore and stiff. Abrasions on various parts of her body were stinging. Even her skin smarted from where the duct tape had been.

A familiar feeling washed over her and the pain began to recede. She was in a light filled, clean apartment she hadn't seen before in any of the other episodes. There was a little red headed girl playing on the floor. Maida was reading on the floor near the little girl. Someone knocked on the door. Catherine opened the door. Then

Catherine was screaming. She heard a gun shot and then another and then another. Maida and the little girl, it was an older Bridget Mary, of course, were crying.

Elizabeth was standing by the elevator when she came back to the present. She heard another gun shot, and then another and then another. These shots were fired in the year 2002. Elizabeth had no doubt that they were coming from the Ruiz apartment just down the hall.

Chapter Fifty-Four

The elevator door opened before her. She couldn't bring herself to get in. She would go back to Dom. He would need her. How awful to have to shoot someone, anyone, no matter what the reason. And he'd have to face the repercussions of that on the very brink of retirement. There would be no doubt that it was a necessary shooting, of course. King probably gave Dom no choice and he had to defend himself. Maybe it was really and finally over this time.

But she was so sick now. Pain was no longer waving from the wings-she felt the full force of it. Nausea, dizziness, and exhaustion colored her view of the walk back down the hall to the apartment. The walls seemed to constrict and the floor appeared to be buckling as she stood in the hall measuring the distance from the elevator to the door of the apartment. She wondered if she could make it. She'd made it from the apartment to the elevator; she could make it back. But the trip from the apartment to the elevator was a blur-she'd had the memory that ended with Catherine screaming, with the three gunshots. Then she heard the three shots fired in the Ruiz apartment.

No one ran out into the hall at the sound of the gunshots. There was no one in the hall or on the elevator. Where was everyone? Maybe most people were at work or school, yes, of course that is where they would be. Others would be fearful to come into the hall after hearing shots fired.

She stumbled down the hall with her good shoulder bouncing off the cool glazed cinder block wall. She stopped and closed her eyes when the pain took over.

Maida Sternberg, as an old woman in her mind's eye, just as she was in the nursing home in Florida, looked directly at Elizabeth.

She said, "One, Two, Three." It was a warning but it made no sense. "Three," Mrs. Sternberg repeated. Something is wrong, Elizabeth thought. But it was all a jumble-Doris explaining how she could be experiencing these memories of another lifetime-was that only this morning?; the "memory" of Catherine giving birth to Bridget Mary, Maida and Bridget Mary playing and then Catherine screaming when she opened the door, and now Mrs. Sternberg warning her. There were three gunshots in her hallucination or memory just now when Maida and Bridget Mary were on the floor of the tenement, when Catherine opened the door. Why was Maida Sternberg saying "three"? She pushed the image of the beautiful old woman away. She had to get to Dom now.

Dom will be angry with me for coming back, she thought. But there is no danger now; he'd shot King. He had insisted that she leave to get her out of harm's way immediately. He didn't need her to go downstairs for back up. He had a cell phone to call for back up. He was just trying to protect her. And that's what he did, as it turned out. He'd had to shoot King while she was safely down the hall.

She was almost at the door. It was ajar.

"Dom," she called. She dreaded going in. Mrs. Sternberg's face was before her again. "Three," she repeated. Elizabeth was cold then and suddenly very frightened. She knew Mrs. Sternberg was trying to protect her, just as Dom had only moments ago. She turned to get away from the door as fast as she could when she heard a moan from inside the apartment. It was Dom; she was sure it was Dom. She had to go inside.

Dom was on the living room floor in the space between where the couch and the only chair had been when Elizabeth first set foot in this apartment. Yes, where the blood was pooling beneath Dom was the spot between where Millie and she had first talked to one another. At once she knew what Maida Sternberg's warning had meant. "One, two, three," and then just "three." A cop would not have fired three rounds at point blank range. Mrs. Sternberg had been trying to tell Elizabeth that King, not Dom, had fired the shots.

Chapter Fifty-Five

Mark took a cab downtown. He had to get to St. James Place. What was Elizabeth thinking to go there? He thought about what Doris had told him about the memories. Elizabeth was having memories about past events, events that tied into her present in some way. Maybe Elizabeth decided to go downtown after her appointment with Doris because she was looking for answers about the "memories." She has to find out the answers, so she can put this behind her.

He got out of the cab in front of the building where Millie's mother had been murdered by Chet King. He shuddered. Sirens registered in his consciousness then, and he started as several patrol cars pulled up in front of the building.

"Officer down, officer down," a patrolman shouted.

He took out his i.d. and entered the building. "Where?" he said as he flashed his shield at the officer guarding the entrance to the building.

"Up on ten," the patrolman said.

The elevators were turned off. Mark took the stairs.

Chapter Fifty-Six

Elizabeth grabbed Dom's cell phone and called for help. "It's okay, Dom. You're going to be okay. Marie will be at the hospital. They'll call her. You're going to be okay." Her tears fell freely onto his wrinkled raincoat, the same one he'd been wearing when she first met him, the one he wore no matter how hot it was.

Dom opened his eyes when he heard Marie's name. He didn't speak at first but he squeezed Elizabeth's hand. "Don't cry, Babe," he finally said. Then he closed his eyes again.

Marty raced into the room followed by a team of paramedics. "What happened here? For God's sake, what happened here?" he said.

"King shot Dom. I wasn't in the room when it happened. It's my fault, Marty."

Marty kneeled beside his partner. "Dom, the guys here are gonna get you all fixed up. You're gonna be okay. Just relax. We'll take care of everything, Pardner."

Marty stood up as the paramedics began to work. "It's not your fault, Elizabeth. It just couldn't be your fault." He wondered then how many times Dom had said that in his long career, recently to Mrs. Ahern, before that to Mrs. Margolis. He wondered how many times he would say it in his own career. He wondered if Dom would ever be able to say it again.

"Where is King now?" Marty asked Elizabeth.

"I don't know. The shots were fired about ten minutes ago."

"My God, Elizabeth, what happened to you?" Marty was staring in horror at Elizabeth's obviously broken arm which he had just noticed.

Mark rushed into the room and paled when he saw the paramedics lifting Dom onto the gurney. "Hang on, Dom. Please hang on for all of us," he said.

"We've got to get Elizabeth to the ER too," Marty said to Mark. Mark stared at Elizabeth's compound fracture for a moment before he realized how badly injured she was.

He put his arms around Elizabeth and stroked her hair. He couldn't speak.

"Let's go," Marty said. They followed the gurney to the elevator and watched as the doors closed. It was a few moments before they were in the unmarked police car going to Downtown Hospital.

Marie arrived at the hospital after Dom had been taken upstairs for surgery. She wanted to speak to Elizabeth.

"Tell me everything that happened, Elizabeth," Marie said.

"I'm turning on my tape recorder, Elizabeth," Marty said. "We haven't heard what happened yet either, Marie," Marty said as he hugged Marie.

"Elizabeth will be going up to surgery herself," Mark said, "as soon as the orthopedic surgeon gets here."

"Do you mind, dear, or are you too tired now?" Marie said.

"No, I'm not tired. I want to tell you and ask you to forgive me," Elizabeth said.

"Wait, Elizabeth. No matter what you tell me, unless you tell me you pulled the trigger yourself, there will be nothing to forgive you for. Dom is a cop. Cops live dangerous lives. I've known and lived with that for the entire time, more than a quarter of a century that we have been married. I always knew this could happen. Now tell us, dear."

"I left Doris's office," she began. "I stopped on Third Avenue to buy a book for Millie. I intended to go home, but I felt compelled to go downtown instead. I took the number 6 train and got off at Canal Street. Do you know about the episodes I've been having, Marie?"

"Yes, Elizabeth, Dom told me."

"I had an episode, or a time slip, a memory, I don't know what, about Catherine, the woman I saw in the very first memory, and the little girl, the child of the woman Sarah, who was killed in the Triangle Shirtwaist Fire." Elizabeth's voice faded. The pain was getting worse with each minute.

"Let's wait until Elizabeth is feeling better," Mark said.

"No, Mark, I want to tell Marie. I want you and Marty to hear this so no more precious time is wasted trying to get King."

"Go on, then, but stop when you have to," Marty said.

"I actually saw Catherine giving birth in a tenement apartment. The infant was a girl and her name was Bridget Mary. Catherine was delivered by a cop on the beat. The little girl was living there with Catherine, I'm guessing, since her grandmother died, but there was no husband."

We have our connection, Mark thought. It was Bridget Mary, Elizabeth's grandmother.

"When I came out of this memory, King was sitting next to me on a bench outside the building. He pulled my arm back and broke it and dragged me to the Ruiz apartment. He needed to conduct some drug business and he left me. Somehow Dom got there. King surprised us. Dom drew his gun and had the situation under control. He made me leave. When I was going to the elevator, I had another memory, of Catherine opening the door of the same tenement apartment where the little girl and the red headed child, Bridget Mary, were playing on the floor. There were three shots fired in the memory, and Catherine was screaming. I came out of it and heard three shots fired again, only this time they were in the present. I thought Dom had to shoot King."

The orthopedic surgeon walked in and ordered everyone out while she did her exam.

In moments, Elizabeth was being wheeled up to surgery.

Chapter Fifty-Seven

The lights in the recovery room were too bright to endure, so she kept her eyes closed.

"Miss Charles, can you hear me?" a disembodied voice asked.

"Yes, I'm awake."

"Good. I'm Erica, and I'm the recovery room nurse. How is your pain?"

"It's bearable. Can you please tell me about Detective Dominic Gentilli?"

"I'm sorry, but I don't have any information on Detective Gentilli."

"Can you please find out how he is doing?"

The nurse ignored her. "Your daughter and stepmother are here and your fiancé."

Millie. And Regina and Mark, who had to take family titles to be allowed to see her, Elizabeth guessed. Did she want Millie to see her like this? Yes, Millie would be frantic with worry; she would need the reassurance of seeing Elizabeth.

"When can I see them?"

"You'll be in your room in about an hour, I think," the nurse said. "They will be waiting for you there. Why don't you try to sleep now? If your pain gets worse, let me know."

Elizabeth immediately drifted into sleep. Mrs. Sternberg was looking at her with sorrow in her eyes. I'm sorry you are going through this she seemed to say. King was in her dream too, turning it into a nightmare. He floated behind her eyes in the darkness, laughing at her and mocking her. Fire blazed up her arm as she came to consciousness. If she asked for painkillers, she wouldn't be able to reassure Millie.

"Is Detective Gentilli out of surgery?" Elizabeth asked Erica.

"No, he isn't, or he'd be in here with you," she said.

Elizabeth bit her lip. She'd have to be patient.

The hour passed, and she was being wheeled to her room. They were all there, Millie, Mark, Regina, Doris, Marty, and Marie Gentilli. She thought she'd have to pretend to smile so that Millie wouldn't be frightened, but her gratitude was so great that her smile came naturally.

Millie and Mark were at her side at once.

"Everyone out while I get her in bed," the orderly said. "In fact, stay out. There are too many visitors in here. Only two are allowed."

"Please let them all stay," Elizabeth said. "Look, the other bed is empty; we won't disturb anyone."

"Okay," he said with good humor, "but everyone out while I get her in bed."

"Wait, I need to know how Dom is," Elizabeth said.

"Still in surgery, Honey. We don't know any more than we did when we saw you last," Marie said.

"Did they get King?"

Marty answered simply. "No," he said. "I wanted to see you and Dom before I went back on the streets, but I think I have to go now. Dom will be so angry with me if I'm here in the hospital instead of out there trying to get King."

Marty left the room followed by the others except for Mark who helped the orderly get Elizabeth into bed. When they were alone, Mark kissed her gently all over her face.

"I was so frightened when I realized where you had gone. Then when I saw you with Dom, Dom shot and bleeding, I couldn't absorb that you had been with that monster, that you had been hurt . . ." He put his hands around Elizabeth's and shook his head, still trying to understand what had happened.

"I know, I know, I can't believe any of this myself. It's okay now for me. I'm okay, really. Do you think Dom will be okay, Mark? I couldn't bear it if anything happened to Dom."

"I don't know. It doesn't look good."

Elizabeth realized that Mark didn't look like the handsome young assistant D.A. she had met last May. Some gray hairs at his temples and worry deep in his brown eyes reflected the toll that the strain of the last few months had taken on him. She knew he could probably say the same thing about her. She wanted to cry then for Dom and for all of them, even for the people who had already completed the trials of the journey of life, Catherine, Sarah, Mrs. Sternberg . . . She was getting melancholy or going crazy. When would this be over? The tears started to fill her eyes.

But the others came in then, Millie shyly approaching the bed with Regina holding her hand. Elizabeth turned away and quickly wiped her eyes. When she took Millie's hand with her own good one, she was able to smile at this beautiful child who had miraculously come into her life.

"Marty told me to tell you that he is going to call Ellen and ask her and Moss to drive up and stay with us for a while. He didn't think you'd mind. Is that okay, Elizabeth?" Millie said.

"Of course, it's okay. It's great. We'll have fun with Ellen."

Doris coughed. "Elizabeth, an envelope was found among your father's papers that I think you should see," she said.

Then Regina stepped close to the bed, and Elizabeth felt a connection with her father.

"Bethie, dear, I hope you don't mind if I call you by your childhood name-that is how your father always referred to you-do you want me to stay at your apartment until Ellen gets there?"

"That would be great, though I do want to go home tonight."

"I doubt the doctor will release you," Regina said.

"Mohammed is downstairs at the elevator to make sure King doesn't come back. I'll stay the night too," Mark said. You'll be safe here."

"What about Millie?" Elizabeth said. "I think Mohammed should be there at the apartment. Actually, I think we both should be."

They hadn't realized that Marie Gentilli was no longer in the room until she returned. She stood in the doorway and said, "Dom didn't make it. He died during surgery. There was nothing they could do."

Chapter Fifty-Eight

"I didn't attend the wake, Mark. I've got to go to the funeral," Elizabeth said.

"Marie will understand. You were in the hospital; you have a serious injury," Mark said.

"I left the hospital within an hour of Dom's passing. I've been home for three days . . ."

"But you were told by the doctor *not* to leave the hospital. You left anyway, and you've been in bed ever since. It's not even your arm that I'm worried about . . ." Mark said.

"I know, I'm sorry I've been so sad . . ."

"Don't apologize, Elizabeth. Please don't apologize," he held her gently in his arms. "How could you not have been sad after all that has happened?" Mark said.

"I'm ashamed that I haven't been stronger for Millie," she said.

"You have always been a model of strength for Millie. What would she think, though, if she had not seen you grieve for a beloved friend? She is grieving for Dom too."

"But she has had to grieve for her mother, then Jane, and now this."

"You have helped her with her losses, all of them. Doris has helped her through each of these losses too, just as she has helped all of us. We had no control over these things. I think Millie is going to be fine. She has to see what grief is though," Mark said.

"There is no doubt she knows what grief is, Mark," Elizabeth said.

"I know, I know," he said holding her and kissing the top of her head.

"I'm going to get dressed for my friend's funeral. Marty will need us there too," Elizabeth said.

Mark nodded. "Yes, of course you're right. We have to go."

Our Lady of Lourdes Church in Queens Village, Dom and Marie's parish, was packed for his funeral mass.

Elizabeth, Mark, and Ellen walked into the church. They agreed that Millie should be at home with Regina. Mohammed and Mrs. Ahern were there with Millie too, and Doris would be arriving by lunchtime.

A sea of blue uniforms and dark suits filled the left side of the aisle. The right side was filled too, with family, friends and neighbors, and as Elizabeth would later learn, many of Dom's AA buddies. Elizabeth, Mark, and Ellen entered a pew in the back of the church. A pale young woman in her mid-twenties wearing a classic black suit approached them.

"My name is Connie Lamberta," she said. "Formerly Connie Gentilli. My mother asked me to look for you; she described you perfectly, but of course, the cast on your arm left no doubt." Connie's smile was sad but her handshake was firm and warm as she extended it first to Elizabeth, then to Ellen and Mark.

"My mother would like you to sit up front with the family," she said.

"We couldn't," Elizabeth said. Mark squeezed her around the waist.

"Please, Elizabeth," Connie said. "My mother knows how you feel. "None of this is your fault; my father was a cop. And it was my father's time. Please."

They followed Connie to the front of the church and she directed them into the second pew behind Marie and the rest of Dom's children. Marie turned around and kissed Elizabeth. "I knew you'd be here for Dom, Elizabeth, even though this is hard for you," she said.

"Hard for *me*, no, it's you, the kids, . . ." Elizabeth said.

"That's why we need to be together. It's hard for all of us," Marie said.

The mass was a celebration of a hero's life. A comforting homily by the priest was followed by a powerful eulogy by Marty. Elizabeth felt Ellen start when Marty marched solemnly from his place with the NYPD to the lectern. Marie cried for the first time during the service when Marty showed his reverence for Dom and the dignity of his career with his words. "My partner," Marty began. "My partner," Marie whispered.

An entourage of policemen carried and escorted the coffin down the aisle of the church as a vocalist sang "On Eagle's Wings." Hundreds of policeman and dozens of police cars lined the street in front of the old church as the NYPD bagpiper played while the honor guard carried the coffin to the hearse.

Dom, Dom, Elizabeth thought. Are you here with us? Can you see all this? Marty approached and shook hands with Mark and kissed Elizabeth on the cheek. He grabbed Ellen and hugged her tightly.

"Your eulogy was such a beautiful tribute to Dom, Marty," Ellen said.

"I still can't believe it; how can he be gone?" Marty sobbed in Ellen's arms. Ellen was crying too.

The cars lined up to follow the hearse. It drove slowly through the neighborhood and passed Dom's house, an old fashioned tradition that moved Elizabeth. So, this is where you lived all the time you were taking care of Millie and me, trying to find King, being my friend. She looked at the comfortable house, built after the war, she guessed, on its thirty-by-sixty plot. It was one of about twenty-five homes on each side of the block in the multi-ethnic working class neighborhood Dom and Marie had lived in and loved since they were first married when Dom returned from Viet Nam.

Next they drove to Calverton National Cemetery in Suffolk County, more than fifty miles from the church. Dom's graveside ceremony combined the religious with the pomp and circumstance of a fallen NYPD detective killed in the line of duty. Finally, his military service was recognized too when a young soldier handed Marie the United States flag, saying it was given with "the thanks of a grateful nation."

The rest of the afternoon was a blur. They returned to the Gentilli home for a buffet after the long ride from the cemetery. Elizabeth met all of Dom's family, many of his neighbors and AA friends and, of course, a countless number of cops.

So many people would miss this very special man.

Chapter Fifty-Nine

Doris spent the morning examining the papers in the box marked, "Mother" that Elizabeth had brought home from the house in Lumberville. The puzzle was almost complete. Eleanor Nolan Charles, Elizabeth's mother, had certainly known a great deal about all the things that were now insinuating themselves into Elizabeth's life.

None of these things were secrets, perhaps, or perhaps they were. In any case, Elizabeth was only three when her mother died, so her mother couldn't have shared the family history with her. Her father, someone who had little or no family of his own, may not have thought this history was important since Eleanor wasn't there to share it with her daughter. Or maybe Michael didn't want Elizabeth to know her grandmother's rather odd history. Doris shook aside this thought. What did it matter that they would probably never know what Michael had been thinking?

She opened her laptop and tried to put together a family tree from what she knew so far about Jane's family. She made a list.

"Facts found in the diary in the mahogany desk, and from Mrs. Francine Levin, Jane's mother:

Esme Jacobs, née Nedbalsky-mother of Rebeccah/Sarah, grandmother of Maida Sternberg, great-grandmother of Francine Levin, great-great grandmother of Jane
b. 1846   d. 1911

Rebeccah Sarah Mendelsohn, née Jacobs-mother of Maida, grandmother of Francine Levin, great-grandmother of Jane, died in Triangle Shirtwaist Fire

b. 1885   d. 1911

Maida Sternberg, née Mendelsohn-mother of Francine Levin and Jane's grandmother, died in nursing home in Florida
b. 1906   d. 2002

Francine Levin, née Sternberg-Jane's mother
b. 1936

Jane Levin
b. 1973   d. 2002

Doris stopped her chronicle and looked up. Now she would list the people on Elizabeth's side. These were the things they learned from what Elizabeth found in the attic of her home in Lumberville, her explorations with Millie in Doylestown, and some of the memories she'd experienced. But first she'd listen to the tape Marty made in the hospital. Elizabeth told her a little about the memory of Catherine Sherlock giving birth to her grandmother, Bridget Mary. After hearing the tape, Doris realized that these last memories Elizabeth had tapped into added a lot to what they already knew. She began to type.

"Facts learned from Elizabeth's memories and research:

Catherine Sherlock-listed as dead in the Triangle Shirtwaist Fire, mother of Bridget Mary who was born almost eight months after the fire, grandmother of Eleanor, great-grandmother of Elizabeth, friend of Rebecca/Sarah Mendelsohn who took Catherine's place at Triangle the day of the fire
b. 1890 d.????

Bridget Mary Nolan née Sherlock (born 11/19/11), daughter of Catherine Sherlock, Eleanor's mother, Elizabeth's grandmother
b. 1911   d. 1963

Eleanor Charles, née Nolan-Elizabeth's mother
b. 1942   d. 1976

Elizabeth Charles
b. 1973"

The next part was a little more tricky, Doris realized. It had to do with the letter Elizabeth found in the attic in the house in

Lumberville. The Fennell family and how they figured in to this would be the key.

"Austin Fennell, was married to Alice Fennell, née Campbell, had one son, Robert William Fennell, who died at age eight, and wrote a letter to Bridget Mary Sherlock, calling her his daughter, leaving her a house and a fortune.

b. 1878   d. 1933

Robert William Fennell, child of Austin who died and whose grave Elizabeth and Millie had visited in the old graveyard of the Doylestown Presbyterian Church

b. 1924   d. 1932

Bridget Mary Sherlock (illegitimate?)

b. 1911   d. 1963"

Doris stared at the screen of her laptop. There were a great many questions yet to be answered.

Chapter Sixty

She knew she was dreaming. Her father was standing next to Dom and they were smiling at her. Then Michael and she were at the Hungarian restaurant in Brooklyn Heights just as they were the last time they were together. Her father was saying, "We'll talk more about it at your place." Then he said, "We have all the time in the world." Dom came to their table and said, "Don't cry, Babe." She tried to rouse herself from these dreams, but she could not. Her body was weighted down, and she couldn't move her arms or her legs. She heard herself moaning but it was so far away. "There is something I want to tell you," her father said. "There is something I want to tell you," he repeated. But he didn't tell her what it was.

She awoke in her den in Mark's arms, "It's okay; it's okay, Elizabeth. You had a bad dream; it's okay." He held her as tightly as her injuries would allow. She relaxed as his voice and the strength of his arms soothed her.

"We fell asleep on the couch," she said then.

"It was late and we didn't want to leave each other. I guess we dozed off."

"It's three a.m.; we've been asleep for hours. I can't believe Dom's funeral was less than a day ago. It seems that the more time that passes, the farther away he will be from us," Elizabeth said.

"It sounds corny, but I don't believe he'll ever be far away from us," Mark said.

"I was just dreaming about him and about my father. In the dream, they each said things to me that they had really said, things they said the last time I was with them. Then my father said he had something to tell me which wasn't something he really said. Maybe they are close by and can come to us in dreams, but not being here, my father not having a life with Regina, Dom not going to North Carolina with Marie to retire . . . It's hard to understand the why . . ." Elizabeth said.

"I feel that way too, not understanding, I mean," Mark said.

"Let's have coffee," Elizabeth said. "I don't think either of us will be able to go back to sleep."

"No, and I want to talk to you about us, about getting married," Mark said.

"Mark . . ." Elizabeth said.

By the time the sun came up outside the kitchen window where they sat at the table, they had finished a whole pot of coffee and had planned a future, albeit a tentative one.

A sleepy Millie wandered into the kitchen first. "Ellen's still sleeping," she reported after she kissed Elizabeth. Mark put his arms out and she climbed onto his lap.

"What would you think of Elizabeth and I getting married and the three of us being a family, instead of a family of two, like you have now?" Mark said.

Millie's eyes widened and her jaw dropped for a second. She quickly recovered from her surprise, though, and hugged Mark tightly. She jumped out of his arms and hugged Elizabeth too.

"I take it you think this is a good idea?" Mark said.

"Oh, yes," Millie said.

"We thought you might," Elizabeth said. "This is a first-I've never seen you speechless, Millie."

Elizabeth felt a twinge of guilt at this happy moment. She wondered if her father and Dom were really here to share it with them. If they were, she knew she shouldn't feel guilty because they'd be happy too.

They heard the clicking of Moss's nails on the ceramic tile in the hall outside the kitchen just before Ellen and he walked in.

Mark got up to pour Ellen a cup of coffee when he realized he had to make a fresh pot. Ellen looked like she needed a cup. Elizabeth and Mark knew she was worried about Marty. He'd left the post funeral buffet at Dom's house early to get back to work on the King case.

Before he left, Marty told them that the lieutenant was holding back nothing to find Dom's killer. When a cop is killed, the entire force is involved in one way or another with finding the killer.

"Can I tell her?" Millie asked.

"Sure," Elizabeth and Mark said simultaneously.

Ellen's eyes filled up with tears as she hugged them. "You deserve every happiness," she said.

Mark thought that with the entire NYPD looking for King, it wouldn't be long now. It couldn't be. They all needed for this to be over. The joy of their decision to get married was overshadowed by sorrow at Dom's loss and the continued threat posed by Chet King, not to mention the episodes, or memories, or time slips.

After coffee, Mark took Moss downstairs for a walk and Elizabeth took a shower. When Elizabeth came back to the kitchen, dressed and ready for the day, Mrs. Ahern was there.

"Ellen went upstairs to get dressed. Mrs. Acevedo just got here and Millie's with her in her room. Don't forget to take these antibiotics. Do you need the pain medication they gave you?"

Elizabeth picked up the juice and the antibiotics that Mrs. Ahern had left for her. "No, I don't need the pain medication," Elizabeth said. "Thank you so much for all your kindness to us, Mrs. Ahern."

"You got a phone call from the office while you were in the shower," Mrs. Ahern said. "Apparently there is some question that they think only you can answer," Mrs. Ahern said. "I set them straight, though. I told them you were recovering from a bad injury and couldn't be disturbed."

"Oh, thank you again, Mrs. Ahern. I think I'll just call them and find out what it's all about," Elizabeth said.

She went into the den to use the phone, amused at Mrs. Ahern's protectiveness, and grateful too.

"Elizabeth, we've got problems. Clients are calling up wanting to know what's going on. They saw all the stuff in the paper about King, about Dom, your picture. Some of them say we are supposed to be a conservative financial planning firm, and if Michael were still here, well, you can imagine the rest."

"How many calls have you gotten like that?" Elizabeth asked her assistant.

"I've gotten at least a dozen this morning. Have you seen the papers?"

"No. I'll be right in. I need to handle the calls myself," Elizabeth said.

She kissed Millie who was just settling in with Mrs. Acevedo. Ellen was still in the shower.

"Where's Mohammed?" Elizabeth asked Mrs. Ahern.

"He's making his morning rounds of the building," Mrs. Ahern said.

"Tell him I went to the office. Make sure he stays with Millie. I'll be back as soon as I can," Elizabeth said.

The shock on Mrs. Ahern's face did not deter Elizabeth. She had to protect her father's firm, his reputation, all he'd worked for. "I'm sorry, Mrs. Ahern. Don't worry. I'll probably run into Mohammed downstairs. I'll probably run into Mark with Moss, too. I'll explain it to them. Don't worry."

Chapter Sixty-One

Should she have left Millie so soon after Dom had died and she herself had been injured? These things must have frightened Millie who had suffered so many losses already. But the news she and Mark shared with her this morning seemed to delight her. And Mrs. Acevedo was there to tutor her. Ellen was there. And when they came home last night Doris was still there. She told Elizabeth how she talked with Millie for over an hour about her feelings about Dom's death, Elizabeth's being in danger and hurt by King. Doris thought Millie was processing these things as well as could be expected.

She got off the elevator. Mohammed wasn't in sight, nor were Mark and the dog. "Bruce, have you seen Mohammed this morning?"

"Sure, Miss Charles," the day doorman said. "He was making his usual rounds."

"What about Mr. Lewis and the big black dog?"

"He left a half hour ago with that dog. Not much space to walk that guy around here. I bet he took him up to Park Avenue where there's more grass."

"Probably. Bruce, could you get me a cab?"

"Sure, Miss Charles." He went to the curb.

A cab soon appeared, and Elizabeth was on her way to the office.

Moss barked frantically and Mark looked up. He spotted Elizabeth getting into the cab a half block from the apartment building. But it was too late. Soon the cab was out of sight.

Chapter Sixty-Two

Elizabeth sprinted into the lobby of the midtown building that held her father's suite of offices. She still didn't think of the business as hers, she realized with a start. Financial planning, no, it wasn't hers and it wasn't her. What would she do with her life after this was all over? Would it be over, ever? Yes, of course, it would. They'd find King. The memories, the time slips, the episodes, whatever they were, would stop after she found out what they all meant. It would be fine. Her life, after . . . The soft ding signaling the arrival of the elevator interrupted her thoughts. She got in and the memory of Dom on the gurney in the elevator of the building on St. James Place assaulted her. She turned her thoughts back to happier things.

They'd be a family, Mark, Millie and Elizabeth. They'd live, where? In Manhattan? She'd never felt at home in her father's apartment. When she was growing up, she lived there five days a week during the school week, but she always felt like the Pennsylvania house in Lumberville was home instead. No, they wouldn't stay in her father's apartment. Mark's apartment? No, it was a bachelor pad, not big enough for the three of them.

What were they doing with their lives? Mark said he was tired of the rat race, of feeling like he wasn't making a difference. And she felt the same way. The financial planning business wasn't for her. She always knew that; her father had known it. Her career in social work with the city was over. Her life as Millie's mother was what mattered now.

Would Mark be willing to leave the city, his life here, to go to Pennsylvania and start over? She sensed that he would. There were lots of possibilities for them to discuss and plan. A feeling of contentment washed over her. They would have a great life together.

She was almost at the double glass doors of Charles Financial

Planning Services when Annette, her assistant, spotted her from the other side. She jumped up from her desk and opened the doors. "Miss Charles, the calls keep coming in. I'm so glad you're here."

And she looked glad. It must be difficult to field those calls. Elizabeth dreaded doing it herself. "It's okay, Annette. I appreciate your handling this by yourself. I still wish you would call me Elizabeth though," Elizabeth added with a smile for the bedraggled young woman.

"No problem about the calls, Miss Charles. I'm sorry I bothered you at home, though, but all the planners are out in the field this morning. I just didn't know what to say to the clients." She laughed self-consciously then. "I guess I just can't get used to calling you by your first name. My mother always taught me to call the boss, you know." She blushed. "You have a million messages on your desk." Annette followed her into Michael's office.

Elizabeth saw the pile of little yellow messages near her phone on her father's big desk. She thumbed though them and saw that all of them were from clients.

"Annette, please don't put any calls through while I'm calling our clients back. Just take messages until I'm finished with this pile."

She picked up the first yellow message slip. Mr. Gerald Ferguson, an old client. One her father revered. She'd start with him.

"It's not that your father didn't have his share of scandal, Bethie," the man said.

What could that mean, Elizabeth wondered.

"I remember before you were born, girl. Insider trading. Yes, Michael had invested a large sum, some two million dollars, I think, and made an enormous fortune. He was accused of insider trading, a tip from a trader friend. Back in those days, it wasn't a crime like it is today. He was never even indicted. I thought he was guilty at the time, I guess, but who knows. I stuck with him anyway. He was as clean as a whistle after that, and he did well by me. Anyway, what's this stuff with you all about?"

Elizabeth's mind was reeling. Two million dollars. Her mother's money from Bridget Mary. Her father doing something illegal? She'd have to clear her head and think about all this later.

"There was a man stalking me, Mr. Ferguson. You know I adopted a child who was physically abused and neglected. She is a child I met while I was working for the city as a social worker. The man stalking me was the boyfriend of the mother of this child. I removed her from her home because she was being beaten. He was so angry with me that he became obsessed with revenge and began to stalk me. One of my friends, and one of the detectives who was working on the case, also my friend, was murdered by this man," she paused for a second to swallow the lump in her throat as she thought of Jane and Dom, "as was the little girl's mother." Oh, God, she was telling him much more than he'd asked or needed to know. She'd have to give the nutshell version to the next person she called.

"Oh, Bethie, how awful. You must miss your father so much right now. Have they caught this guy?" Mr. Ferguson said.

"Not yet, but they will soon, I'm sure," Elizabeth said.

"How is the little girl?" Mr. Ferguson asked.

"She's been struggling with grief and all the trauma, but she is being treated, and more importantly, loved, so I'm sure she will be okay," Elizabeth said.

"I know you are a wealthy woman, Bethie, but if you ever need money to help other kids, like you helped your little girl, please let me know. I'm getting old and thanks in part to your father, I have more money than my kids and grandkids could spend in two lifetimes. I've never been generous, but now, when I sense that my life is coming to a close, I'd like to use it for some good. Think about it, and let me know if you can think of anything."

Elizabeth hung up, shaken by the news of the old scandal involving her father, a man whose integrity was sterling, she thought. What was that about? Then there was Mr. Ferguson's kindness and sympathy to her, and his offer-it was tickling her consciousness, her thoughts less than an hour ago about the meaning of her life, Mark's struggle with the same universal question. She'd have to think about all that later. In the meantime, she'd get through this pile of yellow messages, this time with the capsule version of the so-called stalker scandal.

When she finished the calls, knowing that some people would remain loyal to the firm while others would take their business elsewhere, Annette walked into the office holding a little yellow message.

"You told me not to interrupt you while you were calling the clients back," she said. "Mr. Lewis called. He said he was on his way and that you should wait for him."

"When did he call?" Elizabeth said.

"About a half hour ago, almost as soon as you started calling the clients back. I waited until I saw the light go off on the phone line you were using before coming in to tell you."

Chapter Sixty-Three

Doris stared at the thin envelope that held a piece of the puzzle, an envelope that she found in the "Mother" box and opened on the day that Dom was shot.

She read the words again:

> Elizabeth, I never told you anything about your mother's family. I know now that she would want you to know. But I can't change now. You'll know after I'm gone. I made a mistake that I want you to know about.
>
> About me-I was young and had two million dollars to invest. It was your mother's money, more about that later.
>
> Elizabeth, I wanted to impress your mother. I wanted to show her an enormous return. It was such a waste because she was the most unassuming person. She would have loved me even if I had lost her money. She wasn't greedy and didn't care about the money. It was her mother's money she said. Her own mother didn't even want any part of it. But it was I who was grandiose and greedy. I used a friend and didn't care that I was using him, didn't care that I was breaking the law. Your mother's fortune became a mega fortune. My reputation was under a shadow, but I got away with it. Your mother stood by me, but I knew she was disappointed. It was a mess. The shame I felt about what I did stayed with me though. Then your mother had an idea-we would use the money for good. And we did. The problem was we couldn't give it away without it growing bigger and bigger from charmed investments. I like to think I've used it to do some good things, but it is still there. I had no money when I started out, just lots of dreams of being a success some day.

I never felt I made it on my own, but your mother's love and having you, trying to do good with the money-these things made my life a good one. Losing your mother almost killed me. But loving you and wanting to be the best father I could be made me go on. And as you know, I did live like a wealthy man, the apartment, my lifestyle. I feel some shame about that and for not using your grandmother's fortune as well as I could have for the benefit of others. When I'm gone, you will have to manage it. It's a big job.

About your mother's family. Eleanor came to me when she was barely a woman, with two million dollars. She was so beautiful and innocent. Naturally I asked her where she got it, and she said it had been in her family, in cash, for many years.

It wasn't until after we were married that she told me the story. Her mother, Bridget Mary Sherlock, had been an illegitimate child. On his deathbed, Bridget's father, a married man, felt remorse because he hadn't supported Bridie's mother or Bridie herself. And so he left her two million dollars and our house in Lumberville.

I love you, Elizabeth. I hope you are not disappointed in me.

Dad

Doris put the sheet back in the envelope. She wondered how Elizabeth would react to this letter.

Chapter Sixty-Four

King strode boldly into the office startling Annette. A flash of recognition flickered across her face. She knew he looked familiar, he realized. He marched to her desk, and when he got close to her, he could see that she remembered. He had "mistakenly" delivered flowers to the office last week to familiarize himself with the place. She didn't know that he had successfully used this strategy before, pretending to deliver stolen flowers to gain access where he didn't belong. As he recognized that these thoughts were coming together in her mind, he slapped her hard across the face. King then clasped his hand over Annette's mouth and sneered at her bulging eyes before he delivered the blow that knocked her out. He tied her up quickly with rope he had in his pocket. After he dragged Annette to the rest room and threw her in, he headed confidently down the hall to Elizabeth's office.

"It's over now," he said as he burst into Elizabeth's office. She was sitting at her desk, her face framed in a riot of red hair. She stared at him solemnly without fear.

"Is Annette all right?" Elizabeth said.

King didn't answer.

Elizabeth stood up and walked to the front of the desk. "I'm not afraid of you, Chet King." She glared at King and tried to side step him out of the office. He grabbed her arm.

"Didn't I do enough damage to this arm?" He pulled it up sharply.

Elizabeth didn't scream. "You're a coward," she said.

King's rage exploded from his fist when it connected with Elizabeth's face.

She fought for consciousness, but the pain from the punch and the new injury to her arm made it impossible, and she was out cold.

Chapter Sixty-Five

Doris stared at the first page of the letter in front of her. She pushed a strand of wiry gray hair out of her eyes as she read Bridget Mary Sherlock's words to her daughter, Eleanor. It would provide the answers Elizabeth had been seeking.

She began to read:

"I am writing to you, my daughter, to tell you about my past. My mother, the grandmother you never met, was Catherine Sherlock. When she was a young girl growing up on the Lower East Side, she had a job sewing at the Triangle Shirtwaist factory where she met her dear friend, Sarah Mendelsohn. Sarah's real first name was Rebeccah, but she changed it for the more modern name of Sarah. My mother was a rebel. The first wave of Irish immigrants was no longer working in the sweatshops when she went to Triangle. Most of the girls in the shops were Italians and Russian Jews. But she went there anyway. She didn't want to do the other kinds of work that were available. She loved working with the newer immigrants. Of course she couldn't make enough money at the sweatshop to get out of the Lower East Side and start the kind of life she dreamed of as an educated woman. She had a plan to get out though. Her family thought she was mad to have these dreams and they didn't encourage her. They only ridiculed everything she did. Sarah encouraged her though, and they plotted and researched and figured out how they could both get an education. They were educating themselves using the library, and Sarah planned to go to school when her little daughter Maida was older. With no children, your grandmother Catherine didn't have the same constraints as Sarah, and all she needed was a little money.

Catherine took a part time job as a maid in the home of a wealthy New Yorker named Austin Fennell. Fennell was married and was probably taken by the beautiful young Irish girl, but she wouldn't respond to his attentions. She told Sarah about the unwelcome advances and that she wanted to quit, but the pay was too good and would eventually help her to realize her dreams. Fennell's attentions became more and more intense, though, until finally his passion got the best of him, and he raped her. Catherine told Sarah that she was pregnant from the rape and that she wanted to have an abortion. Sarah tried in vain to talk her out of it, telling her not to destroy her child, saying that she would help her raise the child. But your grandmother felt there was no other choice.

Even then, as throughout history, there were people who performed abortions in secret. Catherine found such a woman, a midwife on Houston Street, who helped unmarried girls in trouble and even married women worn out by childbirth and poverty. The appointment was made. A part of the savings for her education that she had accumulated from the second job would have to be used. The problem was that if Catherine didn't show up for work at Triangle for even one day, she'd lose her place. It was decided that Sarah would fill in for her.

Eleanor, Sarah had worked at Triangle before she was married and knew the routine. They both knew that management wouldn't know or care if someone else showed up in Catherine's place. All they cared about was having a warm breathing body behind the sewing machine."

Doris remembered Esme's diary. She had written how her daughter Rebeccah, who called herself Sarah, had asked her to watch Maida, Sarah's daughter, on March 25th, the day of the fire, so Sarah could help a friend. That friend was Catherine Sherlock who was going to have an abortion that day.

> "The day of the appointment with the midwife came, March 25, 1911. Sarah reported to Triangle in your grandmother's place, Eleanor. Catherine headed for Houston Street. The trouble was that when she got there, she realized that she couldn't go through with it. She thought of Sarah's words, and she decided to have the baby. It was probably Sarah's influence, Catherine's Catholic upbringing, and the maternal instincts she had that made it impossible for her to have the abortion. She wandered around the streets for hours trying to figure out what to do so that she and her child would survive. And while she was doing that, late in the day, the fire broke out, and Sarah was killed in it. Catherine's guilt over Sarah's death must have almost destroyed her."

Doris closed her eyes. Catherine Sherlock went from dreams of an education and getting out of the poverty of the Lower East Side by working hard, to the horror of being raped, to the shock of finding herself pregnant, to the death of her best friend, a death for which she felt responsible.

"Elizabeth 'saw' Esme's death in one of her memories," Doris mused out loud. With Maida's grandmother gone, Catherine had to be strong for both children. She would now have two children to care for, her unborn baby and five-year-old Maida Mendelsohn, Sarah's child. How did she bear the guilt over Sarah's death, the weight of the responsibility for the children; how did she bear the death of her dreams, Doris wondered.

Ah, she did what people have done since time immemorial. She dealt with unbearable pain by taking action, Doris learned as she read on. Bridget Mary's record showed how Catherine fought for the rights of sweatshop workers, how she tried to change the laws, how she worked alongside the society women of the day who marched and protested and used their money and their husbands' influence to change things so that a Triangle Shirtwaist Fire could not happen again.

Doris continued to read Bridget Mary's narrative:

> "Through all this, she managed to continue to work, take care of Maida, and barely get by. When my mother went into labor, Officer McGlinchy came into the picture. He delivered her baby-he delivered me."

Doris remembered how Elizabeth saw it all in one of her episodes.

> "Officer McGlinchy married your grandmother, though she never took his name, a radical thing back in those days. *She remained Catherine Sherlock.*"

Bridget Mary had underlined this. Doris thought about Elizabeth's mother Eleanor reading this and wondered how she had reacted.

> "And she insisted that I, too, keep the name Sherlock. I wonder how her husband really felt about that."

Surely that would mark Bridget Mary as an illegitimate child back in those days, Doris thought. She continued reading to find that Bridget wrote about that too. She said McGlinchy told her from the beginning that Catherine hadn't been married to Bridget's father.

> "He was so matter of fact that I never felt bad about it. It was simply my history. Eleanor, it wasn't until years later that I learned about Austin Fennell, the rape, and the money, but that is not the bad part. The bad part is that my mother was shot to death in front of Maida and me. I'm glad I don't remember it; I was little more than a baby."

Doris felt tears fill her eyes. This compelling narrative made her feel like she knew these people. Catherine murdered in front of the two little girls, how horrible, Doris thought.

> "Catherine was murdered by someone hired by a sweatshop owner. Her activism threatened their way of life. They couldn't retaliate against the wealthy New Yorkers who were fighting to change the conditions in the sweatshops, so they picked on one of their own, the daughter of immigrants, Catherine Sherlock, whose best friend died in the Triangle Shirtwaist Fire in her place."

Doris held her breath as she read Bridget Mary's words.

> "Maida, that poor child. First she lost her father, then Sarah, her mother, then her grandmother, Esme, and then to see Catherine murdered. Eleanor, can you imagine?"

As a psychiatrist, Doris couldn't imagine how she was able to bear all that trauma. Yet, Maida Sternberg raised Jane's mother, Mrs. Levin, and apparently did a good job.

Elizabeth's visit to Mrs. Sternberg in Miami . . . she remembered now. Mrs. Levin's mother had called Elizabeth, 'Bridie.' Mrs. Sternberg had said, 'Bridie, you've come back to me,' when she saw Elizabeth. Elizabeth must look like her grandmother, Bridget Mary Sherlock, called 'Bridie' for short. But how did Bridget know all about her history, how did she write all this down for Elizabeth's mother Eleanor?

The answer was found in Bridie's narrative. Before he died, George McGlinchy told it all to Maida and Bridget Mary. Bridget Mary wrote to Eleanor how she and Maida stayed with Officer McGlinchy until his death from alcoholism nine years after Catherine died. Maida was sixteen, and Bridget Mary was eleven when they learned all this.

Maida had lived through a lot of it herself. No wonder Maida wouldn't talk to Francine Levin about her childhood; it was so sad.

Doris flipped through to the last page. What happened to the girls when McGlinchy died?

It turned out that Maida was adopted by a Jewish family. Bridget Mary never heard from her after she was adopted.

> "I was placed in a Catholic orphanage and was never adopted, Eleanor. When I was grown enough to leave the orphanage, I got a job as a laundress and a cook in various places and went to college at night. I graduated Magna Cum Laude from City College. I got the education my mother had wanted for herself and had then wanted for me. I feel that I had a good life, despite these sorrows, largely because I made something of myself, and also because I had the love of a good man all my life."

A short life, Doris reflected, as Bridget Mary died of cancer in 1963 at the age of 52. The rest of her letter to Eleanor was about Austin Fennell, the rapist who was Bridget's father. Doris skimmed the final pages. She learned how Austin Fennell had found Bridget Mary and had written her the letter Elizabeth found in the attic in Lumberville when he was close to death. He left her the money, two million dollars, and the house.

"Bridget Mary never touched that money; it was intact when she gave it to Eleanor who brought it to Michael Charles to invest," Doris said to the four walls of her office.

Doris's secretary came in. "Doctor Fisher, it's Mark Lewis on the phone. He says it's urgent."

Chapter Sixty-Six

Mark paced in front of the shiny metal doors glancing up frequently to watch the floor numbers light up as the elevator slowly made its way to the lobby.

He jumped on it the moment the doors opened and gritted his teeth as it seemed to crawl up the building to the twenty-seventh floor. He sprinted down the hall to the glass doors of Charles Financial Planning surprised to see that the office lights were off. He pulled on the door handles repeatedly even though it was clear that the doors were locked and the dark office was closed. He pounded his fist against the glass. Where could she be?

He pulled out his cell phone and called Elizabeth's cell phone. No answer. He called the apartment. "Mrs. Ahern, have you heard from Elizabeth?"

"No, Mr. Lewis. She hasn't called here since shortly after she arrived at the office."

He held his breath as he dialed Doris's number.

"She's not here, Mark," Doris said.

"I think King has her. I know he has her. Call Marty, Doris. Tell him to meet us at the apartment. Make sure Mohammed stays with Millie every minute," Mark said.

Chapter Sixty-Seven

Elizabeth knew she had to stay in the moment if she was to get herself and Annette out of this situation alive. King had brought her to the bathroom because he'd forgotten to lock the office and turn off the lights. She knew he'd be back soon.

Annette was moaning softly on the bathroom floor. She would soon come to, and Elizabeth had to be collected enough to reassure her. She dampened some paper towels with cold water from the tap and gently wiped Annette's face. "It's okay, Annette. It's going to be okay." Annette's fingers sought her scalp. She felt around in her thick hair and screamed. Her eyes flew open and then closed as sweat poured from her forehead when her fingers found the painful lump on her head.

Elizabeth heard footsteps. King slammed into the bathroom.

"It's time, Social Worker. It's time for you to pay for what you did to me, coming into my home and interfering with my life," King said, "saying those things about me in court, making me kill that bitch. And you're going to pay right back there in your father's private office."

She knew it would be a waste of time to argue with him, but she wanted to buy time.

"This young woman needs medical attention," she said.

"Are you kidding?" he sneered. "Should I get her the medical attention I got for you on St. James Place?"

Annette had opened her eyes and was staring at King.

"Don't look at me that way, Honey," he said and kicked her hard in the head. Tears of shock and pain poured down Annette's face.

An explosion took place in Elizabeth's brain as she thought of all the crimes against women and children that are so common that they are accepted as normal. The exploitation of the women who burned in the Triangle Shirtwaist fire, Millie's constant abuse, Millie in a coma, Millie's mother's murder, Jane's murder, the children Elizabeth had seen abused and neglected every single day while she was with the Administration for Children's Services, the poverty and suffering of immigrants then and now, the months of being stalked and terrorized by King, the daily news stories of children, boys and girls, being sexually, physically, emotionally abused-all of it was mixed up in her mind as she saw Annette, another innocent woman, brutalized by King.

It looks like King has all the power, Elizabeth thought, as she cradled Annette in her arms, but she knew that he did not.

She couldn't do much about what had gone before or what would come in the future, but she could fight for her life, for Annette's, and somehow, somehow, for what was wrong with a society that allowed people like King to harm women and children.

She looked up at King, and she saw a flicker of fear in his eyes as he somehow recognized what was in hers.

Elizabeth heard the noise outside the bathroom before King did. She held her breath. It was the handles on the glass doors to the office suite being shaken and shaken again.

"You make a sound, and the girl dies," King hissed.

Elizabeth seemed to be observing herself. She saw that she was neither frustrated that she couldn't signal Mark, who was probably the source of the noise, nor was she afraid for her life. They were all with her, surrounding her in goodness and strength, Eleanor and Michael, Catherine and Bridget Mary, Jane and Mrs. Sternberg, Dom.

Chapter Sixty-Eight

As he stepped off the elevator, Mark's cell phone rang.

"It's Marty. Don't leave the building. I'm on my way. Doris is on her way too. He's there; I can feel it."

Was Elizabeth in that dark office? Was she now being harmed by King? More adrenaline pumped through his veins and every fiber of his being wanted to rush back upstairs on the elevator. Instead he ran to the security office.

"Can you let me into Charles Financial Planning on the twenty-seventh floor?" he said as he showed the officer his credentials.

"Is Miss Charles okay?" the officer asked as he grabbed the key from the wall of his office.

Mark and the security officer boarded the elevator. The officer put a key in the control panel that sent the elevator directly to the twenty-seventh floor.

Chapter Sixty-Nine

With a gun trained on Elizabeth, King pulled a roll of clear packaging tape from his pocket. Elizabeth wondered idly if he had brought it with him or if he had taken it from Annette's desk. With only one hand, he taped Annette's wrists behind her back and put a piece of tape over her mouth. Elizabeth's stomach churned as she remembered King using tape on her, her ankles, the gag in her mouth, the duct tape over her mouth, in the apartment on St. James Place.

Annette was unconscious, but she was breathing.

The rattling of the locked glass doors had stopped. Elizabeth thought she heard the elevator doors open and close. King must have heard it too. She knew it had been Mark, and now he was gone.

King opened the bathroom door and directed Elizabeth to go out in front of him.

"After you," he said, mocking a gentleman by bowing and motioning with the gun toward the door. Once in the reception area, he jammed the gun between her shoulder blades and pushed her back in the direction of her father's office down the short corridor.

Stay in the now, Elizabeth told herself. She emptied her mind of the plans, the schemes to escape or overtake him. She knew it would all unfold as it was meant to if she just stayed present.

King continued his obscene imitation of courtesy when they reached the door of Michael's office.

"May I?" he said as he opened the door.

She went in.

"The couch," he said. "You know what you have to do now." He placed the barrel of the gun under the top two buttons of her blouse and jerked the gun up roughly. The tiny buttons immediately gave way and flew in the air, falling noiselessly somewhere on the carpeted floor.

"I have no intention of getting on the couch, not with my clothes on, not with my clothes off," she said.

"You want it the hard way, you'll get it the hard way," he said, but she could see that same uncertainty, the flicker of fear in his eyes, that she had seen earlier. She knew her own eyes were as steely as the energy force that surrounded her. It was energy that was coming from a power greater than herself, and she felt invincible.

"Get on that couch," King screamed. She heard panic in his voice. He reached for her blouse and tried to pull it off. She squared her shoulders and the fabric didn't budge.

She heard the glass doors opening outside. King did not appear to have heard anything. His face was red, and the veins in his neck were bulging. He reached for his belt buckle and got it undone; he unzipped his pants.

"You bitch, it's over now," he said as he tried to shove her toward the couch.

The office door opened as he said these words, and a shot rang out. King screamed in outrage at the pain in his leg from the bullet that had just entered it. He turned and saw Marty standing in the doorway, his gun poised and ready to fire again.

King lifted his gun to return fire when Marty fired again, this time hitting King dead center in the chest.

Mark grabbed Elizabeth and held her in his arms.

"It's over," Doris whispered. She was on the floor, her forefinger on King's limp wrist.

"Marty, you ended it," Elizabeth said.

"It was Dom, Elizabeth. I swear it must have been. How would I have known you were here?"

"Annette . . ." Elizabeth said. They stepped over King's body and ran to the bathroom where Annette was struggling to get free of the tape.

She was okay.

"Will you call me Elizabeth now?" she asked with a weak smile as she held the shaking young woman in her arms.

Chapter Seventy

The first party guests pulled into the driveway for Millie's ninth birthday celebration at a little after noon. Millie was radiant as she greeted Doris, Regina, Mrs. Ahern, and Mohammed who arrived together. Elizabeth was stunned when Marie Gentilli got out of the car too. She'd invited her, of course, and had asked Regina to call her and offer her a ride, but somehow she didn't expect Marie to want to come.

"I wouldn't have missed it for the world, Elizabeth," Marie said. "I wanted to come and see you, meet Millie finally, but also, I wanted to come to represent Dom."

Elizabeth's eyes filled with tears, and the two women embraced.

Marty was already in Lumberville with Ellen. They were walking down the hill from Ellen's house with Moss just as Mrs. Margolis got out of Al and Joe's car with Thunderball. The two dogs greeted each other happily.

"Elizabeth, here comes another car," Millie shouted. Elizabeth didn't recognize the car, which turned out to be a rental. Mrs. Levin got out smiling and carrying brightly wrapped gifts.

"For Millie, for all of you, and for your home," she said when Mark relieved her of the boxes.

Elizabeth clung to Mrs. Levin. She knew Francine Levin had come to see all of them, but she was here too because there was something important that they would do together tomorrow. Elizabeth grasped Mrs. Levin's arm, and they headed toward the rest of the guests. Elizabeth introduced Francine to the ones she didn't know and said to no one in particular, "I hope you're hungry because we have enough food to feed all of Bucks County."

Mrs. Margolis pointed to the shopping bag Al was carrying. "I brought some food too, a little bit of everything," she said.

"I hope it has the chocolate chip cookies," Millie said staring at the bag.

"It sure does," said Mrs. Margolis.

Balloons of all colors decorated the patio, and the music of the Dixie Chicks, a favorite of Millie's, filled the air. Some neighborhood children and children from school arrived too. Even with the kids, the food went on forever. With Francine Levin engaged in conversation with Doris, Elizabeth went into the kitchen to check the food. Regina was there.

"Don't worry," Regina said. "When the financial planners from our office arrive, it'll all be sucked up and gone in no time."

"*Your* office, you mean," Elizabeth said.

"I know it is no longer your business, Elizabeth, but it will always be Charles Financial Planning, a part of your life."

"I'm just glad it's your business now, Regina, that you wanted to buy it. I know my dad would have loved that it is yours now," Elizabeth said.

"Speaking of the financial planners, here they come and Annette too," Regina said.

"How is she doing at the office after that terrible ordeal?" Elizabeth asked.

"She's fine. A hard worker, a cheerful spirit. She holds everyone together. We couldn't manage without her. I think she saw what happened as an opportunity to grow. I know you feel terrible that she had to go through that, but don't worry about her. She's a strong, courageous young woman," Regina said.

Johnny Jackson ran up to Elizabeth. "Elizabeth," he said, "Millie just gave me a chocolate chip cookie from Brooklyn. It's so good," he said.

"You'll never be the same after eating Mrs. Margolis's chocolate chip cookies," Elizabeth said hugging him tightly before he ran off for more cookies.

"How's he adjusting?" Regina asked.

"He's a natural country boy. We thought he'd have a tough time getting used to it here, but he fell in love with the river right away and that made the transition from city to country really easy for him. Mark takes him fishing almost every day," Elizabeth said.

"Do you think the adoption will go through?" Regina asked.

"There is the issue of Johnny not being raised in an African-American home, but Mohammed has agreed to be a role model for him. He's doing a good job, and Johnny loves him. I know if he were married, Mohammed would have wanted to adopt Johnny, but he isn't, and his job keeps him away from home for long periods. Selfishly, I'm glad he's part of our family, and we'll make sure he knows his African-American culture and heritage," Elizabeth said. "Millie loves having Johnny for a brother, and of course, Mark and I love having him for a son. I felt so sad when I left him in the shelter after all he'd been through that May. I always felt sad about it. But that's history, and we got him out of the system and here with us. That night, when I met Johnny, was the last night I saw my father, also history . . ."

"I know, darling Bethie. Your father would be so glad you were able to bring Johnny home to Lumberville, so glad you married Mark and have Millie. It's wonderful."

"And thanks to our client, Mr. Ferguson, and the money from Bridget Mary, we can help a lot more children, the Foundation . . ."

"I know how busy you are with that, with helping children. And Mark doesn't seem to mind leaving the D.A.'s office, does he?"

"No, he's practicing law here in Bucks County and working with the Foundation to help kids. He's busy and feels more fulfilled than he did before. We're both glad we gave up city living, not that we won't always love New York City. It will always be a beloved part of us."

"Do you feel any resentment that your father didn't tell you about your family's past on your mother's side, your grandmother's money, the scandal when he was accused of insider trading?" Regina said.

"Not really. He had his reasons, and I accept that," Elizabeth said. "He was human and made some mistakes, all of which he tried to make amends for."

Dr. Piscali and Nancy Cabello, Millie's doctor, and her physical therapist when she was in the coma, arrived. Nancy showed them an engagement ring from Dr. Piscali.

"We fell in love while we were working with Millie," Dr. Piscali, whose first name was Tony, said. Millie seemed delighted to have been the matchmaker.

Hours later, the well-fed guests drove away, all with promises to call, email, and see each other again soon. The old group remained, Doris, Marty, and Ellen. Millie and Johnny were tucked into bed, two happy but tired party goers who could barely keep their eyes open. Francine Levin had also gone to bed early.

Mark poured some decaf coffees.

"One thing I don't understand," Ellen said, "is how the little boy fit into all this."

"You mean Austin Fennell's son?" Doris asked.

"Yes, do you know, Doris?" Ellen said.

"I can tell you that. That's what I went to find out about right before Dom died."

They were all quiet for a moment, missing Dom. Doris cleared her throat and continued. "Austin Fennell was a scoundrel as we know from how he treated Catherine Sherlock, Elizabeth's great-grandmother. He raped her and left her pregnant with no means of support.

"It was years later when he had a child of his own, his beloved Robert William, that he had a change of heart and realized what he had done, and what he had failed to do by not taking care of Catherine and his own daughter, Bridget."

"How do you know that?" Marty asked.

"You see, Austin killed his own child. Elizabeth and Millie had seen the child's grave in the Presbyterian Church in Doylestown, but they didn't know how he died. When I left Dom's hospital room that day, I was heading for the Bucks County Historical Society to look up the newspaper articles from the days after the child's death. We already had his obituary which didn't shed any light on what was going on with Austin Fennell."

"And what did you find?" said Ellen.

"I found that little Robert William had been killed by his own father."

The room was silent. "It said in the paper, *The Intelligencer*, that Robert William was killed in a motor accident when his father's car drove over him in the driveway of their home," Doris said.

"I can't believe that someone who was evil enough to rape an innocent young woman in his employ could change that much," said Marty.

"It does happen, Marty. Traumatic events can change people immediately and forever. Think of it. How could Fennell bear it, knowing that he killed his own child? Well, he couldn't. He got sick with cancer and died soon after his son," Doris said.

"But not before trying to make amends to Bridget Mary by leaving her money and this house," Elizabeth said.

"It was a sad journey for all those people in the past," Doris said. "Catherine, Maida, Esme, Bridget Mary."

"What do we know about Bridget Mary's life?" Ellen asked.

"Doris filled in the blanks on that when she went to my dad's apartment and really read everything in the box I brought back from here that was marked 'Mother.' Bridget Mary learned about her mother from her stepfather, George McGlinchy, and of course, Maida. She knew about the activism and trying to change conditions in the sweatshops for women and children, her murder by the sweatshop owners," Elizabeth said.

"We can assume some things about Bridget Mary too, or at least speculate," Mark said. "She kept the two million dollars Austin Fennell sent her, but didn't use any of it."

"But she kept the house, and lived in it after she married my grandfather, Kevin Nolan, in 1941. Doris found letters from Bridget Mary addressed to my mother, Eleanor, who was born in 1942. My grandfather was a kind and gentle man, she said, and she'd had a good life with him. My mother was her only child. She missed Maida all her life and tried unsuccessfully to find her," Elizabeth said.

"She said she always had an underlying feeling of sorrow because she lost her mother and Maida. And don't forget she was partially raised by an alcoholic, a sad life for both girls until Maida was sixteen and Bridget Mary was eleven, when McGlinchy died. Then life in an orphanage . . . In the letter, she told Eleanor how sorry she was that she had to be raised by a mother who was always sad. Apparently Bridget Mary suffered from low-level depression all her life from the traumas and deficits in her childhood," Doris said.

Mark had quietly refilled the decaf coffees. "It seems to me that a lot of the things that were 'done' in the past have been undone in the present," Mark said.

"I was thinking the same thing," Doris said.

"But what about the sweatshops?" Marty said. "We see that people are being exploited all over the world and even still, in New York, where this all started. How much progress have we made?"

"Lots of people care and are still working to prevent those abuses. We're using the money from Bridget Mary's original fortune right now to try to help women and children through the Foundation. We can't fix everything, but we can try to do our part, and we are," Doris said.

"Millie and Johnny will be raised in a good home and not have to endure the pain and suffering Maida and Bridget Mary did," Ellen said.

"Even Dom figures into this in a way," Marty said. "It's a stretch, but the good cop who delivered Catherine of Bridget Mary, Officer McGlinchy, was an alcoholic. He didn't go into recovery, and instead, died of his alcoholism. Dom was an alcoholic too, but he was in recovery and made a good life for himself and his family. McGlinchy let Maida and Bridget Mary down by continuing to drink, while Dom was instrumental in saving Millie and Elizabeth."

Ellen put her arms around Marty and he buried his head in her hair to hide his tears.

"And you'll still be a good cop," Ellen said. She looked at the group. "Marty and I are going to get married. He loves his work in

New York and I love my home here. But since I love New York too, and I love Marty, we're going to live in New York most of the time, but come here on his weekends off, vacations. My work can be done anywhere," she added.

Congratulations, hugs and best wishes removed the sadness from the moments before.

"Maybe we have finished my great-grandmother's work," Elizabeth said. "Catherine Sherlock may have come to me to right some wrongs, wrongs from her time that continue today, like the exploitation of immigrants, the abuse of women and children. Our paths crossed somewhere in time, and she was able to communicate with me, reach out to me. The result was the good use of the money that came from the bad thing of her rape."

"I wonder if she was able to come to you, or send you those memories because you were on St. James Place," Doris said.

"St. James Place was known as New Bowery Street in the year 1911," Mark said.

"Just as you saw it on the sign when you had the first episode," Doris said. "That moment in time when you were standing in that spot, where Bridget Mary was born . . ."

"Where Millie was abused and where Millie's mother and Dom were later to be murdered . . ." Marty said.

"We can't know the hows or whys, only that it all happened for a reason," Mark said.

And there is one more thing, something I will do tomorrow," Elizabeth said.

"And we will all be with you when you do it, Elizabeth," Doris said.

"Just like you've always been," Elizabeth said.

Chapter Seventy-One

They were in Brooklyn's Evergreen Cemetery, where the unidentified victims of the Triangle Shirtwaist Factory fire were buried. One of the coffins, unclaimed, the woman inside buried anonymously, would now have a headstone, a headstone identifying her as Rebeccah Sarah Jacobs Mendelsohn, born on February 14, 1885 and died March 25, 1911, beloved wife, mother, daughter and friend.

Elizabeth's mind was flooded with thoughts as she stood before Sarah's grave. Sarah had died in Catherine's place. Jane had died in her place. Sarah's death had left Maida without a mother. Sarah died on March 25th, and Bridget Mary had lived on that day when her mother decided against the abortion.

Francine Levin stared at the gravesite. She was dressed in black, but she was dry eyed. "When Jane was born, Elizabeth, I knew she was not a child for this world. I had a premonition the very day of her birth that this was so. I tried to tell myself it was foolish and to shake off the fear I felt, but it was like when a mother feels like no man is good enough for her daughter to marry. I felt Jane was too good to be here on this earth, that she wouldn't be here for long. I tried to dismiss these thoughts that someday I'd lose Jane. I never told anyone this, not even my husband. I knew he would be appalled that I was so morbid about our own baby. I placed it somewhere in the back of my mind as Jane passed through her infancy, childhood, adolescence, and young adulthood, but it was always there. So when it did happen, when she died, I wasn't surprised. I just knew she had to leave us." Francine began to cry. "But I knew she was sent here for a purpose. Jane's life had a special meaning. Was it to save Millie? Was it to identify her great-grandmother? To finally fix wrongs from the past? I don't know, but I feel at peace on some level." Mrs. Levin smiled then. "Our son, Jane's brother, had twins, a baby boy and a baby girl. They are getting bigger every day and they are a great joy to me."

A few minutes later the grave was unveiled. The rabbi said that Kaddish would be said as usual for Sarah, and there would always be little rocks on the headstone. It was done. Sarah had finally had a proper burial.

Elizabeth smiled at Mark when he put his arm around her and they walked toward the cars.

Mrs. Levin hugged Elizabeth and the others before getting into the rental car to go visit her grandchildren.

"One thing I wonder about. Do you think your mother knew I was related to Bridget Mary, Bridie, when she saw me in Miami?" Elizabeth asked her.

"At first she actually thought she'd found Bridie. She was old and confused and didn't realize Bridie would be much older than you. But when she said to give you the message that she'd see you again . . . I just don't know," Mrs. Levin said. "In any case, she must be glad now. My mother had an air of sadness about her all her life; I'd like to believe that's over, and she is at peace and with Jane, with her mother, with Catherine and Bridie. Her mother has had a proper burial. It's all over."

"I'm guessing you won't hear from the people in the past anymore," Doris said as she kissed Elizabeth and Francine Levin goodbye. Francine's car pulled away and they all waved.

"I'll see you this weekend when I come to Lumberville," Marty said. "I'm off to work now."

"There will be a new member of the family when you come," Elizabeth said.

"I know. Ellen is bursting with the secret. She didn't know how she was going to keep it from the kids this morning while she was babysitting."

"Millie and Johnny have no idea; it will be a complete surprise because I'm sure Ellen won't breathe a word," Mark said.

"I don't know how to thank you all for everything you have done for me, for us," Elizabeth said to Doris and Marty. They smiled and kissed her. Then they left for their lives in New York.

"The shelter in New Hope is waiting for us," Mark said.

"Yes, let's get that new family member. A playful puppy will surely cause some excitement in the Charles-Lewis-Ruiz-Jackson household," Elizabeth said.

Elizabeth turned and looked at Sarah's grave once more. They got in the car and headed for New Hope.

Family Trees

Esme Jacobs née Nedbalsky	b. 1846	d. 1911
Rebeccah Sarah Mendelsohn née Jacobs	b. 1885	d. 1911
Maida Sternberg née Mendelsohn	b. 1906	d. 2002
Francine Levin née Sternberg	b. 1936	
Jane Levin	b. 1973	d. 2002
Catherine Sherlock	b. 1890	d. 1913
Bridget Mary Nolan née Sherlock (born 11/19)	b. 1911	d. 1963
Eleanor Charles née Nolan	b. 1942	d. 1976
Elizabeth Charles	b. 1973	
Austin Fennell	b. 1878	d. 1933
Married to Alice Fennell née Campbell		
Robert William Fennell	b. 1924	d. 1932

Works Consulted

A History of the Doylestown Presbyterian Church. Doylestown: Doylestown Presbyterian Church, 1984.

Allen, Frederick Lewis. *Only Yesterday: An Informal History of the 1920's.* New York: Perennial Classics, 2000.

Allen, Frederick Lewis. *Since Yesterday: September 3, 1929-September 3, 1939.* New York: Perennial Library, 1986.

Lancaster, Clay. *Old Brooklyn Heights: New York's First Suburb.* New York: Dover Publications, 1979.

Mendelsohn, Joyce. *The Lower East Side: Remembered and Revisited.* New York: The Lower East Side Press, 2001.

North, Anthony. *The Paranormal: A Guide to the Unexplained.* London: Blanford, 1996.

Reiss, Marcia. *Brooklyn: Then and Now.* San Diego: Thunder Bay Press, 2002.

Roth, Martin. *The Writer's Complete Crime Reference Book.* Cincinnati: Writer's Digest Books, 1993.

Rogo, D. Scott. *Psychic Breakthroughs Today.* Wellingborough: Aquarian Press, 1987.

Stein, Leon. *The Triangle Fire.* New York: Carroll and Graf, 1962,

Von Drehle, David. *Triangle: The Fire That Changed America.* New York: Atlantic, 2003.

Witheridge, Annette. *New York: Then and Now.* San Diego, Thunder Bay Press, 2002.

Yans-McLaughlin, Virginia, and Marjorie Lightman. *Ellis Island and the Peopling of America.* New York: The New Press, 1997.

Visit Pat at her website:

http://www.patriarileyleyden.com

and visit The Writers Room of Bucks County at:

http://www.writersroom.net

This book can be ordered at:

www.amazon.com

and

www.barnesandnoble.com